Nila's Babies

Nila's Babies

Jac Simensen

Winchester, UK
Washington, USA

First published by Cosmic Egg Books, 2019
Cosmic Egg Books is an imprint of John Hunt Publishing Ltd., 3 East St., Alresford,
Hampshire SO24 9EE, UK
office1@jhpbooks.net
www.johnhuntpublishing.com

For distributor details and how to order please visit the 'Ordering' section on our website.

ISBN: 978 1 78904 121 7
978 1 78904 122 4 (ebook)
Library of Congress Control Number: 2018942989

A CIP catalogue record for this book is available from the British Library.

Design: Stuart Davies

UK: Printed and bound by CPI Group (UK) Ltd, Croydon, CR0 4YY
US: Printed and bound by Thomson Shore, 7300 West Joy Road, Dexter, MI 48130

1

"It's like a big animal attacked her—a dog, coyote, or somethin' like that. Coroner thought she'd been dead maybe four, five days; body started to decompose. Her throat's all ripped up and chewed on. I never seen nothin' like it in all my years takin' pictures of corpses." The coroner's photographer dropped a set of prints on the detective's desk. "Got an ID yet?"

Chief of Detectives Browning turned the set of photos around and quickly flipped through the top few. "Doyle's pulling together the report—I'll give him the pictures."

"Don't bother," the small, scruffily dressed man replied. "I'll email him digital images. These are for my private collection. She was real young—hard to tell now, but good lookin'. Long blonde hair and big—"

"Beat it, Ralph," Browning interrupted. "And take the pictures with you."

"I just wanted to know her name—for my own records, that's all."

"I said, beat it!" Browning stood up and pointed to the door. "I don't waste my time on sickos."

Ralph grabbed the photos. "Big freakin' deal," he said. "See if I do any favors for you."

"Out!" Browning sat down and stabbed at a button on his desk phone.

"Yeah, Billy," Doyle answered.

Ralph slammed the door as he left Browning's office.

"Heads up—that little worm, the photographer with the coroner's office, is on the way to see you. He wants info on that young girl who got mauled in Valley Forge. Don't tell him anything. That's an order."

"I was just comin' to see you about the same thing. Got a voice message from highway patrol down in Florida while I was on lunch break—this case is gettin' really weird. You busy?"

"Come on over," Browning replied. "What was the girl's name?"

"Cartwright," Doyle said. "Amy Cartwright. She was twenty-four."

~*~

Detective Doyle's large bulk hung over the sides of the gray, metal chair that sat next to Browning's cluttered desk. "Got a positive ID right away. Housekeeper came in for her regular weekly cleaning and discovered the body. The victim was an art student. Most of the time she lived alone in an apartment downtown in Philly. She spent occasional weekends at the house—it's her parents' house. The parents are well-off. Old money. They're on an extended visit out of the country—some sort of artsy, charity thing. They've been contacted and are comin' back tomorrow.

"Lotsa surprises in the coroner's report," Doyle continued. He flipped through the printed pages in a manila file folder on his lap. "Cause of death was heart failure. She'd had heart problems and corrective surgery as a child. The trauma to her throat occurred after death."

"Probably rats—rats got in the house after she died and chewed her up," the chief detective responded.

"Nope, not a rat. A human. Human teeth marks. Coroner says there's no doubt they're human. Another strange thing—there's no broken windows or evidence of forced entry. The place was all locked up tight—nothin' bigger'n a chipmunk coulda got in. No sign of a struggle, either."

Browning shook his head in disgust. "Another goddamn sicko. Someone who thinks he's a vampire, no doubt. All these vampire trash movies and books got some nutcase thinkin' about suckin' a young girl's blood."

"Well, it wasn't any vampire. I mean, they were human teeth marks."

Browning smirked. "No shit," he said, sarcastically.

Doyle didn't respond to the sarcasm. "Kid was clean—no drugs and no criminal record. The housekeeper's been with the family for years. She says the kid was an outstanding student and never got in trouble. We're checking out her friends and fellow students. With the house all locked up like that, I'd put my money on someone she knew—someone with a key."

"What about the call from Florida—you did say Florida?"

"Yeah, Florida. A highway patrol sergeant just called and left a message; he was trying to get contact info for the dead girl, Amy Cartwright. He said that her new Corvette was found abandoned at the scene of a robbery-homicide down there—clerk was shot dead inside a liquor store. I'll call the sergeant back soon as we've finished talkin'."

"We gotta keep this away from the press. The story'll go viral if they get a whiff of the vampire angle." Browning pressed another button on his desk phone. "Estelle, call the uniforms downstairs; tell them not to let that guy Ralph—the little creep from the coroner's office—leave the building. Get him back up here right away." He turned to Doyle. "We gotta get those pictures of the girl away from him, now."

2

The tightly drawn curtains efficiently shielded the nursery from the late-afternoon sun. Inside the darkened room, Gordon was trying to coax his baby daughters to sleep. In his soft, baritone voice, he'd read aloud their favorite stories, and then hummed an old Irish lullaby—a song Karen always sang to the girls at bedtime. Karen knew the words, but Gordon didn't, so he only hummed the tune. After a half hour of their father's stories and songs, both twins were breathing deeply, lost in sleep.

Gordon had just finished tucking the girls in when a persistent rapping on the beach cottage's side door threatened to destroy the restful atmosphere he'd created. "Damn," he whispered as he flipped the switch on the baby monitor and tiptoed from the nursery. He softly closed the door and moved down the hall to the kitchen to silence the racket before it woke the slumbering twins.

"I got it," he called to his sister Mary as he passed the living room where she was watching television.

When he opened the kitchen door a shadowed, seemingly disembodied head peered in through the outer screen. "Gordon Hale, is that you? It's Myra Silk, from next door."

Gordon was stunned. He hadn't thought about the old woman in years and assumed she was dead. "Mrs. Silk, I—I didn't know you were back on the island," he stammered. He fumbled with the rusty hook-and-eye latch and then pushed open the wooden screen door. "Please come in."

"We arrived just last evening. Hattie's here too; surely you remember Hattie?"

Gordon didn't remember Hattie, but after an embarrassingly long pause, he said, "Why, Hattie. Of course."

"We didn't open the house last season. We went to Palm Springs instead."

Gordon was thoroughly confused. While he dimly recognized the hunched-over old woman who stood before him, his only certain memory of her was that long ago, his father had sold Mrs. Silk the "big house"—the unwanted mansion next to the beach cottage that she and her nurse had made their winter home.

Mary heard their voices and was drawn to the kitchen. She blankly stared at Myra Silk until Gordon came to her rescue. "Look who's here. It's Mrs. Silk, from the big house."

"Mrs. Silk. Of course."

"I was just telling Gordon that we didn't come to Florida last season. We stayed with friends in California instead. That's why you didn't recognize me."

"Oh, I recognized you all right," Mary lied. "You often had Gordy and me to tea when we were children."

Mary's mention of tea at Mrs. Silk's jolted Gordon's memory, and unpleasant recollections from his childhood flowed into his consciousness: the musty-smelling sunroom in the big house, the collared shirt and uncomfortable shoes his mother had insisted he wear, the tepid milk, and the sawdust-like seedcakes he was expected to finish. Worst was Mary's interminably long piano solo, which she played mechanically, without rhythm, and without pause between stanzas. Tea at Mrs. Silk's was one of the torments that Gordon's overbearing mother had forced him to endure.

Mrs. Silk's jet-black hair and intense blue eyes differed little from Gordon's slowly returning recollections of the somewhat-younger woman who'd been his mother's friend. Her austere, ankle-length dress and severe orthopedic shoes reinforced his childhood memories of her foreboding presence.

She frowned and the deep wrinkles that surrounded her mouth and lined her cheeks ran together.

"I was saddened by the news of your mother's passing. Only a few of the old families are left on Castle Key. I'll miss our get-togethers."

"Thank you for your concern, Mrs. Silk," Mary said. "We miss her terribly—don't we, Gordy?"

"Of course," Gordon flatly replied.

Mary gestured toward the living room. "Would you like to come in, Mrs. Silk? I was just having coffee and watching the news."

To Mary's relief, Mrs. Silk declined. "I don't want to intrude on your Sunday evening. I just came over to let you know that we're here, and to offer Hattie's services for Gordon's poor wife. Hattie's a trained nurse—not an RN, mind you, but just as capable. She gives me my shots every day." The old woman turned toward Gordon. "Beverly, the clerk at Kopel's market, told me the sad news about your wife—brain tumor, she said."

Gordon ignored her question. He only discussed Karen's terminal illness with family and close friends.

Mary broke the awkward silence that followed Mrs. Silk's unanswered question. "Thanks for the offer, Mrs. Silk, but Karen's being well taken care of by Dr. Quigley and a day nurse. Gordy and I manage with the babies."

"Your husband and the boys aren't with you, then?"

"No, they're back in Boston," Mary answered. "And I'm here for as long as Karen needs my help."

"I haven't had the pleasure of meeting the new Mrs. Hale. She's able to get around?"

Gordon took a small step toward the door. "Karen's sleeping, Mrs. Silk. Perhaps another time."

"Yes, all right. I see. Then I'll bid you two goodnight." Mrs. Silk extended her arthritically twisted, claw-like hand first to Mary, and then to Gordon. "Let us know if there's anything we can do for you."

"Thanks," Mary replied. "That's very kind of you, but we're managing just fine."

Gordon pushed open the screen door. Mrs. Silk nodded and stepped out into the long shadows of early evening, the crushed-shell-and-gravel pathway crunching under her orthopedic shoes as she retreated. Gordon hooked the screen door and then closed the main door. He turned toward Mary and scrunched up his face. "Yuck! She's really creepy, like some shriveled-up hag from an ancient horror movie."

Mary shuddered, then turned to the chipped, porcelain sink and aggressively washed her hands with dish soap. "*Psycho*—that's the movie. She's like the mummified corpse in the wheelchair at the end."

"She's not *that* disgusting. How old do you think she is? Her hair's still jet black."

"That's dye, Gordy. She must be well over eighty. She was older than Mother, and Mother would be turning seventy-five the month after next. Even when she was younger, she creeped me out. I never understood why Mother spent so much time with her."

Gordon smirked. "Martinis, no doubt. Mother collected drinking partners."

Mary dried her hands on a dishtowel. "I think I recall Hattie, Mrs. Silk's nurse; she's an albino. Really scary-looking. You remember?"

Gordon shook his head. "Albino? I don't remember her nurse at all."

"Pink eyes and nearly transparent skin?"

Gordon shrugged. "Nope, don't remember…I thought Mrs. Silk was dead. No one's been at the big house since Karen and I arrived last September. There haven't been any signs of life, except for the gardeners."

"There was a van in the driveway, the day before yesterday. It was probably the agents opening the house. You didn't notice?"

Before Gordon could respond to Mary's question, an urgent, woman's cry came from the master bedroom.

"Gordy, help me, I can't see!"

~*~

For a mid-February morning on Florida's Gulf Coast, it was unusually dull and rainy. Gordon and Mary were seated at the kitchen table. Mary was in her PJs, and flip-flops, feeding the twins breakfast. Her ragged blonde hair was still damp from the shower and not yet moussed and spiked into her current style.

The dark bags under Gordon's eyes revealed the emotional stress that had thrown a shadow over his life. He was robotically sorting through the mail that had piled up while he'd been away, carrying Karen's ashes back to Massachusetts, back to her frigid shelf in the Hale family mausoleum. A major snowstorm in New England had delayed Gordon's return flight by six hours and he'd arrived at the cottage after midnight. When, at sunrise, he heard the babies' first chirps, he'd sleepily pulled unwashed jeans and a Red Sox T-shirt out of the clothes hamper and onto his five-foot-ten, athletic frame and then joined Mary and the twins in the kitchen.

Mary set the jar of baby food and a feeding spoon on the stripped-pine table, just out of the twins' reach. "Ever hear of a certified nanny?" she asked.

"Is it anything like a certified lunatic?"

Mary smirked. "A certified nanny is a particularly British way of turning a young woman with a high school education into a pseudo-professional," she told him.

"The Germans do that, as well. They give everyone specialist training and a title—makes for a well-ordered society."

Janna reached across to her sister Julie's highchair and banged her tiny fist on the metal tray. "All right, greedy guts, you're next," Mary told her and turned back to Gordon. "I met one of those certified English nannies when the twins and I were getting groceries at Kopel's. She's well-spoken, probably in her early twenties, and quite pretty, in a chiseled-feature sort of way. Her name is Nila—Nila Rawlings, she said. She's staying up the beach at the Cartwrights', with Amy. Do you remember Amy, Maggie's younger sister?"

Gordon responded to her question with one of his own. "You're not seriously thinking of hiring a nanny for Butch and Barry? They're a little old for a nanny—especially a pretty, young one. They'd probably try to seduce her."

"No, numb nuts, not for Butch and Barry. For you—for the twins."

Gordon put down the letter-opener he was holding and ran his fingers through his sandy-blond hair. "I don't need a nanny—at least, not now. In a couple of months, when we go home, and I get back to the office, then I'll need full-time help. I can handle things here while I get myself sorted out. I could use a house cleaner, though—someone to come in a couple times a week. I thought I'd call Mrs. Kavlosky this afternoon. She was with Mother for years. I imagine she's retired but I expect she could recommend someone local."

Mary covered Gordon's hand with her own. "Gordy, you're seriously underestimating what it's going to take to keep up with these two tykes. Bathing, dressing, feeding, diaper-changing and trying to do all this when you're exhausted from lack of sleep is tough—tough for one baby and doubly so for two. And remember, you don't do these things once a day. You do them four or five times—and on their schedule, not yours."

"Look, my life just turned into quicksand and these little girls are the only solid ground left. I want 'em to know they're still part of a family, that they have a father who loves 'em and takes care of 'em. I can do this."

Mary squeezed his hand. "I understand," she said. "I wish I could stay longer but we have to get ready for the spring shows and Milt needs my help. While he's exceptional at the creative side, he's hopeless at running a business. Milt would give away the shop to the first pretty bride who smiled at him. Look—I have to get back to Boston soon, but I can't go until I know you'll be okay."

Gordon gently pulled his hand away from his sister's. She went back to shoveling puréed peaches into Janna's open mouth. "I think these two are having a contest to see who can eat the fastest."

Julie babbled a long, incomprehensible infant sentence and pointed to Janna, who pushed the peaches out of her mouth with her tongue and grinned.

Gordon yawned. "We'll be okay," he assured her. "I can do this. Besides, I need to start getting ready to return to the real world. While I was back in Concord I organized with the office to review our junior associate's real-estate work, online. I can take care of my girls and get ready to go back to the office at the same time. I'm sure I can."

"Gordy, you don't know anything about babies. During the next couple of months, it's likely one or both girls will get sick. Let me tell you, it's damn scary when a baby gets sick: vomiting, diarrhea, a sky-high temperature, and maybe even convulsions. It frightened the hell out of me the first time it happened to Butch. With two babies, the possibility of an accident is doubled. You, young man, need a certified nanny." She pointed at him for emphasis. "Not necessarily a live-in. Maybe just for the afternoons, so you can take a nap and get your strength and sanity back. I can't go home until I know that you'll have some help nearby in case you need it."

"I don't think so."

"Gordon Hale, I'm giving you 'til lunchtime to come to your senses—and if you don't, I'm gonna call Milt and have him put Aunt Ella on a plane to Sarasota this weekend. Ella loves you dearly and was quite fond of Karen, as well. I'm sure she'd jump at the chance to help until you're ready to go home."

While Mary talked, Janna put her pudgy fingers into the pocket on the bottom of her plastic bib and removed a wad of multicolored baby food. She extended her hand to Julie and the wad fell to the floor with a plop. Both girls looked down to see what had happened.

Gordon made a sour face. "Not Ella. Not here; not again."

"I know Ella's out of touch, but she really is a sweet and loving lady. She'll do anything to help family. Can't she be here just 'til you're ready to come home?"

Gordon shook his head. "Out of touch? She and her cronies think it's still 1950. Not Ella—no way."

"Gordy, you need help."

"Why do you always act like you're in charge of my life?"

"Because, little brother, I *am* in charge—especially now. You probably wouldn't be alive today if I hadn't been around to protect you. Heaven knows, Mother was always too involved in her projects, not to mention her martinis, to do more than pat our heads on the way out the door."

Gordon sighed. "All right, bully, I'll talk to the nanny. Maybe she could work afternoons, just for a while. What's this certified lunatic's name?"

3

Mary was wheeling the two-seat baby stroller along the curving, crushed-shell drive when she and Hattie met. It was at the end of her second circuit out to the main road and back. The warm South Florida air and the motion of the stroller had lulled the twins to sleep. Hattie was standing in a manicured flowerbed behind the lush, three-foot-high sweet-viburnum hedge that bordered the drive. She was cutting flowers and placing them in a wicker carrying basket. Mary saw Hattie first. At just under six feet tall, with pale, nearly translucent skin, pinkish eyes, and a yellow patterned apron with a matching bandana covering her tight, white curls, Hattie was impossible to overlook.

"Good afternoon," Mary called. "Beautiful day."

Hattie wasn't expecting to see anyone in the drive and was startled. "Hey—who ya got there?" she asked with a forced smile.

"These young ladies are the Hale twins, Janna and Julie. I'm Mary, their aunt."

"You ain't from around here, are ya?"

"Why, yes and no. I'm from Boston but I'm staying at the beach cottage now with my brother—Gordon Hale, the twins' father. The Hale family has owned the property for years. I think I remember you from when my mother and brother and I used to stay at the beach cottage when I was young."

"Could be, could be," Hattie said, shaking her head. "My memory's not so good anymore. I can't say that I remember you or your brother. Myra's owned this old house for a long time. We been comin' here most every winter."

"You enjoy being here?" Mary asked.

"Don't much matter. When you're the nurse for a grouchy old lady, one place is pretty much the same as another...How old are them babies?"

"Just over fourteen months. I suspect you've heard that my brother's wife, the twins' mother, died recently. My brother plans on staying here on the island for a few more months before he takes the girls back to Massachusetts."

"Yeah, Myra told me. That's so sad. So, when he leaves you'll be goin' back up north too?"

"No, we're about to hire a nanny to help my brother take care of the girls so that I can head home soon. I have two teenaged boys and a husband to look after."

"I see…So sad about the babies' mother dyin'."

Mary began to push the stroller along the drive. "It was a pleasure meeting you, Hattie. Forgive me for rushing away. I need to get these two in for their afternoon nap. I'm sure we'll see each other again."

Mary reached over the hedge, with her hand extended. Hattie wasn't used to shaking hands, but after briefly hesitating, she took Mary's hand.

"See ya round, Mary from Boston," Hattie said and returned to the flowers.

~*~

The large, rectangular sunroom of the big house looked like a consignment shop. It was choked with bric-a-brac, uncoordinated furniture, and a large flat-screen TV. An oversize, multi-hued oriental carpet dominated the center of the room and was surrounded on two sides by brown leather couches that were crackled with age. Next to the couches were two Mission end tables complete with Tiffany-style lamps. Against the wall with the window facing the driveway sat an ebony grand piano. The piano hadn't been played in a decade. The lid was closed and covered with stacks of books and magazines. A three-tiered chandelier, dripping with dusty Austrian crystals, hung from the high ceiling above the piano. Along the right wall was an arched opening to a hallway. The floor-to-ceiling space along the wall on both sides and above the arch was covered with dozens of framed paintings, drawings, and photos of various sizes—all portraits of women and girls. An ornate Louis-XVI-style games table and two heavily carved walnut chairs of the same period were positioned behind a leather couch.

Myra Silk was seated at the games table, a bottle of crimson nail polish and a set of manicure tools spread in a semicircle in front of her. She was dressed in a Chinese-style embroidered robe, and matching cloth slippers. Her black hair was pulled back in a tight bun. She was animatedly talking on a cell phone when Hattie entered the room through the dining-room pocket doors. Hattie had removed her colorful apron and bandana and was carrying a tall crystal vase filled with freshly cut flowers. She placed the vase on the console table next to the TV. Myra energetically waved her free hand in the air, motioning for Hattie to take the opposite chair.

"Call as soon as you know anything more," the old lady hissed. "Right away—don't worry about the time." She paused to listen. "Yes, yes, I know you are. We'll talk about that later, won't we?" She turned off the phone and set it next to the manicure tools on the table.

Myra's thin lips were set in a deep frown. "That was Clarisse; she says there's big trouble at the clinic." Myra continued staring into Hattie's pink eyes. "Maggie escaped from rehab. She locked the nurse in a closet, stole her purse, and took her car."

Hattie slowly shook her head. "She attack the nurse—go for her throat?"

"She just pushed the nurse into the closet and locked it."

"Hmm. Well, maybe the meds are makin' her less violent... When this happen?"

"Clarisse wasn't positive, sometime over the weekend. They found the nurse, then called Clarisse."

Hattie looked puzzled. "Why they call Clarisse instead a

you?"

"Clarisse is set up as Maggie's Power of Attorney. The clinic thinks she's Maggie's domestic partner. I don't want any legal connection with me."

"Nothin' but trouble—that bitch is nothin' but trouble. We shoulda done it 'fore we left."

Myra glared at Hattie. "For the last time, I needed to get her cleaned up first. Don't bring it up again."

"Startin' when you got her from the pimp, she been nothin' but trouble. Druggie whore—you wouldn't listen. All you could see was that body—that body and that face."

Myra's brilliant blue eyes narrowed to slits. "Show some respect; she's as much my flesh and bone as you are. Not another word or you'll feel my wrath—you hear?"

"Savage, druggie," Hattie mumbled, at a sound level she knew from experience to be too low for Myra's age-impaired hearing.

Myra took a nail file from an embroidered zipper bag. "Pennsylvania. She's in Pennsylvania...At least, she was. Got gas with the nurse's credit card—Clarisse traced the card. You know what that means, don't you?"

"She tryin' to get away from you as fast as she can—that's what it mean."

"You stupid girl! She's going to her parents' home near Philadelphia, to get money from Mommy and Daddy—money for drugs."

Hattie frowned. "We gotta go get her? But we jus' got here, an' I'm tired a travelin'."

Myra continued filing. She was unconsciously shaping her fingernails into points. "She'll come; she bears my mark and can't resist my will. We'll be patient and she'll be along soon. You know I'm right, don't you?"

Hattie saw that Myra was very upset. She knew that when Myra was upset, she could easily become the target for Myra's rage. Hattie didn't like pain and quickly tried to shift the old woman's focus. "I met the Hale boy's sister today—his sister and his two babies. Like you thought, them babies are real young. The sister's name is Mary. She told me she's leavin' for her home in Boston as soon as they hire a nanny. She said that the Hale boy is gonna be takin' his babies back north in a couple months—that doesn't give us much time to get to them."

Myra shook the bottle of nail polish. "One thing at a time," she said in a soft, nervous voice. "One thing at a time. First, we'll take care of Maggie and our little problem. Then, we'll see to the babies."

4

"I can only stay in America for five more months, Mr. Hale. I'm on a student visa and that's when it expires." Nila and Gordon were sitting at the kitchen table.

"Will you please stop calling me 'Mr. Hale'? It makes me feel ancient. I can't be that much older than you. How old are you, exactly?"

"Sorry Mis—Gordon. It goes against my training to use your first name, but I'll try. I'm twenty-three."

Gordon stood, went to the coffeemaker, and filled his cup. He motioned with the pot to Nila. She shook her head.

"I'm not sure how long we'll be staying in Florida before we go back to Massachusetts. Two months, perhaps three at the most. Where will you go when you leave Castle Key?"

"I'll have to go back to London, at least for a while. I've been told that if I don't get myself into any trouble I could stay on even when my visa runs out. Apparently, the immigration authorities seldom come searching for British girls with expired student visas. The problem is that if I left the States after my visa had expired, I might have problems getting another visa in the future."

"You wanna come back?"

"Oh, not just come back—I want to live in America. In Florida. Florida suits me perfectly. Someday, I'm going to live in a little place on the beach. Not Castle Key—it's far too expensive. I couldn't live here even in my wildest dreams. I'm working on a plan to get a green card so that I can eventually stay for good. I'm looking for a sponsor."

Mary bustled down the hall and into the kitchen. "Well, that's settled," she said, putting her hand on Nila's shoulder. "Mrs. Anderson says to tell you how much she misses you." She turned toward Gordon. "It seems that our certified nanny is a superstar; Mrs. Anderson said that she's had lots of staff over the years, but none as capable as Nila."

Nila lowered her head. "Mrs. Anderson is a sweet lady. Perhaps she'll take me on again next time I come over."

Mary patted Nila's shoulder. "I think there's no doubt about that."

Gordon sat down again and faced Nila. "Why did you leave the Andersons?"

"Amy Cartwright invited me to spend a month with her at her family's Castle Key home. I met Amy when she was an art student in London. She was in a drawing class and I was a model. I pick up the odd quid modeling from time to time."

"Oh, how interesting." Mary sat on the chair next to Nila's. "Do you model nude? I've always wanted to model nude but never had the opportunity. I'm too old now—too many stretch marks."

Nila grinned. "Mostly bare bum and breasts," she said. "Actually, I prefer full-nude—it pays more. It's all quite respectable, you know—nothing salacious. You undress, put on a robe, go into the studio, take off the robe, and sit or stand for an hour or so. The professor walks about, and the students draw or paint. The only conversation is if the professor asks you to change position. That's it. Then you dress and go home."

"Don't the male students try to hit on you?" Mary asked.

"You mean chat me up?"

"Right. Chat ya up."

"No, that's never happened. Amy's the only one from class I ever bumped into—in a taxi queue."

Gordon leaned back in his chair. "I assume you gave Mrs. Anderson reasonable notice that you were leaving?"

"That was all worked out in advance before I took the job. I arranged with Amy to stay here with her on Castle Key a year ago. Mrs. Anderson knew from the start that I'd be leaving after Christmas. Amy went home to Philadelphia ten days ago. She said that I could either stay on until the end of the month when her parents arrive or drive up to Pennsylvania with her. I didn't much fancy going to Pennsylvania. She said that this time of the year it's cold and damp, just like London."

Mary interrupted her. "So, you'd be interested in this position for the next few months?"

"Yes, I would. It fits perfectly with my plans and the children are at the age I enjoy the most. I've never taken care of identical twins before. It would be great fun. They're gorgeous—their dark hair and green eyes make a stunning combination."

Mary stood. "That's settled, then. Let me show you the guest room where I've been staying. The guest room shares a bath with the nursery, so it'll be quite convenient for you. You and I can discuss your salary, days off, and so forth. Gordon's hopeless with practical things."

Gordon leaned forward and placed his palms on the edge of the table. "Now, wait just a minute! You said mornings or afternoons. I never agreed to a full-time employee."

Mary put her hands on her hips and turned to Gordon. "Nila's just told you she won't have a place to stay after the end of the month. The guest room's going to be empty; it makes perfect sense for Nila to stay here."

"I'm very flexible, Gordon. I'm sure that whatever level of assistance you require, I can accommodate. I like to spend my free time on the beach, sketching and painting, so I can be out of the house for as long as you wish. I don't really think that there's much chance of finding an inexpensive bed-and-breakfast or bedsit on Castle Key in the high season."

For the first time since Mary had marched Nila into the kitchen, Gordon took a careful look at her. She was a trim five-foot-five, with long, straight brown hair surrounding an oval-shaped face, large dark eyes, a honey-brown complexion, and lips that appeared more accustomed to smiling than frowning. Mary's description was accurate: Nila was quite attractive, in a chiseled-feature sort of way. Taken separately, her broad forehead, strong chin, high cheekbones, and prominent nose might each be considered severe, but together they formed an attractive, character-filled face. It was obvious why she was an artist's model.

Gordon leaned back from the table. "And just exactly what work do you think you'd do here?"

"Well, as I said, I'd be willing to accommodate your needs. Mary's explained that you'd want to take part in the children's care. What I'd suggest is that I get up with the babies in the morning, feed and dress them while you bathe and have breakfast. If you chose to be with them in the afternoon, then I could pop down to the village and do the grocery shopping and any errands you require. You have a car, don't you?"

Mary nodded. "Mother's old Buick isn't much to look at, but it's reliable."

"One thing: I'm a good driver, but I only have a British driving license, not an American one. Amy let me drive her car. It's a sports model, with a gearshift. She didn't think there'd be a problem if I stayed on the island. I'm getting around by bicycle now."

"I don't think the Buick's ever ventured off the island. It was Mother's winter car."

Nila turned toward Gordon. "Cooking isn't usually part of the job, but since I have to feed myself, I'd be happy to cook for you as well. Simple things, mind you—I never learned to cook posh. We could decide who would get up with the children during the night when they need attention. Perhaps we could take turns?"

Gordon shrugged. "I'm used to getting up with them during the night," he said. "We'll see how it goes."

Mary took Gordon's comment as an act of surrender. "Come on, Nila," she said. "I'll show you the guest room."

Mary gently closed the guest-room door and motioned for Nila to sit in the worn, padded vanity chair, the only chair in the room, and then leaned on a tall bedpost. "Nila, besides helping with the twins, there's another reason I need you to be here. I need you to keep an eye on my brother. As you and I discussed, he's been through hell this past year, and I'm concerned that he's kept most of the stress bottled up inside. I'm not sure when, or how, or even if he's ever gonna let it out. Gordy's always been a bit on the wild side—nothing crazy, no drugs or violent behavior—he's just a fun guy who's always joking around. In college and law school he was a good student, but his friends always said that he could smell a party a mile away. He settled down some after his marriage, and even more so when Karen was diagnosed with cancer. Karen was more serious, but she was fun-loving, too. They were a good match. Not long before she died, Karen told me that she couldn't remember the two of them ever having had a deep and meaningful conversation."

"Of course. I've only just met Gordon, but he does seem quite a solemn bloke."

"Exactly," Mary said, nodding. "He's not the boy I've known for twenty-nine years. Karen's brain cancer and death have left him confused and emotionally damaged. Don't get me wrong—I'm not asking you to spy on him. Just be sensitive to his moods and let me know if you think he's acting depressed. That's all. I'll call from time to time and check up on the four of you; you and I can talk then. Here are my contact numbers; you can always reach me on my cell." She removed a business card from the back pocket of her cutoff jeans and placed it on the bedspread. "Are you okay with that?"

Nila scanned the card, which read "Gowns by Milton."

"Is Milton your husband?"

"He is. Milt's a fashion designer. He used to be a costume designer for the film studios and still has a celebrity following. We do wedding gowns and formal gowns."

"How exciting. Perhaps one day he can do a wedding gown for me?"

"Milt would be pleased to create something sensational for you when the time comes. Just be sure to marry well—Milt's services don't come cheap. So, you're okay if I call every week? That won't be an imposition?"

"That won't be a problem. The four of us will get on just fine, I'm sure of it."

5

Detective Doyle held the phone to his ear while he flipped through the stack of gruesome photos lying on his desk, photos he'd retrieved from the coroner's photographer. A call from Chief of Detectives Browning directly to the coroner had insured that no additional prints of the photos would ever be made.

The phone crackled to life. "Sorry I had to put ya'll on hold." A voice with a distinct Southern drawl called out. "It was the Chief, he don't like to be kept waitin'—likes to throw his weight around."

"Yeah, same everywhere," Doyle grunted. "Like I was sayin', Sergeant, the girl you're askin' about is dead. This Amy Cartwright had a heart attack and died. She was only twenty-four."

"Drugs?" Sergeant Crowley asked.

"Nothin', she was clean. She was staying by herself at her parents' house when she died. Took a while before the body was discovered. It had started to decompose—pretty nasty."

"Let me start over, Detective. That interruption got me all confused and—"

"Good idea," Doyle said. "All I got was that you found the Cartwright girl's car at a probable homicide scene."

"That's right. Nearly new Corvette, an expensive, high-performance model, was in the parking lot of a local liquor store in Hopkis, a rural Florida town just a few miles south of the Georgia border. We called in the Pennsylvania plate number and Amy Cartwright was ID'd as the owner of the car. A customer found the young store clerk bleeding behind the package store's counter and called 911. By the time the EMTs got there the clerk was dead. He'd been shot three times at close range. Twice in the chest and once in the neck. The cash register drawer was open, and all the money gone."

Doyle sat up straight. "He was shot in the neck, you said?"

"Yeah, shot in the throat at point-blank range. It was a bloody mess—neck all torn up."

Doyle flipped through the photos on his desk to the image of Amy Cartwright's throat wounds. "You're positive it was a gunshot wound—not caused by somethin' else?"

"What do ya mean? It had to be a bullet wound; it was too torn up to be a knife wound. I don't know anything more—haven't seen the coroner's report yet."

"Was there a surveillance system in operation?" Doyle asked.

"Yeah, there was. The owner of the business is well known around town as a miser and he had put in a cheap, black-an'-white system, so the images of the suspect weren't real detailed or clear. All we could tell for sure was that the suspect was a female—a medium-height female—with long, light-colored, probably blonde hair. No clear facial details are visible."

Doyle frowned. "Not much to go on."

"Hell no," the sergeant replied. "We was hoping that we could find out more from the owner of the Corvette—obviously that ain't gonna happen."

"Obviously. Find anything useful in the car?"

"Weed—a half-dozen roaches in the ashtray. There was a plastic zipper bag in the glove box full of jewelry: rings, bracelets, earrings. Forensics are checkin' the stuff out now to see if any of it is real."

"Look, Sergeant, I'm sorry to be a pain in the ass, but I need to have a written request from your office to release contact info for Amy Cartwright's parents. An email under a letterhead would do. You know, procedure."

"No problem. We just need to find out what to do with the Corvette after forensics release it. I'll get on the email as soon as I hang up. Thanks for your help."

6

It was exactly six weeks since Mary had returned to Boston. Nila and Gordon had settled into a routine. Nila got up with the twins in the morning while Gordon checked his email, made himself breakfast, and then read the paper. Gordon took over in the afternoon while Nila went out to the beach or drove the old Buick into town. In the evening, Nila occasionally threw together a simple meal—more often, one of them picked up sandwiches, burgers, pizza, or a Chinese takeout. Nila was addicted to American fast food. After dinner, Gordon would work on the computer in the small study that also served as a secure hurricane shelter. Nila would put the twins to bed, wash the dishes, and then read or watch television. Sometimes they watched a movie together. Gordon usually got up with the girls during the night when they fussed, unless Nila heard them before he did. Mrs. Kavlosky was happy to be rescued from retirement, and cleaned and did the laundry two afternoons a week.

Nila had just come in from the beach. Although it was only April, it felt like summer, and she hadn't bothered to put a cover-up on over her bikini. She looked in on the twins, who were fast asleep. Gordon wasn't in his study or the kitchen, so she assumed that he must be napping as well. The old-fashioned, yellowed-white wall phone in the kitchen rang and she rushed to pick it up before the noise woke the babies.

"Seven-five-two-double-six-two-four."

"Nila, haven't you learned? The Yanks just say 'hello' when they answer the phone." It was Nila's sister, Della.

"Doo-Doo! How wonderful to hear your voice!"

The sisters chatted for ten minutes, about how Della had finally made the decision to move in with her boyfriend, their mum's health, and business at the family travel agency. Then it was Nila's turn.

"It's quite remarkable—I've never taken care of identical twins before. It's like they're one being in two bodies, as if their brains are wired together. When they play with toys, it's like there's one baby with four hands. And they're so dear. Such beautiful children, almost always smiling and happy."

"Are they really exactly the same? Can't their father tell them apart?"

"Oh no he can't. I'm the only one who can tell them apart. Gordy thinks he can—but he can't. He often mixes them up…By the way, he's asked me to call him 'Gordy.'"

"How do you know who is who?"

"Not telling—it's my special secret."

"You two are still getting on? You and Gordy?"

"Gordy is really sweet. He's polite, funny, and never cross. It's like staying with a close friend."

"Is he still grieving for his wife?"

"Not outwardly—no tears and hardly anything ever said about his poor wife. There's a shroud of sadness hovering around him but nothing more. I don't know whether he's holding it all in or if he's already let it out and is moving on with his life."

"Last call you told me he wasn't bad-looking."

Nila moved the phone to her other ear. "Actually, he's quite handsome and…"

"Hmm, any messing about goin' on?"

Nila chuckled. "Well, under different circumstances who knows? Hold on just a minute." She reached out with her free hand and closed the door to the hall, then lowered her voice to a whisper. "Late Wednesday night, the twins woke me, so I got up to change their nappies—that's another thing: they always need changing at the same time. Really—always. Anyway, it was a hot night, and I was groggy and knackered. Gordy came to the nursery; the only light was from the bathroom off to the side. He saw that I was almost finished and just stood in the doorway. He didn't say anything. As he was going back to bed, he paused and looked at me. 'Thanks,' he said. 'I can see why they pay you to model.' I looked down and realized that I wasn't wearing any knickers!"

"You are joking!"

"Really, no knickers! It's so warm here that I usually sleep starkers, and the top I'd pulled on barely came to my navel."

"That's it? He hasn't followed up?"

"No, he hasn't said a thing."

Nila heard excited squeals coming from the nursery. "Sounds like my princesses are stirring. Better get them ready for their dinner. Thanks so much for the call. I'll ring you up next time. Gordy doesn't mind if I use the phone. He's very generous with his money…I'll call you at the office next Tuesday, like we planned. Love you. Cheers."

The twins were plotting an escape from their cribs and didn't notice when Nila entered the nursery. Julie had managed to pull the fitted sheet from the mattress and had it slung over the crib rail. Janna squatted in her crib, trying to free the sheet from her mattress as well.

"All right, you two imps—I caught you in the act!"

Julie squealed and slapped one hand against the crib rail while she held on with the other hand. Janna tried to stand in her crib but fell over onto her side.

"Maa," Julie called. "Maa."

"No, it's Naa…Naa. Nanny. Nanny."

"Maa," Julie cried again, while Janna bounced up and down, echoing the cry. "Maa, Maa."

Nila shook her head. "Maybe we should settle on Mammy instead of Nanny—you've got the Maa part down to a tee." She shook her hands in the air and rolled her head. "Mammy, Mammy!" she called in a theatrical voice.

Gordon stood in the doorway, grinning. "Where'd you learn about Mammy?"

Nila hadn't heard him approach the nursery. She dropped

her hands and swiveled in his direction. "Couldn't sleep last night, so I watched the end of a dreadful old documentary series about what happened to Negros after your Civil War. Why did white Americans paint their faces black, their lips white, and pretend to be Negros?"

"Oh, you mean minstrel shows? A long time ago white people used to put on what they called minstrel shows—live variety shows imitating black comedians and singers. Nobody does it today. It would be considered highly racist."

"I should think the coloreds wouldn't have much liked being mocked that way. Did the coloreds paint their faces white?"

Gordon grinned. "In America, we say 'blacks' or 'African-Americans.' The terms 'Negro' and 'colored' aren't really used anymore. I don't know what black people did. We didn't have a lot of blacks in the town where I grew up. Not like the South—like here in Florida."

"I have a bunch of colored—er, black half-brothers in Africa."

Gordon screwed up his face. "I thought you were English?"

"I am. Just after my sister Della was born, Dad and Mum packed up the two of us girls and moved from London to Ghana, back to where Dad's family's from. I was only about three or four."

"Your father's African?"

"Hubert. Dad's name is Hubert. He was born in Ghana but has dual citizenship and a British passport. His father—my grandfather—was British. Dad met Mum when he was in London at university, and they married when he graduated. Mum says that he was never happy living in England. She'd spent most of her life within fifty miles of London, her birthplace, but after a while she could see that either she'd have to give living in Ghana a go, or he would eventually leave her. Guess their marriage was doomed from the start. He's a handsome man. I take after him more than I do Mum. Mum's fair—and so's my sister, Della. Dad has a dark complexion—darker than mine. Like I said, Dad's father was British—Caucasian—but my grandmother—her name's Juba—is African. Mum stuck it out in Ghana for just over a year before she left and took Della and me back to London. She said that our grandmother did everything she could to make Mum's life miserable and to chase her away. For a while after we left, Dad used to send Della and me little presents. I was going on five when we returned to England and can only remember bits of our time in Ghana. I still have a small carved wooden bird he sent—a voodoo charm, Mum said. That's my only link with him. I have no real memories of dear old Dad."

"So, you don't have any connections with your father? You don't really know much about his life?"

"Only what I learned from my gran, Mum's mother. Before she died, she told me that after their divorce, Dad married a local woman and had lots of kids. They're all boys, and black as coal, she said. I've always fantasized that one day I'd go to Ghana and find him, put out my hand, and say 'Hi, Dad. I'm your daughter, Naki.' I'll never do it, though. After 'Hi, Dad,' there'd be nothing more for either of us to say to each other."

"Naki?" Gordon said with a puzzled look on his face.

"That's my Ashanti clan name; it means first-born."

"I see," Gordon nodded. "Your parents' story is kinda like my parents' story, but in a different way."

"Oh?"

"Yeah, mostly my parents lived apart, but they stayed married. No divorce. When he was about forty, Father started spending the week living in Boston: working, womanizing, gambling, drinking, and raising hell. He always came home on Saturday afternoon and then went to church with Mother, Mary, and me on Sunday morning."

"He was that religious?"

The left corner of Gordon's mouth turned up in a half-grin. "Not religious at all. We're Unitarians; that barely qualifies as a religion."

Nila frowned. "I don't understand."

"Unitarians believe in one God, if that. It's sort of a minimalist religion for people who don't want lots of rules. Father came home every weekend because he could never admit to himself that he wasn't a doting husband and father. As far as I know, he and Mother slept in the same bed on Saturday nights. From Saturday morning 'til Sunday afternoon, Mother would be sober and cheerful. As soon as he left, she'd start drinking again."

"I still don't understand why he would do such a thing."

"He needed to pretend that we were a happy family. Ever hear of Nathan Hale?"

Nila shook her head.

"Well, old Nate was my great-great-great-uncle and one of the heroes of the American Revolutionary War. He got caught spying on the British troops and they hanged him from a tree. Over the years, there have been lots of famous and infamous Hales in New England: senators, a governor, and a Supreme Court justice. In the self-important, twisted world in which my father was raised, the pretense of propriety was more important than how one lived. Father was a judge—a federal judge—and an important man."

"What about your mother?"

"Mother's ancestors came to this country from Germany a long time ago. They were industrialists who built factories and got rich making blankets and uniforms for the Union troops during the Civil War. She was an only child, so the family fortune—or what was left of it—fell to her. She died a year and a half ago and left this beach house to me and a lake house in New Hampshire to Mary, along with enough stocks and bonds so that neither of us really needs to work again."

Nila shook her head again. "What I meant was: how did your mother put up with your father's infidelity?"

"Father's sins were never mentioned. We all lived with the charade that his important work required him to be in Boston six nights a week. Mother loved him deeply and was willing to accept him on whatever terms he offered."

"Gordy, that's really sad. It must have been unpleasant for you."

"Not really. Mary's seven years older than me. She sorta took over the role of father—and when Mother was blotto, she filled in for her as well."

"That explains why you and Mary are so close."

"She's a mom, a dad, and a sister all in one. Mostly she treats me like her brother, but sometimes like her son. We've been through a lot together."

"How about Karen's family? You've said she had a similar upbringing."

Gordon shook his head. "Karen's mother, Adele, came from an old New England family, but the similarity with the Hales stops there. Adele's an ethereal-type academic who teaches drama at Boston College. She had two kids in her twenties and then divorced and never remarried. Karen was an out-of-wedlock surprise who came along years later. Karen's half-brother is a lawyer like me, and her half-sister owns a real estate business. Unlike their artsy mother, they're pretty much old-school New England conservatives."

Nila lifted Julie from her crib while Gordon picked up Janna. They sat the two babies on the large changing table. "This one needs changing. Yours?"

Gordon pulled Janna's diaper away from her waist to inspect it. "Phew, mine too."

"If you take their nappies off and clean them up, I'll draw a bath," she said.

Nila filled the tub with warm, sudsy water and returned. "Here, I'll take Julie. You bring Janna in."

"I think you got them confused. This is Julie."

"No, Gordy. You've got Janna."

"How can you be so sure? I think this is Julie."

"It's a woman thing. I can tell from their personalities and by the way they move and talk. You've got Janna."

"Maybe we'll cut Janna's hair shorter, and then there'd be no doubt." On cue, Janna smacked Gordon on the nose with her hand. "Ouch, that hurt!"

Nila grinned. "Careful! They understand everything we say."

Gordon shook his head. "All right, no haircuts. At least, not now."

~*~

Nila stepped into the tub, sat, and placed Julie between her legs. She gently poked Julie's navel. "He'll never guess that you're the twin with the slightly convex belly-button," she cooed to the baby. Julie laughed loudly as she splashed her arms in the bath water.

"You can bring Janna in now," Nila called to Gordon.

"Are you decent?"

"I don't know about decent—I'm still in my bikini."

Gordon knelt by the side of the tub and carefully lowered Janna into the water between Nila's legs, facing Julie.

"When you bathe them in the tub like this, make sure you put your back to the spout and taps. They could get a nasty injury if they fell into the spout," Nila said.

"I've only ever bathed them in the plastic tub. That's how Karen and Mary did it."

"They're getting too big for the little tub. Besides, it's much easier to bathe the two at once this way and they enjoy the splashing."

"How long have you been doing this, Nila? Being a nanny, I mean?"

"Since I left school—about five years."

"You learned about childcare at school?"

"No. Actually, I studied for university. Do you know how the

English school system works?"

Gordon shook his head. "Not really."

"I got five A-levels, enough to get into a decent university, but it just didn't work out. Mum got sick, and Della and I, with Mum's assistant, had to run her business: a travel-bookings agency. By the time she got well, I'd lost interest in going to university. So I went to classes and became a nanny. It's fine for now, but I don't fancy doing it for the rest of my life. I expect I'll have my own little ones someday. Maybe beautiful twins, like these two, if I'm lucky."

Julie reached up to grab Nila's hair but instead accidentally pulled down the side of Nila's bikini top. Nila's left breast slid out of the bra. Gordon noticed that, while not particularly large, her breast was well-formed with a brown, perky nipple. He knew that he should look away but found himself unable to do so.

Nila looked down. "Can you pull that strap over my shoulder?"

Gordon fumbled with the strap, but the breast remained exposed.

"Here, hold this squirming baby." Nila pulled the bra top up and adjusted the strap. Gordon was blushing.

Nila smiled. "I might as well show you the other one. Then you'll have seen the whole package."

"I'm sorry about the other night. It was rude of me to mention that you weren't dressed. I shoulda kept quiet."

"It doesn't matter. I would have noticed eventually, when I got back in bed. It was less embarrassing for me that you said something. That way I didn't have to wonder what you saw and what you didn't. Don't think anything of it."

For the last two days, Gordon had thought of little else.

7

"Hello…seven-five-two-double-six-two-four," Nila answered.

"What?"

"This is the Hale residence."

"Who is this? Who are you?"

"This is Nila Rawlings."

"Nila who? Who are you?"

"I'm the nanny."

"Oh, I see. Let me talk to Gordy."

"I'm sorry. Mr. Hale isn't available."

"Oh, he isn't…Where is he?"

"I believe he drove to the village."

"What village? What are you talking about?"

Nila rolled her eyes. "If you give me your name and telephone number, I'll give them to him when he returns."

"When will he be back?"

"I don't know. He didn't say."

"Tell him that Maggie called."

Nila wasn't enjoying the conversation and decided to have a little fun. "Let me write that down… McGee. Is that Mrs. McGee?"

"What? No, it's *Maggie,* not McGee, you idiot."

"I'm sorry, Mrs. Maggie. Does Mr. Hale have your telephone number?"

"It's just Maggie, not Mrs. Maggie. The number's two-oh-seven-six-six-two-five."

"Let me repeat that back to you. Two-naught-seven-double-six-two-five."

"I don't know what you're saying! Forget about the number. Just tell Gordy I'll call back soon."

Nila affected her best minstrel-show accent. "Yes'm, I surely do dat."

Maggie slammed down the phone.

Nila put the phone back on the wall and started to laugh. "Bloody cow!"

Nila was setting out the ingredients for the twins' lunch when Gordon strolled into the kitchen, a large paper bag dangling by the handles from each hand. "You are in for a great treat—Kopel's just got in some fresh stone crabs. Ever had stone crab?"

"Can't say that I have. Is it like lobster? I had lobster once with Amy—it was lovely."

"No, not like lobster." Gordon took a large paper-wrapped parcel from the shopping bag and unfolded it to reveal a dozen off-white and salmon-pink crab claws.

"Those are huge! Where's the rest of the crab?"

"That's it. You only eat the claws. Just one claw—one claw from each crab. When they catch 'em, they break off the bigger claw of the two and then throw the crab back."

"What a waste. You don't eat the whole crab—just one claw?"

"The crab doesn't die—it grows a new claw in a year or two. The season will be over soon, so we were lucky that Kopel's had these."

"I hope you're planning on fixing them. I wouldn't know what to do."

"Sure, I'll fix 'em, they're already cooked. The only preparation is cracking the shells. I'll do that just before dinner. And look what else!" Gordon put his hand in the bag and pulled out several ears of fresh corn.

"That's corn, isn't it? I've never seen corn with the green and hairy bits attached."

"Corn on the cob, with butter and salt—it's ambrosia." He put the crab legs and corn into the fridge and then turned to the second bag. "I got this nice bottle of Chablis, as well. You do like wine, don't you?"

Nila smiled. "I do, indeed."

Gordon put the bottle into the fridge. "This will go perfectly with the stone crab."

"Gordy, the wine is a surprise. I thought that you didn't drink. You haven't had a drop the entire time I've been here."

Gordon started to put the jars of baby food and boxes of baby cereal he'd bought into the cupboard. "If you promise not to tell a soul, I'll let you in on a dark family secret. The Hales are all alcoholics; it runs in the blood. My father was a heavy drinker. Whiskey. I rarely saw my mother totally sober—she was almost always in control of herself but just a bit tipsy. Mary had a drinking incident at Smith—that's a college—and she hardly drinks anything at all now, except at weddings and family events. That's the dark secret."

"And you?"

"I had a few incidents after drinking too much beer in college, but I love wine. My law-school roommate's family was in the wine business, in Oregon. So my legal education included a lot of wine instruction and experience as well as law. Karen and I almost always had a glass or three with dinner. After she died, with our family history, I wasn't sure that I could trust myself not to take refuge in the bottle. So I cleared out all Mother's bottles of vodka and gin and decided not to buy any more wine. That is, until today."

"Why today?"

Gordon shrugged. "I don't know. I guess I just remembered how well a nice white wine goes with stone crab. Maybe I'm feeling more confident about not turning into a street person. I don't really know." He changed the subject. "Are you going out to sketch this afternoon?"

"In a bit. I thought I'd feed the girls first—unless you want to."

"I don't mind. Either way's fine."

"I'll do it in a few minutes. I'm making myself a hot dog on a bun with crisps for lunch. Interested?"

"That would be great—thanks. Did you finish the drawing of the pelicans on the driftwood?"

"It's almost done."

"Can I see it?"

"If you set the table and get out the mustard, or whatever you want for your hot dog, I'll get my sketchbook. Iced tea okay?"

Gordon nodded. "Sure."

Nila returned and set the sketchbook in front of Gordon. "There are a couple of new things in there you haven't seen." She leaned over his shoulder and turned to a pencil drawing of the twins. "I did this earlier in the week, when they were absorbed watching a ladybird crawling up the screen door."

"What kind of bird?"

"No, not a bird. A ladybird—an insect. You know, a tiny little thing with a red back and black spots?"

"You mean a ladybug."

"Ladybird, ladybug…"

Gordon turned the sketchbook toward the light. "Nila, this is really good; this is the best one yet. You've captured their personalities—just look at those serious expressions!"

"I'm happy you like it. I was rather chuffed myself."

"Chuffed?"

"You know, pleased."

"You really are talented. Have you ever thought of pursuing a career in the arts?"

Nila shook her head. "I'm not that good. Really, I'm not. I've seen enough student work in the art school I modeled at to know that I'm about average. Even with lots of instruction, I'd still be average. It's only my hobby—the way I focus on the small bits of life."

"How about if I buy this sketch? It could be your first sale on the road to fame and riches!"

Nila laughed. "How about I give it to you instead?"

"That's very generous of you. You'll have to sign it—it'll be worth a fortune when you're discovered."

"I'm afraid you're probably the only one who'll discover me."

Gordon grinned. "Maybe so."

Nila moved the sketchbook to the kitchen counter and set a plate with a hot dog in a bun and potato chips in front of Gordon. Nila set down a plate for herself and joined Gordon at the table. They ate in silence for several minutes, until the phone rang.

Nila stood and moved toward the phone. "Gordy, I'm so sorry. I forgot to tell you that a woman named Maggie phoned while you were gone. I think she's Amy Cartwright's sister."

Gordon made a sour face. "Did she leave a message?" The phone continued to ring.

"No, she just said she'd call back. I must say, she wasn't exactly pleasant."

"She rarely is, unless she's trying to get her way. Let it ring. I don't want to talk to her."

"She's a friend?"

"Hardly. Maggie is strikingly beautiful, rich, and thoroughly indulged. She thinks that the world and everyone in it—including me—exists for her amusement."

Nila sat down again. "That doesn't sound at all like Amy. Amy's attractive, and obviously not short on brass, but she doesn't flaunt either her looks or her money."

"I don't know Amy. The Cartwright sisters are like Mary and me in reverse order. Maggie's my age—about eight years older than Amy."

"You've got that wrong—Amy's the same age as me. If you're the same age as her sister, then that would make Amy about six years younger."

"Whadya mean?"

"I'm almost twenty-four and you're almost thirty—so there are about six years between us. It would be the same for them." The phone stopped ringing.

Gordon wiped his lips with a paper napkin. "Just six years,

huh? What I was trying to say was that Amy was very young when I stayed here in the summer. I only remember her as a skinny little kid."

"I thought that you only spent winter school holidays here. Isn't that what you told me?"

Gordon shook his head. "I went into forced exile the summer between my junior and senior years at college. I got a DUI—do you know what that is?"

Nila nodded. "Drunk driving."

"Right, drunk driving. The court took away my driver's license for twelve months. It was a second offense and the judge was going to put me in jail for a month, but Uncle Duncan, our lawyer, convinced him to put me under house arrest in Castle Key for the rest of the summer. So, Mary and Mother put me under the supervision of my maiden aunt, and sent the two of us here to the beach cottage: no license, no car, no beer, no social life, and no fun. At that time, Castle Key was a pretty quiet place for a nineteen-year-old without a car, even more so than today. Aunt Ella was an effective prison warden and took my court-imposed sentence quite seriously. But, after her evening sherry, she was always asleep by ten."

"But you didn't have a car."

"No, but Maggie did—a classic Jaguar roadster. I met her not long after my sentence started. I was walking on the beach. She was with a couple of girlfriends, sunning at the back of the Cartwrights' pool house—you know, by those huge royal palms."

Nila nodded.

"I waved, and they waved back, so I joined them. Maggie was sensational—long blonde hair, pretty face, perfect figure, skimpy bikini, bronzed all over, and wide brown eyes. My senses were overwhelmed, and I instantly fell in lust."

Nila laughed. "And did this goddess reciprocate your lustful desires?"

"Hold on—I'll get to that. After a couple of gin and tonics, I explained my situation and Maggie volunteered to pick me up out at the main road that night. Maggie knew every bar and disco on the west coast of Florida where underage kids could get a drink and dance. We spent the next seven weeks exploring them all."

"Your aunt never caught on?"

"Never. I was sorta like a vampire who had to be home before the sun came up. Out at eleven and always home in bed by three or four. Mrs. Kavlosky figured things out, but she never told Aunt Ella."

"Mrs. Kavlosky saw you in Maggie's car?"

Gordon chuckled. "Not exactly. When she was doing the wash, she discovered some Trojans I'd left in my trouser pocket."

"Trojans?"

"You know—rubbers."

Nila looked puzzled. "I don't understand why would you have rubbers in your pocket."

Gordon reddened. "Birth control," he said.

"Oh, you mean condoms! Rubbers are erasers, like on the ends of pencils."

Gordon shook his head. "So much for speaking the same language."

"So I take it from the condoms—rubbers—that Maggie did return your lust?"

"All summer long."

"I don't get it. Maggie was beautiful, sexy, and rich. She rescued you, took you to all the fun places, and had sex with you—I take it the sex was okay?"

"Terrific."

"Then why do you say she's not your friend?"

"Simple: I never really knew her. All we did was party, drink, and screw—that means sexual intercourse."

Nila nodded. "We say shag, but screw's universal."

Gordon leaned back in his chair. "Aunt Ella had a medical problem and needed to go back to Boston in mid-August, so Mary took over for the last few weeks of my sentence. Unlike Aunt Ella, Mary didn't give a rat's ass if I rode around in Maggie's car as long as I didn't drive, so I was able to spend some time during the day away from the house with Maggie. My God, she was like Jekyll and Hyde. In the light of day, Maggie became nasty with her parents and housekeeper, rude to shopkeepers, and even demanding of my attention—a thoroughly unpleasant person. She even looked different—cruel and hard."

"That's quite a transformation."

Gordon shook his head. "Not really. Up until then, I'd only seen her for a few hours at a time and always when we were having fun. Never in the daylight and never in real life. A few days before I was to return home, she asked me when we were going to announce our engagement. At first, I laughed, but then realized that she was actually serious. I told her that I had another year of college and then law school ahead of me before I could even think about marriage, to anyone. She exploded. She screamed that I had used her and howled the worst profanities you could imagine. I came back here and told Mary the entire story. Mary just laughed and told me to forget about Maggie. We flew out the next day."

"You never saw her again?"

"Never, but I heard a lot from her. First the letters: one letter would profess her deep love and passion, and the next would say how she hated me for stealing her virginity." Gordon smirked. "I chuckled at that one."

"How long did she keep writing to you?"

"For two or three months. She sent letters to me, to Mary, to my mother, to the dean of the college...Then the phone calls began. Her father's lawyer called, threatening a lawsuit. I started to get paranoid and even imagined that someone was following me. Mary and I went to see Uncle Duncan; he's the managing partner of our family's law firm, the one where I work now. Duncan is well-connected—he made a call and the letters and phone calls stopped. That was it. I never heard from Maggie again, until now."

Nila stood and began to clear the table. "What a bizarre tale. I had an ex-boyfriend once who wouldn't leave me alone, but nothing like that. Are you going to talk with her?"

"I don't think so. What could it possibly accomplish?"

"Maybe she wants to express her sympathy over Karen's death, or maybe to apologize for her past behavior?"

"That doesn't sound like Maggie. And just talking about her creeps me out."

"What should I say if she calls back?"

"Would you mind telling her that I don't wanna talk to her?"

"I wouldn't mind at all."

"She's likely to heap abuse on you."

"Not a problem. I'll just ring off."

Gordon took her hand. "Thanks, Nila. I appreciate your help. I really do appreciate you."

Gordon released her hand, and Nila carried the dishes to the sink.

"Gordy, why don't you come out to the beach with me? After I feed the girls, we can slather them up and take out the playpen. I'll put a sheet over the top to keep them out of the sun. You can read while I finish the pelicans. Wouldn't that be fun? Some fresh air would help clean out your unpleasant thoughts. Why don't you give it a go?"

Gordon smiled as he looked at Nila standing at the chipped, porcelain sink washing dishes: her long, well-formed legs, her shapely rear and slim hips, her brown hair (now with highlights from the sun). Mary had been right; he really did need a certified nanny.

Nila turned toward him just in time to catch his appraisal. She smiled. Gordon smiled back.

8

Nila was using a pliable eraser to create highlights and soften the pencil lines on her drawing. The white pelican that sat frozen on the page of her sketchbook had long since departed from the twisting driftwood branches. With her pencil, she planted several sea-grape bushes behind the driftwood.

The twins were rolling on their backs in the playpen, softly cooing and trying to stuff their toes into their small mouths. The stand of queen palms on the right partially shaded both the playpen and Gordon, who was perched in an uncomfortable-looking, folding beach chair, reading some documents that Nila had picked up from the post office the day before.

The turquoise waters of the Gulf lapped against the beach. The air temperature was in the low eighties, and the water temperature was slightly lower. It was a perfect, chamber-of-commerce, early summer, South Florida day.

"Gordy, did you put sunscreen on your feet? They're looking a bit rosy. Sunburned feet are the worst."

Gordon leaned down and spread a towel over his feet and ankles. "You're right—it happened more than once when I was a kid."

Nila put down her pad and pencil and swiveled around on the beach blanket to face Gordon.

"How long have you been coming to Castle Key?"

Gordon slid the documents he'd been reading back into the manila envelope and dropped it on the sand next to his chair. "Ever since I can remember. My grandfather built the big house in the thirties. The beach house came later, after World War II, I think. When I was small, we used to stay at the beach house—Father as well. Grandmother and Grandfather would hold lotsa parties at the big house and there were always people going in and out. My grandparents died within a short time of each other.

I was young and I don't remember them well. Father didn't want the big house, so he sold it to Myra Silk. The lawns and gardens are well-tended and the house looks like it's been recently painted, so I guess Mrs. Silk still cares about it, even though she seldom stays there anymore."

"Your family used the beach house for holidays?"

"Just Mother, Mary, and me. Like I told you, by then Father was staying in Boston most of the time. It was sad, because Mother really loved him—adored him. She was devastated when his liver gave out and he died. 'Til the day she passed, I never heard her say a single bad thing about Father, although he gave her lots of reasons to be bitter."

Nila pursed her lips together. "Mum's the same—never a strong word for my dad. The first year after we came back from Africa, she always told Della and me—and the neighbors, too—that he was fixing up the family farm in Ghana and would be sending for us soon. Then she just stopped talking about him. Eventually, she got a divorce, but never remarried, although she does have a steady boyfriend now…Did Karen like Castle Key and the beach house?" she asked, changing the subject.

"Last September, shortly after we found out about her cancer, was the first time she came to the island. Before then, we were always too busy. We met only a year before we married, and then there was the planning for the wedding and honeymoon. Three months after the wedding, we discovered she was pregnant. Then, when we got the prognosis that she had less than a year to live, Karen said that she needed to get away from Massachusetts. The way she put it was that she could see pity in everyone's eyes, and that made her afraid. She was a very brave woman. She wasn't more than nominally religious but she said that she knew that her life had a purpose and she was sure that it was bringing the girls into the world. She said that having achieved her purpose, she could peacefully flow back into the river of life that brought her here." Gordon's voice cracked. "And that's exactly what she did." He stood and lifted the corner of the sheet that covered the playpen. "They're out cold. We should take them back to the house soon, don't you think?"

Nila ignored his question. "You don't talk about Karen very often. Is it still too painful?"

Gordon looked out at the water and smiled. "Karen and I knew each other for about three years. Three years from our first meeting to the end. We were very much alike: same family background, same type of schooling, and similar politics. We even shared quite a few friends. That's how we met—through a mutual friend." Facing Nila, he lowered himself onto the beach blanket. "Karen was feminine, intelligent, caring, and very sexy. She was all the things I had always looked for in a woman. I loved her almost from the first time we met. The thing is that I was just starting to get to know her when she died. We had very little history—I don't have a large reserve of memories to draw on. You've never been married, have you?"

Nila shook her head.

"Ever get close?"

She shook her head again.

Gordon gently ran his finger along the edge of Nila's bare foot and gazed at the water. "Maybe you could take one of the girls in now. I'd like to sit here for a few minutes. I'll bring the other along soon. You can just leave everything. I'll come back for the playpen and cooler."

~*~

Julie was asleep. Nila had the baby tucked up on her right hip, with Julie's head resting on her shoulder. When she entered the kitchen, the phone was ringing. Nila took a deep breath and exhaled through her nose. They got few calls during the day—this one was likely to be unpleasant.

"Hale residence."

"Oh, it's you again. Put Gordy on."

"Is this Maggie Cartwright?"

"Of course it's Maggie. Put Gordy on."

"I'm sorry, Miss Cartwright. I gave Mr. Hale your message and he told me that if you called again, I was to tell you that he didn't wish to speak with you."

"What? Who in the hell do you think you are? Go find Gordy and put him on this instant!"

Nila moved the phone away from her ear. The screaming and profanity continued. Nila placed the phone back on the hook. She walked to the nursery and carefully laid Julie into her crib. The baby yawned but didn't open her eyes. Nila stroked Julie's dark curls. "Sleep, sleep, my pretty one," she whispered. Nila exited through the hall to the kitchen but left the nursery door ajar. The phone started to ring again. Nila decided not to answer. After fifteen rings, she lost patience, lifted the phone from the hook, and placed it on the table. As she walked to the bathroom to wash the sand from her feet and legs, she could just make out Maggie's shrill voice behind her.

When Nila returned to the kitchen, the phone had gone quiet. When she placed it to her ear, she heard an oscillating tone. She shrugged and placed it back on the hook. She waited for the phone to ring again, but it remained silent.

~*~

"This one's zonked," Gordy said.

Nila held out her hands and gently lifted Janna from her father's arms.

"It's the warm air and the sun," said Nila. "I feel a bit drowsy myself. Let me put her down and then I can run out for the post. You have any letters going out?"

Gordon shook his head. "Not today. If you don't mind, I'll go. I need to stop at the hardware store to get a hammer for the stone crab. I thought we had a toolkit here somewhere but I can't find it."

"A hammer? You're joking!"

"Nope. That's why they're called stone crabs. You'll see."

Nila started for the nursery with the baby, then turned on her heel. "Maggie called—twice. I gave her your message, and your prediction about smoke coming from the phone was correct. When she called the second time, I just left the phone off the hook. I guess she gave up screaming after a while."

Gordon put his hand on Nila's arm. "I'm sorry—it was thoughtless of me to put you through that. If the phone rings while I'm out, don't answer it. When she calls again, I'll talk with her. It'll be a very short conversation. Okay?"

"It wasn't uncomfortable. I've heard worse. Think I'll take a catnap while you're gone. The little ones should be out 'til dinnertime."

Gordon gently squeezed her arm and headed for the garage. "Oh, your sketchpad's on the table. I brought in everything except the playpen and cooler. Leave them—I'll get 'em when I come back."

~*~

Nila took the towels and beach blanket outside and shook out the sand. She listened for the distinctive exhaust notes of the old Buick as Gordon turned from the driveway onto the main road, then slowly walked the short distance back to the beach, grasping the fine sand between her toes. She perched on the cooler, gazed out at the calm Gulf waters, and let her mind wander.

Nila understood that she was purposely suppressing her growing affection for Gordon. Although Gordon was obviously still emotionally wounded, his recent behavior left no doubt that he was sexually attracted to her. But was it really her, she thought, or could it be any good-looking young woman with whom he shared such constant, close contact? For the last nine weeks, the two of them had seen or spoken to few people besides each other—the post office and the shops were the outer boundaries of their world. What would be the outcome if she followed her own rising desires, responded to Gordon's gentle advances, and they wound up in bed together?

The shadow of a low-flying gull momentarily blocked her view of the water and interrupted her thoughts. "Not now. I'll sort myself out tomorrow," Nila said aloud.

She stood up, stretched, and then dragged the playpen back to the house and into the living room. When she stepped back through the French doors into the kitchen, she sensed that something was different. There was an odor in the air: Sweat? Musk? Douche? That was it: the bittersweet, antiseptic smell of an old woman. One of the twins began to cry. Nila moved quickly to the open nursery door.

Although she had never seen her before, Nila instinctively knew that the creature hovering over Janna's crib was Maggie. The beautiful, sexy Maggie that Gordon described had degenerated into a living cadaver. She stared at Nila through blood-shot, rodent-like eyes. Her dark roots had grown out three inches and made it look like her long blonde hair was pasted onto a dirty scalp. Her clothing was several sizes too large and hung on her body like rags draped over a scarecrow.

"Get away from that baby!" Nila screamed in a voice she barely recognized as her own.

Maggie turned her head toward Nila. "Stay where you are, you little whore. Been playin' house with Gordy?" Her voice was emotionless. "Get Gordy. I'm here to collect what he owes me."

Nila took a step toward Maggie but stopped short when she saw the gleam of a silvery object in Maggie's right hand—scissors! Nila remembered that she had left scissors on the kitchen table when she removed the sketch of the twins from her pad. Janna began to cry again.

"Get him," Maggie almost whispered. "I wouldn't want to do something nasty to this child."

Nila was paralyzed by the sight of the scissors. "He's not here. He's gone out in the car to the shops."

"I saw the old car was gone, so I guess you're not lying. Then we'll just have to wait for him to come back."

Adrenaline surged through Nila's body. Her heart was pumping at full throttle. She forced herself to slow down and think. Maggie was somewhat taller than she was, but surely she couldn't be any heavier or, in her ragged condition, any stronger. Maggie stood perpendicular to the crib, with the scissors in her right hand. There were less than ten feet separating them—in two steps Nila could be on her and between the crib and the scissors. Julie reacted to Janna's cries and started to fuss. Maggie clearly hadn't noticed the second crib and baby in the room. She was momentarily startled and turned to her right toward Julie. Nila saw her chance and rushed at Maggie. She grabbed the scissor-wielding right hand in her left and forcefully jammed the butt of her right hand into Maggie's face, as she had been taught in self-defense class. She felt Maggie's nose crumple under the impact. Maggie staggered backward, dislodging Nila's grip on her right hand in the process. Bright crimson blood spurted from Maggie's smashed nose.

"You filthy bitch!" she screamed. Blood flowed over her mouth and dripped onto the front of her pale green dress. "You'll pay for that, you slut."

The twins began to wail.

Maggie stepped forward and stabbed toward Nila's abdomen as if she were wielding a sword. Nila turned to the side and shifted her weight to her back foot, narrowly avoiding the point of the scissors. Maggie turned the scissors to the right toward Nila and stabbed her in the side, just above belt level. Nila felt a searing pain as the scissors entered her body. She reacted quickly, grabbing Maggie's outstretched right arm with her left and bringing her right fist down hard on Maggie's wrist like a hammer. The force of the blow dislodged the scissors from Maggie's hand and Nila's side, and the scissors fell to the floor. When Nila stooped to retrieve them, Maggie fell on her. She opened her blood-smeared mouth and attempted to bite Nila's throat, but before Maggie's teeth could find a soft target, Nila headbutted her. Nila's forehead struck Maggie's jaw, and Maggie fell on her side.

As Nila sprang up with the bloody scissors in hand and moved protectively between the two cribs, she pressed her left hand against the wound in her side. It was bleeding freely. Maggie stumbled to her feet and staggered through the nursery door to the hall, to where a black purse lay on the hall table. Without a word, Maggie reached into the purse and pulled out a small handgun. The next two minutes were seared into Nila's memory where, in slow motion, they would replay for months.

Maggie pointed the gun at Nila. A man's voice somewhere behind Maggie rang out. "Police! Drop the gun—now!"

Maggie turned the gun toward the voice. One shot rang out, and then another. Maggie's throat exploded, nearly separating her head from her torso. Her legs crumpled under her and she fell backward onto the floor in the hall with a sickening crack as her skull hit the ceramic tile.

Nila felt faint. She dropped the scissors, slumped to the carpeted floor, and rolled onto her side. Her blood spread into a pool as it soaked into the carpet.

Janna and Julie stopped crying. Janna pointed to Nila sprawled on the floor. "Mama," she said. "Mama."

9

The ambulance arrived in less than five minutes. Nila was still unconscious. The EMTs checked her blood pressure, placed a compression dressing on her wound, and quickly moved her to a wheeled gurney and into the ambulance. Gordon carried the twins from their cribs to the playpen in the living room—the girls were alert, but silent.

"You go ahead with the ambulance, Mr. Hale," the deputy sheriff urged. "A female deputy will be here real soon to see to the girls. I'll stay until she comes."

Gordon, still in a state of shock, nodded, exited the house and climbed into the back of the ambulance as it pulled away with lights flashing.

~*~

Myra Silk and Hattie, drawn to the beach house by the sound of gunshots and the howl of the sirens, were standing in the kitchen with a deputy sheriff.

"You're sure you'll be okay with the children, Ma'am?" the deputy asked Myra. "Deputy Williams should be here any minute now, and then she'll take over."

"You go on after the ambulance, Officer," the old lady replied. "Hattie and I will be just fine. Won't we, Hattie? Hattie's a nurse, you know."

The tall, pale woman nodded. "Jus' fine," she said.

"If there are any problems, the deputy in the car outside can help. He's waiting for the medical examiner to arrive. Please don't touch the body, or attempt to clean or move anything."

"Don't be concerned, Officer. Hattie and I will look after the children until the deputy arrives."

Deputy Sheriff McGill turned on his heel and exited through

the kitchen door.

"No time to waste," Myra Silk exclaimed, as she walked briskly down the hall. Carefully avoiding the pool of blood surrounding Maggie's head, she lowered herself with surprising agility next to Maggie's body.

"The needle," she said impatiently, extending her hand.

Hattie opened her colorful, beaded bag and handed Myra a two-inch-long needle—a needle with a T-shaped black wooden handle. Myra raised the hem of Maggie's blood-stained green dress above her waist, pulled down her panties, and deftly began to puncture the skin on Maggie's belly, just above her vulva. After finishing her grisly task, Myra took the hem of Maggie's dress and wiped away the small amount of blood that had accumulated on the design, and then extended her arm once again to Hattie.

"Now, the power," she said.

Hattie took a small vial from her bag and squeezed a few drops of an ink-black liquid onto the punctures Myra had made on Maggie's belly. Myra rubbed the liquid into the skin with her index finger and then wiped off the excess with Maggie's dress.

Hattie looked down at the body. "Perfect," she said in a soft voice. "Her eye." And indeed, the mark was a well-drawn, miniature eye, no more than an inch wide.

Myra extended her hand. "Help me up," she whispered. As soon as she stood, she bent over and inserted the needle into Maggie's right eyeball. She removed the needle and then quickly held it above the new tattoo on Maggie's belly. A single drop of fluid fell from the needle to the tattooed eye.

"Hah! She can see again," Hattie cackled.

Myra pulled Maggie's green dress down over her new tattoo, then turned toward the hallway.

"Now for the children. Hurry!"

The twins were both awake and sitting upright on the floor of the playpen. As Hattie approached, Julie started to wail. Myra reached down and picked up Janna, who immediately joined Julie in her loud cries.

"The needle," Myra hissed, her hand outstretched.

The rusty spring on the kitchen screen door squealed and then the door slammed.

"I'm Deputy Williams," the pudgy, uniformed blonde said with a smile as she entered the living room. "Thanks for helping, I can take over now—I have little ones of my own."

10

"She's quite fortunate. If the puncture were half an inch lower, the blade would have entered her liver. That would have been serious. Scans show no internal damage. What sort of sharp instrument was it?"

"Scissors," said Gordon.

The doctor scowled. "Nasty."

"Nasty's the right word."

"She's your wife?"

Gordon shook his head. "She's our nanny—she takes care of my baby daughters."

"I see; that explains it. She was in shock when they brought her in and kept asking for her babies, over and over."

Gordon felt the muscles in his throat constrict and tears sting his eyes. "There was an intruder in the house, and Nila protected the girls. They're fine—nothing happened to them. Can I see her?"

"She's had a transfusion—she lost a fair amount of blood. Other than that, and the hole in her side that we've stitched up, she should be fine. We need to keep her overnight—possibly even for two nights. With puncture wounds, there's heightened risk of infection. Also, I want to be sure that there are no lasting effects of the shock. She's sleeping, so it would be best if you waited until morning to see her. Come after breakfast; she should be alert by then."

"Can I just stick my head in the door? It's been a crazy day. I'd feel a whole lot better if I could just see her breathing."

"Sure, I'll walk with you to the nurses' station and ask someone to escort you to her room. Don't wake her. You'll be able to talk with her in the morning."

Gordon nodded. "I understand. Thanks."

The doctor opened the door to the surgical consulting room.

Sheriff's Deputy McGill and another uniformed policeman rose from their chairs, which were just outside the room.

Deputy McGill motioned toward the consulting room. "Is Miss Rawlings going to be okay, Mr. Hale?"

Gordon smiled. "Yes, Deputy. Thanks to you, she's going to be okay."

The deputy returned Gordon's smile. "That's good news. Mr. Hale, this is Detective Lieutenant Tildon from the County Sheriff's Department. He'll be handling the investigation."

Detective Tildon offered his hand and Gordon shook it. "Mr. Hale, I know you've had a traumatic day. Do you think you could answer a few questions while events are still fresh in your mind? I promise—no more than twenty minutes. Then Deputy McGill will drive you home."

"My girls?"

"Deputy Williams is with them, Mr. Hale—she has children of her own. I just spoke with her, and she said that your girls have had their dinner and are sleeping. Would you like me to call her again, so that you can speak with her yourself?"

Gordon shook his head. "I don't think that'll be necessary."

The doctor looked at his watch. "If you gentlemen will excuse me—Mr. Hale, I'll leave instructions at the nurses' station for someone to take you to see Miss Rawlings when you're ready." He pointed to the consulting room. "Officers, you can use this room for your interview."

Gordon shook the doctor's hand. "Thanks, Dr. Cooper."

Detective Tildon took a seat behind the small desk, and Gordon and Deputy McGill sat on the wicker chairs in front of the desk. The detective took a small digital recorder from a leather case. "Mr. Hale, I'd like to record this conversation. Tomorrow we'll ask you to sign a transcript. Is this okay with you?"

Gordon nodded. "Sure."

"Mr. Hale, you're the owner of the house where the incident took place?"

"Yes. I inherited the house from my mother. It's been in my family since it was built."

The detective asked Gordon a number of background questions and then came to the purpose of the conversation. "Mr. Hale, is this your permanent residence?"

"No. My permanent home is in Concord, Massachusetts." Gordon went on to describe the circumstances of Karen's illness and death and his time at the beach house with Nila and the children.

"Your nanny, Miss Rawlings, is British?"

Gordon told them the details of Nila's time in America and of her visa status.

"Do you have access to her passport?"

"She showed me her visa when I first hired her. I'm sure she keeps her passport in her room."

"Do you think you could find it for us when the deputy takes you home?"

"I guess I could, but I'd rather not. Can't it wait until Nila returns to the house?"

"The sooner we can establish positive identity, the better."

Gordon nodded. "Let me think about it. I don't like the idea of rooting through her things."

"How well did you know Margaret Cartwright?"

"She's dead, I take it?"

Lieutenant Tildon nodded. "Right."

Gordon told the story of his DUI, the Castle Key exile, the torrid summer romance with Maggie, and the unwanted letters and phone calls that followed.

"So, you haven't seen Miss Cartwright since you were nineteen?"

"That's right—not once. As I told you, we had a summer fling, nothing more than that—at least as far as I was concerned."

Gordon put his hands on his knees and leaned forward. "I have a question for you: What in the hell was Maggie doing in my house with a gun in her hand?"

Tildon took off his glasses and began to wipe them with a tissue he had pulled from a box on the desk.

"Looking for money, Mr. Hale—money and anything valuable. Miss Cartwright was seriously addicted to heroin. Seems that she hadn't had a fix in some time and was getting desperate. Looks like she came here to loot her parents' house but got chased off by the security system. We're getting information from Florida Highway Patrol that she may have killed a liquor store clerk up near the Georgia state line four days ago and got away with a few hundred dollars and the Chevy that's in your driveway. Seems like she holed up somewhere upstate for a few weeks before driving to Castle Key…There are arrest warrants out for her in New Orleans as well."

Gordon grimaced. "Good God."

"We're just starting to piece the story together. Deputy McGill will tell you all we know when he drives you home. Heroin turns people into animals, Mr. Hale, animals. Just before she came to see you, she tried to rob Mrs. Stickles, who runs the bed-and-breakfast over by the Castle Hill Inn. Miss Cartwright had been staying there overnight. Mrs. Stickles is a tough old bird; she pushed the fire alarm rather than cough up her cash. Miss Cartwright ran out the door with a gun in her hand. That's when Deputy McGill spotted her. After he called in the plate number, we knew that we had a stolen car and probably an armed felon to contend with. The deputy followed her to your house and was waiting across the road for backup to surround the place when you pulled into your driveway. I think you know the rest."

Gordon shook his head. "Not in my wildest dreams," he mumbled to himself.

"Mr. Hale, I have just a few more questions and then Deputy McGill will take you home. Is that okay?"

Gordon nodded.

"It's important to the outcome of this investigation that you answer as clearly as possible. Do you understand?"

Gordon nodded again. "Yes, I do."

"Can you tell me what happened when you pulled into your driveway this afternoon? What time was it?"

Gordon sat up straight in the chair. "About 3, or 3:15. The first thing I saw was the old Chevy. I didn't think anything of it—I assumed that someone had come to the wrong address, or gotten the beach house confused with the big house. Since we share a common driveway, it happens every once in a while. I parked the Buick next to the other car and entered the house through the back kitchen door—no one ever uses the front door."

"Did you see anyone?"

"No. I put the mail and the packages I was carrying on the kitchen table. About ten or fifteen seconds after I entered the house, Deputy McGill came to the screen door. He put his finger up to his mouth, and I could see he had his gun drawn. Just as the deputy entered, there was a lot of noise coming from the nursery. The hall that leads from the kitchen to the nursery is about thirty feet long—I was standing in the kitchen, at the end of the hall."

Lieutenant Tildon interrupted. "Where was Deputy McGill?" he asked.

"He had entered the kitchen and was standing behind and to the right of me, looking down the hall toward the nursery."

"You're sure about that?"

Gordon nodded. "Positive."

"And then?"

"A woman in a green dress staggered out of the nursery. She had her back to us—I don't think she saw us in the kitchen."

"Why do you say she didn't see you?"

"As I said, she had her back to us and her focus seemed to be the nursery. She grabbed something from the hall table just outside the nursery door. When she turned toward the nursery, I could see that it was a gun."

"Where was she pointing the weapon?"

"Into the nursery."

"The nursery and not the kitchen?"

Gordon nodded.

"Mr. Hale, could you please answer audibly for the recorder?"

"She was pointing the gun into the nursery."

"And then what happened?"

"Deputy McGill shouted for her to drop the gun."

"What exactly did he say?"

"He said, 'Police, drop it! Drop the gun!'"

"You're positive that's what he said?"

"Positive."

"Did Miss Cartwright drop the gun?"

"No. She turned and pointed her gun down the hall at us—the deputy and me."

"And then?"

"She fired her gun. Maggie fired at us."

"There's no doubt in your mind that Miss Cartwright fired her weapon first?"

"No doubt at all; Maggie fired first. The deputy returned her fire. He hit her in the throat and she fell to the ground. For a few seconds, I just stood there while Deputy McGill pushed past me and kicked the gun away from Maggie's body."

Tildon turned off the recorder. "Thank you, Mr. Hale. I'm sorry we had to trouble you. Deputy McGill will take you home when you're ready."

Gordon let out a deep sigh. "Thank God the deputy saw her getting into the Chevy."

~*~

Gordon stood a few feet from Nila's bed, looking down at her. The sheets were pulled up to her neck and only her head was visible. Her long brown hair cascaded over the side of the pillow and her complexion was pale—probably, he thought, from the blood loss. Her full lips were turned upward in what seemed to be the beginning of a smile. A tear ran down Gordon's cheek, then another, and he began to sob. The nurse moved into the room, gave him a few tissues from the bedside table, and gently steered Gordon into the hall. "Mr. Hale, would you like to find a place to sit down?"

Gordon continued to sob and slowly shook his head from side to side. "We almost lost her—I almost lost her."

11

"You was real lucky we got to the druggy bitch's body 'fore the cops took her away—real lucky. It'd be a real pain in the ass keepin' you pumped up long enough to prepare another girl. You sure she's still under your control?"

Myra sighed. "She bears my mark. I marked her before we put her in rehab. She's mine, alive or dead."

Hattie shook her head. "I'm not so sure about that. Why'd she go to the little house, 'stead a comin' here to you?"

"I'd forgotten that Maggie had a sexual relationship with the Hale boy. About ten years ago when the contractors were putting a new roof on this old house, I'd come here in the summer without you to check on the construction. I saw her with him—she was magnificent! The next winter, his mother told me about the casual sex between the two of them and I decided that I needed Maggie. She was beautiful and sensual and very reckless—just what I wanted. That's when Clarisse started tracking her."

"So, you think she was comin' to you?"

"I'm sure she was being drawn to me, but the power of her sexual memories took her on a temporary detour next door. Our Maggie is an erotically driven girl. That's one reason I choose her—it's time to put some fun back in life."

Hattie frowned. "What they think about you takin' on the druggy bitch?"

"It's none of their business—and none of yours, either, you stupid girl. I told you to stop calling her a druggy, you hear?"

Hattie didn't like the emotional buildup in Myra's voice and changed the direction of the conversation. "When is she comin'? This would be lots easier if she was still alive."

"I worried they might take the body over to the mainland, so I made her leave the place where they took her and go hide in the mangroves until tomorrow night. She'll come here tomorrow night. You be ready; you hear me?"

"You sure you be strong enough to do it all at once?"

"I'll be ready—you just get everything organized. I'll be ready."

~*~

The twins were fast asleep, and Deputy Williams was on her way home. While Gordon and Nila were at the hospital, the police had photographed and documented the gruesome scene in the hall and the medical examiner had removed Maggie's body. Mrs. Kavlosky would clean up the blood and gore in the morning. The nursery carpet would need to be replaced.

It didn't take Gordon long to locate Nila's passport. It was in the first drawer he opened—the top drawer of the cherry dresser in the guest room. Next to the passport, he noticed what seemed to be several hundred dollars in cash rolled up in a rubber band. Beneath the passport, he discovered an unfinished letter addressed to Nila's sister in London. It was the sort of airmail, onionskin-paper mailer where you wrote your message on the inside of the envelope and then folded the whole thing back up into a featherweight package.

Back in the kitchen, Gordon handed the passport to Deputy McGill, who promised to return it the next day, and then left.

Gordon looked at the stack of mail on the kitchen table. It was as if it were still afternoon and he had just come home from the post office. He opened the bottle of Chablis that he'd bought to drink with the stone crab, poured out a generous glass, and then dumped the remainder of the bottle into the sink. The wall clock in the study softly chimed twelve. Gordon smiled. The clock was one of the few possessions that Karen had shipped from their Concord house.

Gordon sat at the kitchen table and, out of habit, twirled the wine glass in his right hand. He mechanically sorted through the pile of mail; there was nothing of interest. The mind-bending emotions of the day had helped Gordon finalize the answers to two of the three questions that had obsessed him for weeks.

He and the twins weren't going back to Concord. They were going to stay in Florida. Although he couldn't rationally explain the decision to himself, he knew they belonged here—the three of them. They weren't going to live in the beach house, either. He would build or buy a bigger family home somewhere in the area, but probably not on Castle Key. Uncle Duncan was in full agreement with Gordon's proposal to establish a branch of their law firm in southwest Florida. Gordon's specialization in property law was an ideal fit with the Suncoast housing boom. The firm had already assisted one Boston developer with a Florida project and had developed contacts with law firms in Charlotte and Sarasota counties. There was the inconvenience of taking the Florida bar exam, but it was only an inconvenience.

Gordon had decided that he wanted Nila to be his wife. He had explored every dimension of this decision with the painstaking thoroughness of a legally trained mind. He was sure that Nila wasn't a replacement for Karen. Gordon had loved Karen; he still loved Karen. Karen was his physical, spiritual, and intellectual partner. Their minds had continually parried together. They read books together and analyzed the characters and their motivations. She read passages aloud from the Victorian romance novels that were her academic specialty. Karen could sense Gordon's every need and see through the surface of his moods. He could do the same for her. He experienced maximum sexual fulfillment watching Karen's face as he guided her to orgasm, while—with her words as well as her touch—she would drive him to the peak of sexual excitement before they came together in an explosive climax. Yes, Gordon was sure that Nila wasn't a substitute for Karen. He didn't need a replacement; he would carry Karen in his memory and in his heart until he died. He also knew that his heart was young and that much love remained—love that needed to be shared.

Nila was most unlike Karen. Where Karen was a curvy, effervescent pixie with milk-white skin, jet-black hair, and green eyes, Nila was quiet, soft-spoken, and slim, with brown hair, amber eyes, and honey-brown skin. He knew that his decision to remain in Florida and his decision to ask Nila to be his wife were intimately tied. Karen was the perfect life partner in New England. Improving the decoration of their eighteenth-century colonial home, skiing on winter holidays, hosting family gatherings and parties for friends and business associates, and juggling the demands of both an academic career and a suburban household. Nila would be a life partner for the warmth, sunshine, and casual informality of the Gulf Coast. Her languid movement was a tropical ballet and her bright laughter was the sound of warm water rushing over an island waterfall. To be in Nila's presence was to find pleasure in the small details of living—bathing the babies, peeling vegetables, or sketching on the beach. She performed each task with grace.

Gordon was strongly attracted to Nila's body and the feminine aura that surrounded her. He felt sure that they would be sexually compatible and fantasized how they would make gentle love on the beach, in the pool, and in his empty bed. Despite their differences, he knew that Karen would have approved of Nila. Karen would have been pleased by the tenderness with which Nila cared for her babies.

At the end of the day, the decision was made. But did Nila have the same feelings for him? She had known him for only three months. Would she agree to marry him? They got along well; there was never a cross word, or a mean remark. She had said that she wanted to live in Florida. He felt sure that she had come to realize that his inheritance had made him financially independent and that he could provide her with physical, as well as emotional, security. There was no doubt that she loved the twins. He knew that the only way he could know Nila's feelings toward him was to ask. He was afraid that she might smile, pat his hand, and say, "I'm sorry, I can't." He feared that the feelings she showed toward him sprang from sympathy—or even worse, from pity.

He finished the last sip of wine and took the glass to the sink. The months of abstinence from alcohol, combined with the emotional stress of the day, made the small amount of wine have a greater impact than it might usually. Gordon felt a pleasant glow spread through his torso.

Then he remembered Nila's letter. He grinned. A letter to her sister might contain some hint of Nila's feelings. Gordon crept to the guest room and extracted Nila's letter from the top drawer. He slid open the second drawer: underpants and bathing suits. The bathing suits he recognized, but the underpants were a new experience—cotton thongs with a Hello Kitty face printed at the crotch. He laughed out loud and then closed the drawer.

Back at the kitchen table, Gordon carefully unfolded the unsealed mailer. Nila had filled half of the space with her neat, perfectly uniform handwriting. Although she regularly phoned her mother, Nila wrote as well as phoned her sister.

My Dearest Doo-Doo,

Boring, boring, boring—another perfect day in paradise. Temp about 26, sunny all the day long, tropical birds singing in the gentle breeze. I can't possibly imagine how I will survive when I return to Dear Old Blighty (as Nana would say). Speaking of coming home, I'll ring you next week to work out the details. I'm thinking of taking the train or bus to New York rather than flying—might be an interesting way to see more of America. I have about $800 in cash and have another $1200 in the bank. I was planning on converting the $1200 to sterling traveler's cheques so that I would have some money available as soon as I get back. Will $200 be enough for my air ticket? I assume you can still arrange the same cash transaction with the airline people? Anyway, we'll chat next week: as agreed, I'll ring you at the office at half-five your time.

I'm thrilled that the business is doing so well (as I will need a job). It was clever of you to branch out into bookings to India and Pakistan besides Africa and the usual European holidays: then you were ever the brilliant daughter.

I was glad to hear that Mum's sciatica (sp.?) isn't giving her too much grief. She must be thrilled to be in the office again full-time; not sure about your feelings, though?

It's wonderful that Nick's fixed it so she won't have to sell the house. Have you ridden in the new mini-lift yet?

Life with my babies continues to be magic. I love them as if they were my own. I can't imagine us parting; I blank it out of my mind. As I said in my last letter, Janna is becoming the leader. Yesterday she called me Mama for the first time. It thrilled me and broke my heart at the same time. She hasn't said Mama in front of Gordy yet…

I hope she never does—I'm sure that it would cause him pain. Speaking of Gordy, he continues to be the perfect friend. He's always cheerful and attentive to my needs and moods. I can tell from his behavior that he's sexually attracted to me. I'm trying very hard not to fall in love with him. He'll make some lucky girl a wonderful, caring husband. I wish that girl could be me, but unfortunately, the timing's all wrong: him returning to Massachusetts, my visa, and then he's clearly still very much in love with his poor wife. Perhaps if I keep in touch he'll invite me to come back and care for the children in Massachusetts? From his description, it doesn't seem that I'd fancy it much—wet and even colder than winter at home. Must say, though, regardless of the weather, I'd jump at the chance to be with Gordy and my darling angels. We shall see what happens.

I'm knackered so I think I'll end for tonight. I'll finish writing tomorrow with another day of boring experiences and then pop this in the post.

Gordon refolded the letter, returned to the guest room, then carefully placed it under Nila's passport in the top drawer of the dresser.

12

Hattie pulled back the musty-smelling, dark-green curtains that covered the French doors in the dining room—doors that opened to a masonry staircase leading to the walled garden below. The tarnished brass curtain rings scraped against the buildup of grime and dust on the metal curtain rod and let out a discomfiting screech, sounding like fingernails scraping along a chalkboard. Hattie knew the curtains and doors hadn't been opened in years. The locks on the doors easily slid back, but opening the doors themselves required the force of her hip and knee. She stepped down the broad stairs into the walled garden, her black, ankle-length robe fluttering in the light breeze. In the background, she could hear the Gulf waters lapping against the beach. Hattie's tight white curls glistened in the light of a nearly full moon, an orange-yellow moon that had risen only a few degrees above the horizon. Her pale face and hair were in stark contrast to the full black robe that hung loosely on her muscular body.

A weathered stone-and-concrete wall surrounded the rectangular garden. The east wall, the wall nearest the main road, included a wrought iron gate, which, other than the doors from the dining room, offered the only access to the garden. The manicured lawn ran from the house to the mulched beds along the wall. Dominating the far bed were four clusters of Christmas palms, each cluster with either two or three trunks rising well above the six-foot wall. The red seedpods that appeared each December and gave the Christmas palm its name were now long gone. At the center of the lawn was a paved area and what at first appeared to be an oversize birdbath. It was actually a table—a three-by-three-foot, round marble slab that rested atop a carved marble column. Set back and facing the table along each side were three stone benches, each wide enough to seat two. A tall, deep-green viburnum hedge rose above the outside perimeter of the wall and added to the garden's feeling of seclusion. Flanking the stairs leading down from the house were two greater-than-life-size, antique, iron statues, which were Arab-costumed black-a-moors who held electrified torches above their heads. Other than the moon, they were the garden's only source of illumination.

Hattie walked to the nearest stone bench, where a metal box rested on the seat. She retrieved a small bundle from the box—a bundle wrapped in black felt. She unfolded the felt cloth and removed a one-piece wooden icon—an icon no more than ten inches high. The icon was brightly painted, with two heads—one with a smiling face, the other with a face that was twisted with rage. Both heads emerged from a single torso painted to mimic an eyeball with a bright-red iris. Two arms and two legs came out from the eyeball. Hattie placed the carving on its legs, upright, in the center of the table, facing the wrought iron gate. Finally, she draped the black felt cloth over the idol, picked up the metal box, and returned to the house.

The master bedroom was permeated by the subdued but unmistakable odor of decomposing vegetation. The property agent that Myra Silk had paid to look after the house during her absence had been negligent and hadn't noticed the failing air-conditioning compressor that serviced the upper floors of the mansion. As the compressor slowly died, the rising temperature and humidity in the second story provided an ideal habitat for the mold spores that thrive in subtropical climates, and the spores had reproduced by the trillions.

The air conditioning had been repaired and the mold in the carpets and draperies was in retreat. After breakfast, Hattie had sprayed all the upstairs rooms with a floral-scented spray. At first, the spray had disguised the musty odors, but by afternoon the combined odor of lingering mold and scented spray had become the acrid-sweet smell of a vase of wilted flowers.

Myra was naked and lay on top of the green silk bedspread,

white towels under her butt and crotch. She was on her back; her skin was the color and texture of a wrinkled sausage casing. Her pendulous breasts drooped over the sides of her rib cage, and her thick pubic bush was silvery gray. Curiously, she did not have a belly button. The ravages of arthritis had transformed her hands and feet into bony, animal-like talons. She was spread-eagled in the center of the bed, her wrists and ankles bound to the four bedposts with nylon cords.

Hattie fussed with a vial and syringe. "I don't think you're up to this," she said. "We should do it like we used to—with a knife."

"Do it, now," Myra hissed without opening her eyes. "There's no time left. It has to be tonight!"

"Have it your way, old lady, but if your bones bust outa your skin, remember that I warned you—you hear?"

"Do it!" Myra shouted. "Do it now!"

Hattie tore open the foil envelope from an alcohol swab. "Don't know why I bother with this. There's more germs inside a you than there is on the outside." She swabbed the area around Myra's navel-less belly. "You ready?" Hattie asked.

Myra gritted her teeth and nodded.

Hattie picked up the syringe with a two-inch needle from the nightstand and in one deft movement darted it into Myra's belly. Myra screamed. Her wrists and ankles jerked hard against the confining ropes. Hattie ignored the continuing screams and slowly injected the blue-green fluid. When she withdrew the now-empty syringe, a spurt of bright-red blood followed after the needle. Hattie pressed a wad of surgical cotton to Myra's belly and taped it in place. Myra's screams turned to whimpers but her arms and legs still flailed against her nylon bonds.

Hattie took a damp cloth from a plastic container and began to wipe the sweat from Myra's face. "Tha's it, we ain't doin' this so late again—never."

Myra's eyes remained closed and her breathing was labored.

"Wake me—in one hour—exactly," she panted.

Hattie gathered up the medical equipment, and as she left the room, Myra began to snore.

~*~

Although each transformation was somewhat different, when she re-entered the bedroom Hattie knew what to expect. "Wake up, Lilith," she cried as she slapped Myra Silk across the face. "This ain't pretty," she called. Myra's teeth had turned black and her aged, wrinkled skin was now gray and reptile-like. Black claws had begun to emerge from under her fingernails and toenails.

It took all of Hattie's considerable strength to drag Myra's nearly comatose body from the bed and dress her in a white robe. Hattie struggled with Myra down the grand staircase, through the sunroom and dining room and out into the garden. Out of breath, Hattie lowered the body onto a stone bench, the bench that faced the east wall and the wrought iron gate. Myra's brilliant blue eyes were slits, and her breathing was labored.

Hattie removed the cloth that covered the two-headed idol. The idol began to mumble an unintelligible, repetitive phrase. She shook her head and looked down at Myra. "Don't know why we have to have that filthy thing on the table."

Myra weakly responded, "The Du-Mon amplifies and focuses my powers—that's why."

Hattie continued to shake her head. "Filthy thing!" she repeated. "You ain't gonna fall off that bench, are ya?"

Myra almost imperceptibly shook her head.

"Don' move none," Hattie said as she walked toward the far wall and opened the rusty gate. To her surprise, the gate opened without squealing. *Gardeners must oil it up*, she thought.

Hattie returned to the stone bench and huddled close to Myra's hideous body. The night air was cool, but still comfortable, and the stone bench had retained much of the sun's warmth. Hattie knew that this was the tricky part. They could sit here for minutes or for hours, perhaps even until sunrise—it all depended on the uncertain strength of Myra's powers. The cold-blooded moon was now high in the night sky.

Around the edges of the garden, unseen legions of insects scratched out their mating invitations. Myra leaned heavily against Hattie's left side. The stone bench was growing uncomfortable and Hattie's bony butt was aching. She guessed they'd been waiting for over an hour, when suddenly—with no sound or warning—a naked woman appeared at the gate. She strode through the open gate without hesitation and continued to walk across the grass toward the stone table that Hattie had turned into an altar. The woman stopped in front of the table and inclined her head toward them, as if her pupil-less, white eyes could still see. Her blonde hair was greasy, tangled, and hung limply over her shoulders. Her face was expressionless, and her pale feet, legs, and hands were muddy and covered with bloodless scratches, as if she had walked through a field of brambles.

As the woman approached, Myra's body became rigid and her breathing became even more shallow. The two-headed icon increased the volume of its chants, a separate shout issued from each of its heads. When the woman reached the altar, Myra sprang up from the bench. Hattie rose to assist her, but Myra roughly pushed her assistant back onto her seat.

Myra faced the woman. "You've been very naughty, haven't you, Maggie?" she asked in a powerful voice. "You should have known you could never escape from me. You know you are mine—my daughter who must serve my needs." Myra slowly walked toward the woman. "And after all of my careful planning, you ran and then you killed—killed twice and without my permission. You'll need to be severely punished, won't you? Purged. Eliminated."

The scratched and muddy woman stared sightlessly ahead with no reaction.

"You've made the transition needlessly complicated. You're a wicked, wicked girl." Myra was now only a foot from the woman's side. She stepped closer, grasped the woman's wrists, and pulled her body around so that the two stood face to face, only inches apart. Myra spread her arms, and the flowing white robe fell from her shoulders onto the concrete. She stood naked in the moonlight—her back hunched from the ravages of osteoporosis, her pendulous breasts sagging nearly to her waist, her gray, lizard-like skin and the extensive varicose veins on her legs and butt accented by the overhead moon. Myra started to laugh. At first, her laughter was light, but it quickly became loud, guttural, and animal-like. The icon joined the laughter. The sound stilled the insects' calls, bounced off the garden walls, and returned as frightening echoes. Myra threw back her head.

"Now, you evil girl! Do it now!" she screamed at the sky. Without hesitation, the vile woman seized Myra's throat with her teeth and began to violently twist her head like a predator tearing meat from a fresh kill. Myra's ancient body writhed back and forth in the woman's powerful jaws. Bright-red arterial blood began to drip from the corners of the woman's mouth and flowed down her sallow breasts and belly. Quickly, the trickle of blood became a steady stream. The woman grasped Myra's shoulders and tore at her throat with renewed energy. Myra's arms thrashed in the air and her legs collapsed beneath her. Then the woman released her grip on Myra's throat, letting Myra's torn body fall to the ground.

Hattie stood. She removed her gown, carefully folded it, and placed it on the stone bench. Her naked, muscular body glistened like polished alabaster. Carefully stepping around Myra's corpse, she walked toward the blood-spattered creature. Hattie looked into the gruesome woman's face. Her eyes were no longer white and sightless—they were now bright blue and fixed on Hattie.

"You're there, Lilith?" Hattie asked.

"I'm here," a youthful, resonant voice replied.

Hattie smiled, kissed the woman's bloody lips, and embraced her.

"What we do with the body?" Hattie whispered in Lilith's ear.

"We'll cut her up and burn her—burn her tomorrow. But now you must clean me up. Ah, what a joy to have a young body again! Even a body so broken and damaged."

"We'll get Maggie's body all fixed up. In a couple of months, you'll be even more beautiful than she ever was—you'll see."

Lilith moved her hands around Hattie's waist to her butt and pulled Hattie tightly against her.

13

"Nila, come on! Our reservation's for 7:30—get a move on."

"I'm just setting out some things for Sally, should the girls awake and need changing. Won't be a tick," Nila called from the nursery.

Gordon opened the kitchen screen door and looked at the sky. Dark clouds were forming. *Good chance of rain,* he thought. *Better bring an umbrella.*

He stepped back into the kitchen just as Nila entered from the hall. "Do you know where the umbrella—" He stopped in midsentence and whistled. "My, aren't we spectacular!" He took her hand and twirled her about.

"You like the dress? It isn't too tartish, is it?"

"Sensational!" Gordon was impressed. He'd never seen Nila in anything other than shorts, jeans, or a bathing suit. The off-white, form-fitting dress was suspended on a pair of spaghetti straps and belted at the waist. Her hair was drawn back in a braided bun and she had applied just a touch of rouge and pink lip gloss. Except for her jeweled Moroccan sandals, she could easily be dressed for a night out at any of Boston's chicest venues.

Nila adjusted Gordon's tie. "And don't you look smart? See? I told you that tie would go well with your jacket."

"I thought I'd temporarily escaped neck-ties and jackets. Castle Hill Inn's the final bastion of blue-blooded snobbishness in the area."

"Don't fuss. You look elegant and sophisticated, even if your khakis are a bit tatty."

Gordon grinned sheepishly. "Want to see my silent protest to overbearing formality?"

"Your what?"

Gordon pulled up on the side of his trouser leg, revealing penny loafers and bare ankles. "No socks!"

She shook her head. "Gordy, you can be so infantile. The umbrella's on the back seat of the car."

Sally emerged from the nursery. Nila turned to her. "Sally, we'll be in the main dining room at Castle Hill," she said. "I've left the number on the pad on the kitchen table. We'll be back no later than ten."

Sally laughed. "My cousin manages the front desk. I know how to get hold of you if need be. Have fun and don't worry about a thing."

Nila slid into the passenger seat. "Ouch! Did that a bit too fast."

"Your injury still hurting? Sure you're ready for this?"

"Not a problem. The doctor said that I can do anything I fancy—no restrictions. The internal stitches aren't quite dissolved and pinch a wee bit when I stretch or bend quickly, but I'm just fine."

Gordon turned out of the driveway, onto the main road. They drove in silence for a few minutes.

"Gordy, do you have a specific date yet when you'll be returning home? It's just that I need to call my sister quite soon and book my air ticket. She gets a very special rate for me. It's a bit of a fiddle—I have to give her a few weeks' notice."

Gordon tightened his grip on the wheel. "I thought that we'd discuss our plans over dinner. But now's as good a time as any, if that's all right with you?"

Nila was puzzled. "Of course. Any time you wish."

Gordon took a deep breath. This was not at all how he had planned to start the conversation. He glanced over at her; she was looking directly at him. "Well, you see—it's like this. While you were in the hospital, the twins and I had a very serious conversation and came to several important decisions."

She smiled. "Oh, did you now?"

"Yes, and some of our decisions concern you."

"Do tell."

"First of all, the babies and I are not going home. We decided that we are already home. As they both pointed out, they've lived here for much of their lives and wouldn't want to leave the warmth and the sun for some place unknown. I had to agree—made sense to me. I've arranged with Duncan to start up a law practice here—not in Castle Key but in a nearby town. Also, I think we'll need to build, or buy, a new house—a proper family house."

"Not on the beach?" she asked, interrupting him.

He bit his lip. "I think in a neighborhood where the girls can have regular friends and go to good schools—but we'll keep the beach house, of course, for weekends and holidays."

"Oh, I see," she said rather flatly. "When did you organize all of this?"

"Just in the last few weeks."

She nodded. "I see," she said again.

He downshifted before a curve and then glanced at her. Her expression was neutral. "There's more." Gordon felt his mouth grow dry; it seemed his tongue had doubled in size. "The girls told me they deeply loved you and wanted you to be with them always. They said they want you to love and protect them, forever."

Nila chuckled. "Which one of them said that?"

"It was Janna, of course—but then Julie added that she felt the same way."

"And what did you say?"

"Well, I told them that could only happen if we were a family—if you and I were to marry. I explained to them that I've fallen in love with you and intended to propose to you tonight over dinner. But I cautioned them that it would be quite possible that you might not feel the same about me. I mean, I know that you love them but...?"

Nila swiveled in her seat toward him. "Are we almost there?"

He was puzzled by her question. "Just a few minutes away.

Why?"

"I just wondered how long I had to decide. Let me make sure I understand. You and the girls are going to stay in Florida. You're going to set up a law practice and build a family home—probably not on the beach, but keep the beach house as well?"

He nodded. "I thought that maybe you'd like to redecorate the beach house, put in air conditioning, a modern kitchen, and..."

Nila shook her head. "One thing at a time. You want me to marry you so that I can be the twins' mother?"

"No—that's not it at all. I want to marry you because I've fallen in love with you and want to be with you for the rest of my life."

Nila frowned. "You're sure it's *me* that you love? You're not looking for a mother for the girls and a replacement for Karen?"

"Nila, I want to love you, adore you, protect you, and spoil you forever. I know that since we've only known each other for a few months, my feelings may seem kinda crazy but when I considered my emotions carefully, I had a full-fledged panic attack thinking about us separating—you leaving me and flying back to England. So I stopped thinking and decided to go with my heart. You see? That's what I'm learning from you."

"Gordy, you're daft," she said with a smile.

"I was never looking for a replacement for Karen. I wasn't looking for anyone—not even a certified nanny. I planned on being on my own with the girls for several years. I would go back to Boston, throw myself into my work, spend evenings, weekends, and holidays with the twins, teach them to swim, ski, and do homework. It sounded like a good plan. Then I started learning from you and began to ask myself some questions."

Nila frowned. "I don't understand. What could you possibly have learned from me?"

"Mainly to get off the agenda."

"The agenda?"

"Uh huh. Since I was a young boy, I've been on an agenda.

First, it was following all the steps necessary to get into my grandfather's prep school, then Amherst, Harvard Law, and finally making partner in the firm—haven't done that yet. Karen had an agenda as well—hers was a Ph.D. and, eventually, a career as a professor. What I discovered—what I've learned from you—is that if you always follow an agenda you stuff your real life in between the agenda items, where it can easily get lost."

Nila interrupted. "I'm not sure what this has to do with me."

"I've watched when you get up with the first light and take your tea outside to the lanai."

"It's coffee, actually—I don't like hot tea."

Gordon shrugged. "Coffee, then. I watch you sitting on the tall chair or on the step and I'm sure I can read your mind. You're thinking about the light, the cool of the morning, the gull cries, the osprey's scream, or the wind in the palms. That's all you're doing. You're not thinking about how the weather will affect your plans for the day. You're not wondering if the pool needs more chemicals, or if you left the car without any gas—which you did!"

"I'm so sorry. I didn't notice."

"Exactly my point. That's how you do everything. You take pleasure in the moment, not in planning for the future. That's what I'm learning from you—to love each moment."

Nila was perplexed. "You're right. That is true about me, but no one's ever thought that was a positive thing. Mum and teachers were always on to me for not having focus, or goals. I couldn't be bothered. It's most confusing that you'd want a scatterbrain for a wife. What else do you like about me?"

"I made a list of all the things I love about you—your smile and your beautiful, sexy body are at the top of the list, of course. And I've just added that provocative dress. I could recite the whole list for you—however, it's pretty long, and since that's the hotel ahead, I'd have to talk very fast."

Nila shook her head. "Gordy, you're impossible. Everything

you do involves a list, an analysis, or a carefully worded opinion."

Gordon frowned. "You don't wanna see the list?"

Nila's bright laughter filled the car. "Of course, I wanna see the list. More precisely, I want you to read it to me—on bended knee would be appropriate."

"Does that mean you might say yes?"

"You know that I love Julie and Janna. As for you, Gordon Hale, I think that there's a chance that I could fall for you, as well. As the pitchmen say on American TV, 'Wait—there's more! Three for the price of two.'" She put her hand on his knee. "I do have a concern, though."

Gordon turned into the parking lot. "Oh? What's that?"

"It's a bit delicate, me having a proper upbringing and all, but—well—we haven't done any of the things that lovers do. We've never been on a date until tonight. We've never made love or even kissed. It seems like you've got it all backward, you telling me that you love me first."

Gordon pulled to a stop, turned off the ignition, exited the old Buick, and walked to the passenger side. He opened the door, and Nila stepped onto the crushed-shell drive. "Well," he said. "This is our first date, and there's no reason why we can't promptly address your other concerns afterward. Can you think of a reason?"

Nila put her arms around his neck and kissed him—a long, lingering kiss. She held both his hands and stepped back. "That's number two," she said with a mischievous grin.

14

Gordon had a serious erection. His penis had begun to engorge shortly after he dropped Sally off at her home, when he started imagining Nila waiting for him, naked, in his bed.

It had been a long time—eight months—since Karen had summoned up the strength for their final act of lovemaking. He considered the next morning to be the beginning of her downhill slide to blindness, then coma, and death.

He'd had a wet dream the night he saw Nila standing naked from the waist down at the changing table in the nursery. He'd often mentally removed her bikini while she sunbathed by the pool or the beach—and since he'd seen her sweet, shaved vulva, and bare, perky breast, his sexual fantasies had become intense.

He noticed he was going over the speed limit and glanced at the speedometer—he was going 50 in a 30 mph zone. He hit the brake and slowed to 35. Although he was sure he was under the blood-alcohol limit, he didn't like the idea of explaining the circumstances under which he'd quaffed champagne at dinner to a suspicious deputy sheriff.

Early in the meal, Nila had begun to tease. She held a lock of her long hair between her thumb and forefinger and repeatedly stroked her cheek and lips with it. She sipped champagne from a crystal flute and then provocatively gathered the drops that remained on her full lips with the tip of her pink tongue. She slid her foot out of a Moroccan sandal and stroked Gordon's ankle with her bare toes. "No socks," was all she said.

When the waiter brought the dessert menus, she had left her menu unopened on the table. She fixed her eyes on Gordon. "Later," she purred, "at home."

Gordon was in such a hurry to leave that the waiter had to follow him to the parking lot to return his American Express card.

The halogen floodlights nearly blinded him as he turned into the drive. He'd had the lights and a security system installed before Nila came home from the hospital. "Came home"—he loved the sound of that phrase. This would be her home, his home, and the twins' home: a real home once again, at least until they decided where to build.

He punched in the security code, opened the door, switched off the bright lights, and then reactivated the system. Soft music spilled from the iPhone docking station in the den. It was playing an oldie: "Nights in White Satin" by The Moody Blues. He looked down; the bulge in his trousers was obvious.

Nila wasn't in his bed, but the bedspread was folded, lying neatly on a chair, and the sheets had been turned down. He removed his shirt and trousers and draped them over the back of the chair, slid out of his jockey shorts, and then got into bed.

He didn't hear her enter the room. He smelled her scent before he saw her—it was a fragrant blend of sunscreen, soap, and conditioner, mixed with her natural body oils. She stood in the doorway that led from the bath in a pale-yellow nightdress, backlit by the night-light. The nightdress was suspended by a chain of tiny, fabric flower buds that curled around her neck. The hem ended at the top of her thighs, in a similar flower-bud border. Her long hair fell over her shoulders and covered her breasts. She spread her arms. "You approve?" she asked.

Gordon was speechless. He smiled and shook his head from side to side. "My God, you're beautiful!" was all he could say.

"I bought it the same place I got the dress. Woman's intuition told me that I might need something sexy sooner rather than later."

Gordon grinned. "It's perfect."

Nila coquettishly tilted her head to one side and pushed back her hair. "If you like the wrapper, let's see what you think of the candy." She reached behind her neck, released the clasp, and the nightdress fell to the floor with a silken rustle.

The dark nipples of her medium-size breasts were teasingly erect. Her long, well-formed legs led to a bare vulva, her labia vertically mimicking the sensuous pout on her mouth.

Gordon raised himself on one arm. "You're magnificent—exactly as I'd fantasized!"

"Move over," Nila replied with a grin. "Let's see what you've got hiding under the covers." Nila put one knee on the bed and started to pull back the sheet.

"What's that?" Gordon playfully poked low on her belly with his index finger. "A tattoo?"

The tiny image a few inches above her vulva was faded and barely visible.

"That's my apparition. She protects me from those who might injure me. My grandmother put her there with a needle when I was a child, when we lived in Ghana. It's a cat, or maybe even a tiger. See, you can just make out the whiskers. I used to see the outline quite clearly, but now it's faded and nearly gone. Grandmother didn't tell Mum she was going to tattoo me and it was the last straw—the thing that made Mum take Della and me away from Ghana, away from Dad, and move back to England."

Gordon pulled back the covers and put his arms around her neck. "Got any other surprises?"

She climbed into the bed and pressed down on top of him. "You have all night to find out."

~*~

Gordon heard a loud banging noise. He thought he was dreaming. He'd heard Nila get up to go to the twins sometime in the middle of the night, but he'd gone back to sleep before she returned to bed. That was before she decided to wake him. He'd spent the next hour feverishly revisiting the crevices and contours of her soft body.

He heard the noise again—it wasn't a dream. Someone was

pounding on the kitchen screen door. He gently moved Nila's hand from his shoulder. She didn't stir. He looked at the bedside alarm clock; the digital display read 6:42. He slid from the bed so as not to wake her and looked back at her naked body. She lay on her side, her face toward him, her dark hair framing her face. *God, she's beautiful,* he thought. He longed to reach out to stroke her magnificent, bare butt, but the knocking resumed.

Gordon found bathing trunks on top of the hamper of soiled clothes and pulled them over his still somewhat engorged, and especially sensitive, penis.

Deputy McGill had his hand raised to rap on the screen door again when Gordon opened the main door.

"Sorry to wake you, Mr. Hale. I need to speak with you—it's urgent."

Gordon unlatched the screen door. "Oh, it's really that urgent? Come on in, Officer; I'll put on some coffee."

"None for me, thanks," McGill responded. "I'm finishing my shift and about to go home."

"Suit yourself." Gordon turned and shuffled toward the coffeemaker.

The deputy stood behind a kitchen chair with his hands grasping the chair's back. "I'll come right to the point, Mr. Hale. Have you or Miss Rawlings heard from anyone regarding Margaret Cartwright—her family, or anyone else?"

Gordon turned and sleepily shook his head. "No, no one. What's this about?"

The deputy did not answer his question. "How about Miss Rawlings? You told us that Margaret Cartwright's younger sister was a friend of Miss Rawlings. Has she called Miss Rawlings?"

"I'm sure she hasn't. Nila would have said something."

The deputy looked uncomfortable. "Would you mind asking Miss Rawlings if she's had a call? It's very important."

Gordon nodded toward the bedroom. "I think she's still sleeping. We had a late night."

"Would you please check, Mr. Hale? I wouldn't barge in on you like this if it weren't urgent."

Gordon was both irritated and puzzled.

"Let me start the coffee and then I'll see if she's up."

~*~

Gordon entered the bedroom and heard the toilet flush in the adjoining bathroom. Nila was washing her hands when he entered the bathroom. She was naked, with her long hair thrown back over her shoulders. His penis involuntarily throbbed when he looked at her breasts in the mirrors above the twin sinks. "How are you this morning, sex goddess?" he said to her image in the mirror.

She flashed a grin. "I'm just a wee bit knackered, pleasantly so. Let me brush my teeth and I'll meet you back in bed. The twins won't likely be up for another hour; we can try something different." She turned from the mirror to face him. "Won't be a tick."

At first, Gordon had been taken aback by Nila's enthusiastic approach to sex—it seemed in direct contrast to her demure personality. He put his hand on her hip and lightly kissed her cheek. "Throw something on, the deputy sheriff's waiting in the kitchen; he wants to talk with us about Maggie."

"Maggie? What about Maggie?"

He shrugged. "He's being mysterious. He asked me if Maggie's sister had called you. She didn't, did she?"

Nila shook her head. She turned back to the sink. "I'll be right there. Just give me a minute."

The coffeemaker had just started to beep when Nila entered the kitchen. She'd pulled on one of Gordon's long white T-shirts and tied her hair back in a ponytail.

The deputy was seated at the table, and Gordon was putting two coffee mugs on the countertop.

Nila extended her hand and the deputy rose to take it. "Morning, Officer. What brings you out so early?"

The deputy visibly softened. "Forgive me for intruding so early in the morning, Miss Rawlings; it's about Margaret Cartwright. You're feeling better, are you?"

Nila sat and motioned for the deputy to do the same. "Thanks to you, I'm alive and on the mend. Gordy said you wanted to talk about Maggie."

"Has anyone called or spoken with you about her—maybe her sister?"

Nila shook her head. "I've been debating whether to call Amy—she's Maggie's sister. But I haven't had the nerve—I'm not sure what I'd say. And no, no one's called. No letters or emails, either. Why do you ask?"

Gordon set a mug of steaming black coffee on a paper napkin in front of Nila. "Sure you don't want some?" he asked the deputy.

The deputy drummed his fingers on the table. "You got me; I can't resist the smell of fresh-brewed coffee. Just a splash of milk, please." He paused to collect his thoughts. "Something strange is going on, Miss Rawlings, Mr. Hale. The medical examiner wasn't able to positively identify Margaret Cartwright's body. There was no ID of any kind in her purse and no fingerprints in the stolen car."

Gordon interrupted him. "There must have been prints on the gun. She wasn't wearing gloves."

"She had no fingerprints. I mean, no prints on her fingertips—they were all blank."

Gordon set a mug on the table in front of the deputy. "Strange. I remember reading a spy novel once where the bad guy had his prints surgically removed."

"The medical examiner thought of that possibility. But he said that there was no evidence of surgery. It was like she was born without fingerprints."

Nila raised her hand to her mouth, then lowered her head and closed her eyes.

"Highway Patrol haven't called back yet with contacts for Margaret Cartwright's relatives. Beside her probable involvement in the robbery-homicide upstate, the only new information is that the New Orleans Police have a rap sheet on a Margaret Cartwright. She was a high-priced prostitute, and her last known address was in New Orleans. Either of you have any ideas?"

Nila removed her hands from her face and shook her head. "Several months ago, just after she arrived back home in Pennsylvania, I talked with her sister Amy on the telephone. Amy attends an art school in Philadelphia. I don't remember the name, but it was an important school—one that offers graduate degrees. I suppose you could track it down. Actually, I do remember one thing Amy told me when I was staying at the Cartwrights' beach house: she said that she had a sister who lived in Louisiana. She didn't say her name, just called her 'my sister.' She said this sister was estranged from her parents and that she—Amy—hadn't seen her in several years. That's all she said about her."

Deputy McGill removed a notebook from his breast pocket and took some notes. He turned to Gordon. "Mr. Hale, would it be correct to say that you've never had any relationship with Margaret Cartwright in her professional capacity?"

Gordon wrinkled his brow. "Professional capacity? Oh—you mean as a hooker!" He laughed. "Like I said, haven't seen her since I was nineteen. There was lots of hot sex back then, but none since."

The deputy placed both palms on the table and stared at his mug of coffee. "Someone's taken her body from the clinic. It happened late last night, or early this morning. There were no signs of forced entry and no clues—none at all. Her body just vanished. It's as if she got up, walked out, and left the door open."

"Good Lord!" Gordon exclaimed. "Who'd do something sick like that? Was she on one of those sliding shelf things, like you see in the movies?"

The deputy frowned. "There's a temporary morgue here on the island—just a cold storage locker at the rear of the clinic," he replied. "Her body was gonna be transferred to Fort Myers for autopsy this morning."

The deputy put his notebook back in his pocket and stood. "Forgive this early intrusion on your day. Frankly, I've never had to hunt down a corpse before. Please call me right away if anyone contacts you or if you have any ideas that might be pertinent to the case—anything at all."

Gordon and the deputy shook hands, the deputy said goodbye to Nila, and Gordon walked him to the car. When Gordon reentered the kitchen, he found Nila sitting with her elbows on the table, her chin resting in her hands.

"Creepy shit," he said. "Who'd steal a dead body? Maybe a psychotic grave robber," he added, answering his own question.

Nila sighed. "C'mon, let's make some breakfast, and then we'll have a chat—a nice long chat."

~*~

"I'm beginning to enjoy these sausages; I guess they're an acquired taste," Nila said, as she set a plate of scrambled eggs and breakfast links in front of Gordon. "The chipolata at home are different—less meat and more filler. Different spices, too."

Gordon refilled Nila's coffee mug. "Anything else you miss, besides the sausages?"

"Not really; just Mum and Doo-Doo—that's what I call my sister Della."

"I know. You told me."

"I don't remember telling you her nickname."

"Well, you did. Otherwise, how would I know?"

Nila smiled a little. "Yes, how would you know?"

They locked eyes for an instant, and Gordon's smile grew to match Nila's. He picked up a fork and poked at the mound of eggs. "Telepathy, no doubt," he said.

"Yes," she replied. "No doubt."

"I think we should have our wedding in England," he said, changing the subject. "We should have a formal affair in an old church, with a big reception afterward. That's what you'd want, isn't it?"

Nila, who was swallowing scrambled eggs, choked. She raised the paper napkin to her mouth and coughed for several seconds.

"You okay?" he asked, getting up and thumping her on the back.

She nodded. "You just caught me off guard, talking about weddings. I'm all right now." She sipped some coffee.

Gordon took his seat. "Sure you're all right?"

"Just fine."

"So, you'd be okay with a wedding in England?"

"Gordy, I haven't even thought about a wedding—not even once. Everything's happening so fast; you only asked me to marry you last night. I don't know. A wedding at home would be lovely, but America will be my home now. I think we should do it here, in Castle Key. I do get to become an American citizen, don't I?"

Gordon smiled. "Of course, but it will take some time to jump through all the bureaucratic hoops. I'll email Stephanie at the firm. She handles immigration and naturalization issues, and she'll advise us on how to get started with the process."

"Gordy, I'm surprised. Under the circumstances, I'd think you'd want something low-key, like at a registry."

"What circumstances?"

"I'm not sure how to put this. With Karen's death so recent, wouldn't her family find it distasteful for you to marry again so quickly, and in a formal ceremony? And what about Mary?"

Gordon shook his head. "Mary's your champion. She'll be happy with whatever we decide. As for Karen's family—aside from her mother, it doesn't matter what they think."

Nila saw Gordon's serious expression and assumed one of her own. "Please, can I have more coffee?"

He filled both their cups. "Karen's stepbrother and stepsister are angry with me. Karen was much younger than her siblings. She was a love child who was conceived during her divorced, middle-aged mother's brief relationship with a younger colleague; Karen never met her father. Her siblings were married and out of the house with their own kids and careers when Karen was growing up, so the three of them weren't close."

"You're not on good terms with her stepbrother and stepsister?"

"After the diagnosis, Karen decided that she needed to get away—away from her family and away from Massachusetts. This house belonged to me and winter was coming, so it wasn't a difficult decision to pack up the girls and move to Florida. Adele, Karen's mother, came with us for the first week and helped us get settled. Adele's the ethereal, artsy type and is completely caught up in her work at the university—but aside from being flaky, she's a normal, pleasant woman."

Nila interrupted. "She's been back to the cottage?"

"She came down two more times last fall to babysit the twins while Karen and I went on short trips. She called Karen every day right up until Karen went into coma. I'm still in touch with Adele. We're not what you'd call close, but we get along. But, at Karen's funeral, her brother and sister were quite unfriendly. I think that in some strange way, they blame me for Karen's death. Nothing was said, but they were very cold to me."

Nila carried Gordon's plate to the microwave. "Let me heat this up for you."

"Thanks," Gordon replied. "I email pictures of the girls to

Adele every now and then. She has seven grandchildren in Massachusetts to fuss over, but I'm sure she'll come visit the twins at some point. That's all you need to know; there's really no need for us to talk about this again."

The microwave beeped, and Nila removed Gordon's plate. "Eat, before the eggs get rubbery." Nila set the plate in front of Gordon and took her seat. "You eat, I'll talk." She poured the last of the coffee into Gordon's mug. "You haven't given me much time to think this proposal through, but I need to tell you what I'm feeling. I love you—of that I'm sure—and I love Julie and Janna as if I were their own mother. I'm excited about building a new life with you—even though, except for love and happiness, and perhaps a few more little ones, I have no idea of what that life will include." Gordon started to speak, but she held up her hand. "Not yet, not 'til I'm finished."

"Just trying to find out how many little ones to expect," he said with a laugh.

She tilted her head to one side and grinned. "Judging from your performance last night, I'd say a dozen. Now don't interrupt again. Promise?"

Gordon crossed his heart.

"This is the important bit. Our love—our life together—will be all new to me: housekeeping, and taking care of my husband's needs. All new. Not so for you—you've already loved someone, loved truly and deeply, and you had started building a life together. It's most important for you to know that I want you to always remember that love—I want you to remain in love with Karen. Karen gave you Julie and Janna and now she's allowing me to share them. You and I and the girls will be building on the love that you and Karen established, not starting over again." She smiled. "That'll make my job lots easier."

Gordon reached across the table and took Nila's hand. A tear ran down his cheek.

15

Hubert Rawlings sat at a scarred, century-old, teak writing table and stared blankly through the French doors into his mother's flower garden. It was the rainy season in southern Ghana and the exotic African jungle plants that Juba had collected over decades flowered in profusion. Without his mother to constantly nag the gardeners, Hubert knew that her garden would now begin a gradual descent into weeds. In her garden, like everything else in her life, Juba Rawlings had always insisted on excellence. Because of her extensive charitable work, especially founding the Children's Hospital, Juba had been widely respected throughout Accra, and her funeral had been nearly a state occasion. Even His Excellency, the president, had made an appearance at her grave.

Hubert was struggling to find the words to describe the emotions he was feeling after a life spent under the thumb of his domineering mother. Words entered and exited his consciousness, such as guilt, pain, admiration, and hurt. The word 'love' never appeared—love wasn't an emotion that he and his mother shared.

The Rawlings had been fixtures in Ghana's business community and society since 1874, when the British pulled together a number of West African tribal territories and created the Gold Coast crown colony. The first generation of Rawlings to settle in the Crown Colony was English; the following generations to bear the Rawlings surname were an amalgam of European Caucasians, including British, Portuguese, and Finns. Hubert's father, John Rawlings, was a successful businessman with a talent for recognizing and exploiting imminent change. In 1954, four years before the creation of an independent Ghana, John married Juba Nkrumah, a strikingly beautiful sixteen-year-old girl from a deep-rooted, politically well-connected

Ghanaian family. John and Juba moved effortlessly in all circles of Ghanaian society, and their timber and cacao businesses prospered. Hubert was born a year after their marriage. Because Hubert's birth was so difficult for Juba, he would be the couple's only child, and this was the source of bitter disappointment for the rest of Juba's life. Juba desperately needed a girl—a female who would carry on her ancient family line.

Hubert was eighteen when, against Juba's objections, his father sent him to England to study engineering at Imperial College, University of London. Hubert was a serious student. He got good grades and returned to the family home in Accra, Ghana, each summer. Two months before his scheduled graduation, Hubert's parents received a letter and a wedding invitation. Hubert enclosed a photo of his blonde English wife-to-be, but failed to mention that she was carrying his child. Juba Rawlings was enraged. She'd already selected Hubert's future wife—Morowa, her second cousin's beautiful, well-educated daughter. Juba had also purchased a building lot in a fashionable district on the edge of Accra where the newlyweds, with her financial backing, would build their first house. Juba immediately booked herself and John on the next weekly flight to London.

When they arrived, Juba summoned Hubert to a breakfast meeting in her suite at the Dorchester, where Juba mounted her campaign against her son's marriage plans. He wouldn't be able to support a wife and family in an incredibly expensive city like London. Hubert countered that he had an excellent job offer from an international investment company in the City, and that his fiancée was already running her own small, but profitable, travel agency. John launched the second round of attack—he needed Hubert's help in the fields and factories. Hubert apologized for disappointing his father, but emphatically stated that he'd chosen to be a player in the high-stakes, international finance world and intended to remain in London. Juba tried the emotional appeal of an abandoned mother. Hubert had to suppress a smile, and quickly moved the conversation along. That evening, when Juba and John met his fiancée Carrie over dinner, all further attempts to bring young Hubert back to Ghana ended. Carrie was unusually attractive, intelligent, and polite—but more importantly, she was obviously pregnant.

John Rawlings was among the last of a dying breed of colonial British men—gentlemen who believed they had well-defined responsibilities regarding women they'd knocked up. There was no doubt in John's mind that Hubert would—of necessity—marry Carrie.

After the dinner, John forcefully informed his wife that the matter of their son's marriage was no longer open for discussion. Juba gave up arguing and turned her considerable energies to shopping. The couple flew home with six more cases than they'd brought. A few months later, John returned to London for the wedding, but Juba insisted that the pollution in London had inflamed her asthma and remained at home in Ghana.

Shortly after Hubert and Carrie's wedding, Nila Rawlings was born. Nila was a pretty child with large amber eyes and a complexion close to Hubert's honey-colored skin. A year later, another daughter arrived. She was another pretty child, but with chestnut-colored eyes and a light complexion nearer to her mother's. She was named Della. John and Juba Rawlings remained in Ghana and never visited London again.

A year into his new career, Hubert began to lose his enthusiasm for the high-stakes world of finance. The greed and cutthroat competitive behavior of the City was in direct opposition to the Ghanaian values of community and family that had shaped his life. As Hubert's infatuation with high finance diminished, the irritations of city living—pollution, noise, and overcrowded subways and buses—suddenly became more noticeable. When Della, his second daughter, was born—unlike with his first child—he found the baby's nighttime feeding and constant crying to be unbearable. He had a brief affair with a young Jamaican girl who was illegally working as a barmaid. When she was fired and left London to stay with a girlfriend in Leeds, Hubert frequently got drunk and wallowed in guilt. Carrie understood; she knew Hubert was miserable. She knew their lives would have to change. It was late afternoon and Carrie was home with the girls when she got the call. John Rawlings, Hubert's father, was dead—crushed to death by a teak log that had fallen from a moving truck. As she hung up the phone, she knew that she and Hubert and the girls would be moving to Ghana.

~*~

Hubert hadn't heard Morowa enter the room and flinched when she spoke. "I've finished upstairs; it didn't take as long as I expected." She set several sheets of lined paper on top of the leather blotter on the desktop.

"I'm sorry?" he replied.

"The inventory of your mother's jewelry and clothing. I finished the inventory."

"Oh, right. Any surprises?" He lifted the top page and scanned the itemized list without actually reading any of it.

"Not really. There were a dozen pieces of fine jewelry in the safe. The four pieces she willed to Naki were the only ones I hadn't seen before. Since she was so tall and slender, her clothing's not likely to fit anyone in the family. Some are lovely, old, vegetable-dyed fabrics that I can have resewn."

"Anything left in Father's room?"

Morowa shook her head. "Except for the furniture and the bedding, it's bare. It took her long enough to decide to clean out your father's things, but when she finally did, she was thorough. When are you planning on leaving?"

Hubert turned his head to meet her gaze. "Tomorrow morning—I don't want to put this meeting off. I managed to get a message through to Ringwald; he'll meet me at the camp."

She placed her hand on his shoulder. "I'm going with you, of course."

"You don't have to," he said.

"Yes, I do. Ringwald is my blood relative, as well as yours. Besides, he'll be more comfortable if we speak Akan, and you know you're hopeless."

Hubert smiled, pushed the desk chair back, stood, and embraced his wife. "I'm really apprehensive about this whole damn thing. It's like my mother is reaching out from the grave, still expecting us to give her a granddaughter, and trying to control our lives."

Morowa gently stroked his cheek. Her long, mahogany-colored fingers contrasted with her ivory-colored nail polish. "With Ringwald's help, we'll deliver the jewelry to Naki and cast Juba out of our lives. Then we'll burn this house to the ground and be done with her!"

Hubert pulled her close and kissed her on the forehead.

~*~

Hubert and Morowa left the smells, noise, and overcrowding of Accra behind as the Range Rover flew down the six-lane N-1 highway. They traveled more slowly on the progressively poorer regional roads, and finally, crawled deep into the forest on an unpaved logging trail. Hubert had driven the trail for decades, and automatically shifted through the gears, anticipating most of the deep ruts and potholes in the well-worn track. The forest had belonged to his family for four generations. What had once been a native teak forest was now a scientifically managed plantation.

At the end of the trail were three substantial buildings with metal roofs: a bunkhouse, a mess hall, and an infirmary for the loggers who harvested the valuable timber. There was also a fourth building—an attractive superintendents' lodge.

Hubert cut the engine and then stepped down from the Range Rover onto the crushed-stone-covered courtyard that fronted the buildings. He looked around and, seeing no one, opened the SUV's hatch. A twelve-gauge, pump-action shotgun lay on the black carpet, within easy reach. Morowa, who was also an excellent shot, remained in the vehicle with a .38 Special revolver clutched in her right hand. The jewels in the velvet pouch that she'd stuffed into her handbag were easily worth a couple of hundred-thousand US dollars, and even though they were on their own property—a property patrolled by armed security guards—Hubert had discussed the jewels with Ringwald on the questionably secure satellite phone and they knew that brutal things sometimes happened in the forest.

A compact, muscular, white-haired man came out the front door of the superintendents' quarters and stepped onto the wide front porch. He wore a clean, sleeveless white T-shirt, black sweatpants, and bright-green wellington boots. Incongruously, he clutched a large pink linen napkin in his left hand. "Welcome," he called in the Akan language. "You're early. I wasn't expecting you until afternoon."

Hubert waved, then closed the SUV's hatch door while Morowa returned the revolver to the glove box and stepped down from the vehicle. She held her handbag tightly against her chest.

"It's past one, Ringwald, you old fool," she laughingly responded in Akan.

Ringwald pointed to his watch and shook his head. "I'm always off time. It broke last week and I haven't got it fixed, but still put it on out of habit."

Hubert bounded up the three wooden steps to the porch and grasped the old man in a bear hug. "Uncle, you never change. Even when I was a child, you were an old man with white hair."

"You be respectful, boy. Now that your mother's gone, I'm the leader of the clan—at least until you two get your act together."

Morowa embraced Ringwald and kissed him on the cheek. "You look much more like yourself without that moth-eaten adinkra robe you wore to Juba's funeral. I think that was the only time I've ever seen you without your wellies."

"Come in, dear children." He held the napkin in the air. "As you see, I was just sitting down to lunch. Come in and eat with me. Alexandria has prepared waakye with red-red—better than any food you'd be served in the pig troughs you city people call restaurants."

Alexandria, Ringwald's longtime housekeeper and cook, stood in the kitchen doorway. She was a short, squat woman with short silver-gray hair and a large mouth. She nodded unsmilingly to the group and then wordlessly disappeared into her kitchen.

Hubert wasn't fond of waakye, a Ghanaian staple made from beans and rice and often accompanied with a spicy sauce of prawns and tomatoes, but he knew that for a guest to refuse food would be a gross breach of etiquette and vowed to himself to eat as little as Ringwald would allow.

To his great surprise, Hubert enjoyed Alexandria's waakye and, at Ringwald's insistence, ate a second helping.

After Alexandria had silently cleared the table, poured coffee, and retreated to the kitchen, Ringwald laid out a black felt cloth in front of Morowa.

"I can restrain my curiosity no longer; let us see what treasure you have brought." Turning toward Hubert, Ringwald continued, "And now, so that this highly educated foreigner can fully understand the important things I must tell you, we will speak only in English—and," he added in Akan, in a loud voice, "so that when Alexandria eavesdrops, she will not understand."

Morowa removed the velvet pouch from her purse, and laid out the four pieces from Juba's jewelry collection—a ring, two pendants, and a necklace—onto the black felt cloth. "As Juba directed just before she lapsed into a coma, we've brought the jewelry she left for Naki for you to explain the significance of the pieces."

Ringwald stood and hovered over the jewels for only a moment. "The orange diamond," he said. "The pear-shaped, orange diamond in the gold ring setting."

Morowa picked up the ring and held it up in the sunlight streaming in from the front windows. It's pure, vivid, orange color was dazzling. "I'm surprised," she said. "It's lovely, of course, but I thought you'd select one of the bigger, more valuable, stones." She pointed to a pendant. "This, for example, must be five carets."

Ringwald's laugh—a deep, throaty snort—seemed out of place coming from such a small, squat man. "I select nothing. This orange diamond is a power stone. The rest are but baubles."

"Power stone?" Morowa asked. "What's a power stone?"

"I'm not really sure. All I can remember from long-ago family conversations is that a power stone has no intrinsic force by itself. But, when the stone is worn by someone who possesses potent force, the stone amplifies that person's ability to exercise their powers."

"How did Juba come by this power stone?"

Ringwald stroked his beard. "According to Ashanti legend, thousands of years ago, when this stone was torn from the ground, it was rough, uncut, and—of course—much larger than it is today. Five centuries ago, it became the property of the king of the Ashanti and was incorporated into a warrior headdress, which was passed on to future kings. It was said that the stone would gather power from the strength of each ancient warrior who possessed it and transfer that power to its next owner. But, as you both know, other than land, inheritance among the Ashanti flows through the matriarchal line. So, technically, the stone has always been the property of women. But, as I just told you, my belief is that the stone has no intrinsic powers of its own. In the mid-nineteenth century, during one of our wars with the British, the stone fell into the hands of a Dutch trader, who had the stone cut and set into the ring you see before you."

"Then how did the ring become my mother's?" Hubert asked. "I never saw her wear it."

"The story that has passed down through our family is that your great-great-great-grandmother bargained with the trader for the ring. But when she was unable, or unwilling, to pay his price, she slit his throat and took the stone. It's a great story, but I have my doubts as to its truth. I suspect that someone in the family bought it. Now, you must both listen carefully to what I have to say in my poor, mission-school English. If you do not understand, you must question me at once. You got that?"

Hubert and Morowa nodded.

"To begin, I will tell you of times long before my sister Juba—your mother and mother-in-law. I will also tell you why I believe Juba became a cold, frustrated, and controlling woman, and why she willed the power stone to Naki.

"You, of course, know the story of Adam and Eve. That story is a Christian story. Jews have their stories and the ancient peoples who came before the Christians and Jews had similar stories, too. You must learn that these stories are false. Creation did not happen as the Christians and Jews say it did. The correct stories of the beginnings of man have been preserved in Ashanti lore—the stories of Elemi and Eleda, the two gods of creation. However, the Eden the Christian stories tell of was a real place—a place nearby, here in what the English named West Africa." Ringwald paused. "Do you understand what I'm telling you?"

Hubert nodded. "When I was a child, I learned about the ancient gods Eleda and Elemi."

"What does this have to do with Juba, or with Naki?" Morowa asked.

"Be patient while I tell you of the Ashanti creation stories, and then you will understand," said Ringwald. "To amuse the gods, Elemi created the earth, the seas, and the heavens, and then moved on to other worlds, leaving Eleda behind to create the creatures of the earth—the fish of the seas, the birds that fly in the sky, and, lastly, humans. When Eleda was finished, he blew life into each one. As with all true gods, Elemi and Eleda are each male and female at the same time. However, when Eleda created the creatures of the earth—including man—Eleda made them incomplete so that each male and each female would be inferior to the gods. Of course, this is what drives men and women to crave sex—it is the desire to become complete, to try to become like the gods, if only in a brief moment of ecstasy."

Morowa snickered and then covered her mouth with her hand. "I'm sorry, Uncle," she apologized. "I'll behave."

Hubert shook his head and gave Morowa a mock-reproachful look.

Ringwald continued. "Eleda named the first man Alos and the first woman Lilith. There was no tree of forbidden fruit, nor any serpent, nor were Alos and Lilith ashamed of their nakedness. The Christians made all that up much later for their own purposes. You see, the Jews and Christians were terrified of the sexual power that women had over men. They needed to marginalize that first woman as naïve and easily tricked by the forces of evil. As with all the other creatures of the earth, Alos and Lilith produced offspring—first twin boys, and then a girl."

"So, this Lilith was the biblical Eve?" Morowa asked.

"Hold onto your pants. There's more coming—you're understanding my English?" Ringwald asked Hubert.

"Uncle, I'm amazed by your vocabulary. Your English is excellent."

Ringwald grinned. "When I was a young man, I read many books written in English, and other languages as well. Not everyone needs to go far away to university to become educated, you know. Right, where was I? Ah, yes—Lilith had a voracious sexual appetite and bore Alos more daughters and sons. When her twin sons grew into men, she began to copulate with them as well as with Alos. From the union with her sons, Lilith produced a girl child who was born with pink eyes and nearly translucent skin."

"An albino?" Morowa interrupted.

Ringwald nodded. "An albino girl. Alos was alarmed by the appearance of the child and forbade Lilith from copulating with their grown sons, but she laughed at him and continued to do so. Alos grew jealous and angry with Lilith and called out to Eleda to constrain her. Eleda heard Alos' call and, while the couple slept, spoke to Alos and Lilith at the same time. Eleda appeared to Lilith in a stern, male visage, and to Alos as a beautiful woman. Eleda told Lilith that she was forbidden from copulating with her sons and that she was to take the pale girl to the sea and throw her into the waves. Eleda told Alos that he was obligated to sexually please Lilith in any manner she chose and whenever she wished."

Morowa laughed. "And that was his punishment?"

Ringwald ignored her question. "When they awoke, Alos and Lilith shared with each other what Eleda had told them. Lilith took the pale child and started for the sea. But, instead of destroying the child as Eleda had ordered, Lilith took two of her daughters, along with the baby, to a cave in the nearby woods, where she instructed her daughters to care for their pale sister. Then she returned to Alos and told him that the baby had been swallowed by the sea. Eleda immediately knew of Lilith's deceit and became enraged that she had so disobeyed the will of the gods.

"In this angry state, Eleda appeared to Alos and Lilith in the form of a hideous serpent. Alos was so greatly terrified that he fell to the ground, shaking and crying, but Lilith stood firm and said nothing. Because of Lilith's deceit, Eleda had decided to destroy all living things and to begin creation anew without humans, but when Eleda saw Alos' pitiful weakness, the god relented. 'You, Alos, I will spare,' Eleda said. 'But Lilith, you are banished from this place and, in punishment for your deceit, you are condemned to eternal life—barren, eternal life. When your body becomes ugly and old, full of pain and suffering, you will exchange it for the body of one of your female descendants—one of the daughters of your sons and daughters. The pale child whom you refused to destroy will live forever. She will accompany you in your wanderings, so as to remind you of your vile defiance of the gods. Since you have been too indulged to learn to care for your own needs, your maid-servant may come with you.'"

~*~

Morowa shook her head. "And so you're gonna tell us that Juba was a descendant of this Lilith?"

Ringwald laughed. "Indulge me yet a while longer." He leaned back in his chair. "So Lilith and her pale daughter were forced to forever wander the earth. Eleda decided that instead of destroying all living things, the god would just remove all memories of Lilith from everyone."

"So, Lilith wasn't Eve?" Morowa asked.

Ringwald shook his head and sighed. "Is this woman always so impatient?" he asked Hubert.

Hubert grinned. "Always."

Ringwald held up a finger in front of Morowa's face. "Now comes Eve," he said. "After Lilith was banished and memories of her were erased from every living being's mind, Alos was lonely and became depressed. Eleda saw Alos' despair, took pity, and decided to create a new mate for him. And so, Eleda created a new woman, blew life into her, and named her Eve. Eve was smaller than Lilith and very beautiful. In their time together, Eve and Alos produced many daughters and sons. As they came of age, the sons and daughters of Lilith and the sons and daughters of Eve reproduced and began to populate the earth."

Ringwald turned toward Morowa. "Now for Juba," he said. "Eleda found humankind's preoccupation with sex tiresome, and desired to rejoin Elemi to see what Elemi was up to. So, Eleda called in the Esu, a clan of lesser gods, and directed the Esu to watch over the humans and, above all else, to maintain harmony. Then Eleda left the earth, never to return. You got it so far, impatient Morowa?" he asked.

She nodded.

"As is always the case, when humans aren't closely supervised, they get into lots of trouble. First off, Alos and Lilith's twin sons fought over the attentions of their sisters, and eventually one twin killed the other. That, of course, is the origin of the biblical tale of Cain and Abel. Next, Lilith sensed the absence of Eleda and attempted to return to the place the Christians call Eden. When Lilith approached the dense, thorny hedge that Eleda had placed around Eden to bar her reentry, on the other side of the hedge she spied the first daughter of Eve, who was named Nanina. Lilith called out to her, Nanina approached, and the two spoke together through the bush. Lilith told Nanina that she, and not Eve, was the mother of all humankind and begged Nanina's assistance in helping her find a way to get into Eden through the thorny hedge. Lilith told Nanina that if she could not reenter Eden and take her rightful place as Alos' mate, she would wreak vengeance upon all. Nanina was frightened by Lilith and told her father, Alos, of the encounter. Since Eleda had stripped Alos of all memories of Lilith, Alos was thoroughly confused by Nanina's story and called out to the Esu for help.

"The Esu were perplexed. They knew that Lilith was a threat to the harmony that Eleda had charged them to maintain, but being only minor gods, they lacked the power to undo Eleda's acts of creation by destroying Lilith. They considered what to do and decided to give Nanina the power to protect humankind from Lilith's threats of vengeance against the descendants of Alos. Since Lilith was doomed to eternal life, and would continue to be a threat to humankind, the Esu further agreed to allow Nanina, before she died, to pass these powers on to her daughters, and her daughters to their daughters, and so on."

"So, according to your story, Juba was a descendant of Eve's daughter, Nanina, and Juba possessed the same powers the Esu had given to Nanina. That's it, right?" Morowa asked.

"Exactly so," Ringwald replied. "Understand that the ancient powers passed to Juba were only those powers required to protect mankind from the ravages of Lilith—Juba had no other occult capabilities. She was not a sibyl or enchantress."

"And was Juba unique or are there other descendants of Nanina who share the same powers?"

Ringwald stroked his white beard. "There is no way for me to know the number, but I suspect that there are many, many descendants of Nanina who walk the earth today; tens, or perhaps even hundreds, of thousands. Most have no knowledge of their gift. But, because Juba was of the Ashanti, it was different with her. She learned the creation stories and was taught about her powers to protect against Lilith in her childhood."

Hubert sighed and then slowly shook his head. "My dear uncle, it's a fascinating story and, in its colorful detail, it's worthy of the complex Ashanti tradition. But you don't seriously expect us to believe that these tales actually happened—and that Juba, my mother, inherited special powers from Eve's first daughter?"

"Ah, my overeducated nephew, it is of no concern to me if you believe all that I have told you, or not. Lilith and Hattie, her pale daughter, were condemned by the gods to eternal life and they both walk the earth today, just as you do. In addition to Ashanti lore, if you study ancient history, as I have, you will discover in the writings of Mesopotamia, Babylon, Assyria, and Egypt, many tales of how Lilith, Lilit, or Lilitu captured the souls of infant children and destroyed them. The Christian Bible, in the book of Isaiah, talks of a female demon and calls Lilith 'the screech owl' or 'night hag.' The ancient manuscripts tell of an aged, worn-out Lilith taking over the bodies of young women."

Morowa rose from her chair and then squatted in front of Ringwald, her face only inches from his. "Still, nothing you say explains why Juba, my mother-in-law, was such a bitter, controlling woman, why she was so disappointed that Hubert and I had no female child, or why she was cold and unfriendly to our boys. What you have told us is that Juba would have been able to pass on her powers to a daughter, but she had no daughter—and only one son, my husband."

Ringwald scowled. "I know precisely when my sister Juba became such an embittered woman—she first began to change after her husband was killed. Then, when Carrie, Hubert's first wife, took Hubert's girls back to England, Juba's personality completely shifted. Even as a small child, Juba was always intense and serious, but she wasn't nasty. I believe that she was deeply frustrated that she was unable to pass her ancient powers on to a daughter. But, you see, when she has no daughter, each female descendant of Nanina, before her death, can pass her powers to the nearest female blood relative. Since the two of you had no girl child, for Juba, that blood relative would be..."

"Naki," Morowa whispered.

"Yes, child," Ringwald confirmed. "That would be Naki, her first granddaughter."

~*~

Morowa waved goodbye to Ringwald while she pushed the switch to raise the Range Rover's side window, and then abruptly turned toward Hubert. "You don't believe a word of that nonsense, do you?"

Hubert grinned and exhaled. "Hold on a minute while I turn this tank around." He circled the courtyard, waved to Ringwald, tooted the horn, and then drove back toward the trail.

True to her nature, Morowa didn't pause for breath. "Of course, when I was a child, I heard the Ashanti creation stories—the stories of Eleda and Elemi—but Lilith, Alos, Nanina, and your mother? Do you think that Ringwald just made that stuff up?"

Hubert changed gears in the Range Rover. "I don't think he made it *all* up. From my childhood, I can remember stories about Lilith—stories my Ashanti relatives told while sitting around their fires at night. This Lilith they spoke of was a monster—a monster with a woman's body and claws on her feet and hands. A monster who preyed on young children. Lilith was the terrifying star of many of my childhood nightmares."

"But Nanina, and your mother, and her passing her powers to Naki—you've heard that stuff before?"

"Never, but it might explain a lot of things—things about my mother and her obsession with having a female grandchild."

"You really think Juba might have had some sort of protective powers—powers she inherited from Eve's daughter, Nanina?"

"Of course not, but if Juba believed that she had powers—powers she was required to pass on to a female relative—that might explain her obsession, her cold, unfeeling treatment of her grandsons, and how she turned on you when you told her that you couldn't bear any more children."

"So maybe that's why she tattooed Naki before Carrie took the girls away—backup in case you and I produced no granddaughters?"

Hubert nodded. "And maybe that explains why my mother left her jewelry to Naki and why she made me swear that after her death, I would have Ringwald identify the power stone and personally deliver the jewelry to Naki. A long time ago, at university, I had to take a course in psychology, and I still remember something we were taught. If a person becomes obsessed with an unsubstantiated belief, to that person, the belief becomes just as real as would any concrete, observable fact. Perhaps that's what she—" Hubert paused and focused on the rearview mirror. "What's this?" he asked. "Ringwald's jeep is coming up behind us. Did we leave something? You got the jewels, right?"

Morowa leaned forward and opened her purse. "They're right here," she replied.

Hubert downshifted and began to slow.

Morowa turned and looked back at the battered jeep that was quickly closing on the Range Rover. "That's not Ringwald!" Morowa shouted. "There's another man driving, and someone in a head scarf sitting next to him. I think they're going to crash into us."

Before the jeep could ram into the Range Rover, Hubert stepped down hard on the accelerator, the churning tires threw up a cloud of dirt and gravel, and the Range Rover shot forward.

"This doesn't look good," Hubert said—and, as if to support his understatement, three gunshots rang out and the Range Rover's rear hatch window exploded.

"Holy shit!" Morowa shouted. "They're trying to kill us!" She reached into the glove box and pulled out the revolver.

"Don't shoot! That old Colt is only accurate at short range; you'd just be wasting ammunition. Hold off until they get real close."

"Okay," she replied. "What are we gonna do?"

"Think you can crawl between the seats and get to the shotgun?"

"Sure," was all she said as she began to slide her torso through the gap between the front seats.

"Leave the handgun on the front seat, and try not to get cut on the broken glass back there."

Kneeling on the floor, her torso resting on the rear seats, Morowa pulled down one side of the split rear seatback and then crawled into the hatch. "Got the shotgun," she called, as two more shots rang out.

"Stay there and keep down on the floor. I've got an idea. A couple of hundred yards ahead, an old trail cuts in from the right, and then quickly switches back to the left. I can take the turn-off at enough speed so that they'll have to stop and back up to follow. That'll give us time to negotiate the switchback, stop, and wait there for the jeep to catch up. Since the switchback is a very sharp turn, they'll have to slow way down, and then, when they're close, you can go for them with the shotgun."

"Okay—sounds like a plan. I'll stay on the floor, and you shout when they're in range."

Hubert was impressed with her calmness, but then he'd always known Morowa was an unusually strong woman; she was descended from an ancient line of female warriors.

"Right, the turn-off is coming now. Brace yourself."

Hubert cut the wheel hard to the right and shot off the main trail, onto the overgrown secondary trail. He downshifted, carefully maneuvered the big SUV around the sharp turn, and then jerked to a stop. "They missed the turn-off," he called. "Should be along in about a minute. Wait until you can make out their faces and then go for the passenger first—he's the shooter. Then just empty the whole chamber into the cab. I'm gonna be on the ground behind the driver's side door with the .38, just in case one of them manages to get out alive. Okay?"

"Got it," Morowa called, as she extended the shotgun through the jagged remains of the hatch window.

Exactly as Hubert predicted, the jeep slowly turned the sharp corner and was less than fifty feet away from the stopped Range Rover. Morowa started to squeeze the trigger, but then froze; she recognized the passenger. It was Alexandria. The glint of the sun's reflection off the rifle in Alexandria's hand snapped Morowa out of her momentary paralysis. She fired the shotgun at Alexandria, then pumped it and fired again. She turned her attention to the driver and fired off three quick bursts, then fired the final round back toward where Alexandria had been sitting. Hubert ran to the side of the jeep and pointed the .38 into the front seat. He pulled back and tucked the handgun under his belt. The .38 wasn't needed—the blasts of the shotgun had reduced the two occupants to bloody carcasses.

Morowa climbed out of the Range Rover and cautiously looked through the shot-out windshield into the jeep. "Who's the man?" she asked.

"Hard to tell now, but I think he was Alexandria's youngest son. Looks like Alexandria could understand English a lot better than Uncle Ringwald thought. We'll need to go back and check up on the old guy."

Morowa nodded. "Let's hope his blood isn't on these diamonds, along with theirs."

16

Gordon was unloading bags of groceries from the new SUV when Deputy McGill appeared in the driveway. The deputy was obviously off duty—he was dressed in faded jeans and a green Miami Dolphins T-shirt.

"Hey! What're you doin' around here, Deputy?" a puzzled Gordon asked.

"Hey, Mr. Hale. I moonlight for my brother-in-law. He's got a property-maintenance-and-surveillance business here on the island and just last week he got a contract on the house next door. We put up the storm shutters this morning, so I thought I'd take a minute to drop over and see how Miss Rawlings was doin'. Hope I'm not interrupting anything. When I saw that SUV out there, I thought you might be havin' company."

"Grab that last bag and come on in. Nila's in the kitchen with the girls," Gordon replied.

Nila was spoon-feeding cereal to a hungry Julie. Janna was cranky and refusing to eat. "You're not interrupting a thing," she said, having heard them talking. "And we don't have guests. That's my new car—Gordy bought it for me. I love it. It shifts all by itself and has all sorts of gadgets—even air-conditioned seats."

"It's a beauty, Miss Rawlings. My girlfriend loves Lincolns."

Gordon filled the deputy's coffee cup. "Deputy, I think we've been through enough together that we can use first names now, especially since you're off duty."

The deputy nodded. "I'm Joshua. My girlfriend, Tyrece, calls me Josh, but everyone else on the island calls me Mick."

"Mick, Mick, Mick," Julie called out as she banged her small fist on the metal high-chair tray.

"I guess you're Mick," Nila said with a grin. "Lately, Julie's discovered she's a parrot, not a little girl."

"So, Mick, you said you have new information about Maggie?" Gordon asked.

"Not exactly. It's about her sister, Amy. You haven't heard from her, Nila?"

Nila shook her head. "Not a word."

"She was your good friend?"

"Was?" Nila asked, her voice rising. "She's dead?"

Mick nodded. "I'm sorry to have to be the one to tell you—Amy Cartwright died of a heart attack."

Nila covered her eyes with one hand and started to sob. "Gordy, could you take over here, please?" She dropped the spoon on the table and walked to the sink. When she turned back toward the table there were tears rolling down her cheeks. She raised a dishtowel to her face.

Gordon stood and embraced her. The twins silently stared at Nila and Gordon with troubled expressions on their small faces.

After a few seconds, Nila lowered the towel to her chin. "When did it happen?"

"About a week ago, at her parents' home in Pennsylvania, near Philadelphia. I haven't seen the official report just yet. We shoulda received it from Highway Patrol by now—I'll check it out when I go on duty tonight. The sergeant I spoke with said that there's no question it was heart failure. She'd had a past history of heart problems and had heart surgery as a child."

"That's so sad," Nila sobbed. "She told me about the heart surgery—she was born with a hole in her heart and had surgery as an infant. Amy was such a lovely woman in every way—talented and with so much promise. We weren't exactly close friends. I'd only known her for a little over a year, but I'm sure we would have become much closer. We were like each other in so many ways."

Janna began making the little unhappy noises that were always the prelude to a full-fledged howl. Nila wiped the tears from her own face and resumed her seat in front of the two high chairs. The twins stared into her face.

"It's okay," she said to them with a smile as she retrieved the feeding spoon.

"Mama nadda, mama nadda!" Janna shouted.

"Mama nadda," Julie took up the chant as she bounced in her chair.

Gordon moved to Nila's side and stroked the back of her neck. "Here, I'll take over."

Nila turned toward him. "I'm fine. I can do this—it was just the shock. I've never had a friend die before." She patted his hand. "Thanks, but I can do this."

Mick turned around in his chair. "There's just one more thing I think I should tell you."

"About Amy?" Gordon asked.

"Actually, it's about Margaret Cartwright. When she robbed the liquor store and shot the clerk, she left a car behind—a nearly new Corvette convertible that was registered to her sister in Pennsylvania. The Corvette was out of gas. Maybe that's why she took the clerk's old Chevy. So, it's possible that Margaret Cartwright was at her parents' home in Pennsylvania at about the same time her sister Amy had the heart attack. Maybe she saw that her sister was dead and stole the car. Kinda strange coincidence, isn't it?"

"Do the Pennsylvania police think there's a connection with Maggie to her sister's death?" Gordon asked.

"I don't think so. As I said, they're convinced that Amy Cartwright died of heart failure. After I read the report tonight, I'll give you a call if there's anything else."

The deputy stood up. "I'd better get back next door and help Tony put the ladders on the truck. My shift starts at six, so I can still get a few hours' sleep before I go on the road. That's if Tyrece doesn't have a honey-do list for me. I'll give you a call tomorrow if anything interesting turns up in the report."

"They're gone now, the old lady and her nurse—the tall, pale woman?" Gordon asked.

"I don't know about the old lady. She must've left earlier. Just after we got here this morning, a limo picked up the pale nurse, and a younger woman. She was pretty skinny—short brown hair, with dark glasses, a long dress, and a big floppy hat. They didn't answer when I hollered hello. The old lady wasn't with them."

Gordon frowned. "That's curious. Hattie, Mrs. Silk's nurse, left a text on my cell phone sometime last night saying they were leaving early this morning. They had some unexpected business back in Louisiana and didn't know when they'd be back. I'm glad they're out of here. Mrs. Silk gives me the creeps—always has."

"Something else kinda strange," Mick said. "There's this big fifty-five-gallon steel drum around the side of the house in the walled garden. It was all charred and burned-out like, and all the grass within about ten feet of the barrel was black, as well. Looks like somebody had a very hot fire goin' for a couple of days in a row. The inside of the barrel was all swept out, and no trace of whatever they was burning was left."

Gordon stood and walked toward the door. "Like I said, I wish my father had never sold Myra Silk the house."

17

Most everyone in Tortola knew about the Purple Palace—three connected, single-story, concrete-block buildings nestled between the coast road and the sea, not far from the west end of the island. Maybe at an earlier time the palace had actually been painted purple, but it was now sky blue. The color had changed but not the name. Dr. Ponder, his wife, and two children lived in the largest of the buildings. Another housed a clinic with his examining and operating rooms, and the last building consisted of four luxurious, private hospital rooms. To the rear of the buildings were a large kidney-shaped swimming pool, a shady cabana, a well-stocked open-air bar, and numerous lounge chairs and large umbrellas. Ponder employed a staff of seven: a reconstructive surgeon, an anesthesiologist, two operating room nurses, a practical nurse, a chambermaid/cook who also served as a poolside bartender, and a waitress. The medical professionals had all been recruited from the UK. Although Ponder had long ago moved to the British Virgin Islands from the UK, he had a strong Central European accent and no one knew his exact country of origin. His young, dark wife was a *Belonger*, a native of the BVI. The Ponder family kept mostly to themselves, but because of Ponder's charity work at Tortola's only hospital, an annual scholarship he funded for a local student to attend nursing school in nearby Puerto Rico, and his wife's generous contributions to her church, the Ponder family were held in high esteem throughout the community.

Most of the visitors to the Palace were women—wealthy middle-aged women who came for tummy tucks, face lifts, liposuction, breast augmentation or reduction, vaginal tightening, nose jobs, and a host of other cosmetic or elective procedures. After their surgeries, these women would usually stay at the clinic for a few days, chill by the pool, watch TV, or read while the staff pampered them and monitored their healing. Occasionally, someone famous or notorious would reserve the entire clinic for the time of his or her surgery and recovery. A second group of both women and men came for reconstructive surgery: scars, burns, and gunshot wounds. A still smaller number of patients sought Dr. Ponder out for his recognized expertise in altering and changing faces and identities. For these services, Ponder's fees were hideously expensive, and advance payment was required in dollars, euros, renminbi, certified diamonds, or gold.

It was May, during low season on the island, and the Purple Palace had only two resident patients. Lilith, now in Maggie's body, lay on her back on a padded lounge chair next to the pool. Lilith's nose, chin, and throat were bandaged; she'd been through several surgical procedures and had more to go. They'd fed her a high-calorie, high-fat diet before the surgery began and she had put on ten pounds. The clinic brought in a professional beautician who recolored and restyled her short brown hair, salvaging the hack job Hattie had done before they left Castle Key. Her nails had been done and her skin treated with luxuriant oils and creams. The scratches on her ankles and legs had healed. The strong painkillers they gave her turned the world where she lived into a soft, quiet, and unthreatening space.

Hattie rolled the large umbrella in its heavy stand closer to Lilith. "The big nurse said no sun on your face—the doctor's gonna do your ears and hairline tomorrow and he doesn't want you sunburned."

"Go check again."

"I just checked twenty minutes ago. Sara said she'd bring it out here to the terrace as soon as it comes."

"Go check. Sara's lazy and won't move her fat ass until she has to."

Hattie shook her head and sighed in frustration. "All right, all right, but I know it won't be here yet. They said 3:30 on the phone and it's just past that now. Everything happens lots slower down here."

"Go check!" Lilith spat out.

"Doctor told you not to raise your voice," Hattie replied as she rose from her chair and stepped toward the sliding glass door. As she approached, the door slid open and a large brown forearm and hand reached out through the opening with a red-and-white cardboard mailing envelope.

"This what all the fuss about?" the owner of the arm asked.

Hattie grabbed the envelope and returned to the chair next to Lilith's.

"Hurry," Lilith told her.

Hattie pulled the opening strip on the top of the mailer, extracted a manila envelope that contained a sheaf of papers, and dropped the empty mailer onto the ground. She began to read to herself.

"What's my name?" Lilith demanded.

Hattie grinned. "I don't think you're gonna like this! You're De-von! De-von Anne Sinclair. De-von Sinclair—it sounds like a stripper, or a porn star!"

"How do you spell De-von?" Lilith anxiously asked.

"Just like it sound, D-e-v-o-n, De-von."

"That's Devon, not De-von, you stupid girl!"

Hattie frowned. "Why you say that?"

"Because if it were De-von it would have a hyphen, or a capital V. It's Devon, like the county in England."

"Oh," Hattie said. She continued to read aloud, the animation now gone from her voice. "Well, Miss Devon, you're from Baton Rouge. Your parents are dead and you don't have any brothers or sisters, neither. You went to LSU and have a masters in ancient history."

Lilith laughed louder than she was supposed to and then clutched her throat with both hands. "Damn, damn," she hoarsely whispered.

"You all right?" Hattie asked without sympathy.

Lilith nodded. "Vocal cords still sting," she mouthed. "Ancient history, huh? Clarisse has a twisted sense of humor."

"Where was I?" Hattie ran her finger down the page. "Oh, yeah. You're thirty-one, never been married, and you're independently wealthy. Your father owned some mines and left you lots a money. You wanna hear more?"

"What are all the papers?"

Hattie sorted through the documents. "Let's see: a birth certificate, university diplomas, and a driver's license. This here's a passport but it don't have a picture."

"We'll take care of that when the doctor's all through and we get these bandages off."

"There's an income tax return for last year and one for the year before. These here are a deed and all the real estate papers for the house in Castle Key. Myra Silk sold it to you for 1.8 million."

"What else?"

"Lots more stuff." Hattie sorted through the papers. "Social security statements, medical insurance cards, AAA membership card, three credit cards, stockbroker's statements, bank statements, photos of an older couple with a dog—probably your parents. Then there's this bunch a pages stapled together. It says, 'Devon Anne Sinclair—Family History.'"

Lilith smiled. "And poor old Myra?"

Hattie thumbed through the pages. "Death certificate and an obituary clipping from a New Orleans newspaper. Myra died two days after she sold you the house—clipping says it was a stroke. Listen to this part of the obit." Hattie chuckled. "'Myra Silk's family had all predeceased her. Only Devon Sinclair, her young friend and neighbor, and Hattie Shiffer, her long-time nurse and companion, were at her hospital bedside when she passed.'"

Devon smiled as broadly as her swollen, recreated lips would allow. "Clarisse does excellent work."

Hattie nodded. "Any of this stuff real?"

"Yes, most of it. Each time I change bodies, Clarisse does extensive research. She finds someone dead, and suitable for my purposes—someone like Devon. Then she collects ID and documents, like birth certificates and driver's licenses, from the various city and state agencies—agencies that haven't been notified of Devon's untimely passing. Once she's got the ID, she just creates the rest of Devon's life. Myra's death certificate and the newspaper clipping are forgeries, of course. What's the picture on the driver's license look like?"

Hattie sorted through the documents again and found the laminated card. "Not good. Big nose and thin lips. The blue eyes are the only things that looks like you—but then, I don't really know what you're gonna look like when they take them bandages off, do I?"

"They'll redo the license photo when they do the passport. Ponder has people in St. Thomas who'll take care of everything; it's all part of the package. Ponder will start on you Monday, Hattie. He's gonna make you a sex goddess: perfect tits, sculpted ass, and green contacts."

"But I still gotta be albino?"

"Maybe next time when you change, you could be my twin? How'd you like to be my pale twin?"

"As long as I was good-lookin' that'd be jus' fine."

"Next time we're gonna be twins. Both of us," Devon Anne Sinclair hoarsely whispered.

18

"Mary sends her love and this kiss, too." Nila bent over the back of Gordon's chair and kissed his neck. "She said to tell you that she's sent an email about the house. She needs to get your approval as soon as possible. You didn't tell me you were selling the Concord house."

Gordon pushed away the spiral-bound manual he'd been reading and swiveled the desk chair to face her. "No, I guess I didn't. I've been preoccupied with studying for this damn bar exam. I thought I could blow it off with a quick review. Since Massachusetts has one of the more stringent processes, I assumed that the Florida bar exam would be a piece of cake. I was wrong—there are enough detailed differences that it'll require more prep time than I expected. Not a big deal, though."

"I'm sorry I interrupted. Would you like me to go away?"

"No, never!" Gordon almost shouted as he wrapped his arms around her slim body. He pulled her onto his lap and awkwardly kissed the tip of her nose.

"Is this part of your exam prep?" she asked, laughing.

Gordon slid his right hand under her halter top. "Actually, I'm studying to be a gynecologist, and I need more hands-on practice." He ran the tip of his finger over her already-erect nipple.

"You're randy this afternoon."

"*Randy*—that's one of your better English terms. It sounds so much more erotic than *horny*. Horny conjures up visions of dirty old men. Randy, randy, randy," Gordon said in three different tones of voice. "I like the sound of that much better." As he talked, he slid Nila's halter top up, over her breasts.

She raised her arms above her head. "Skin the bunny," she said. Gordon maneuvered the halter top over her head and through her arms, then began nuzzling her breasts.

"Girls asleep?"

"No, they're in the playpen out on the lanai—likely to be occupied for a bit longer." She stood and dropped her shorts and cotton thong to the carpet. "Another few months and they'll be tearing about the house on their own. That'll stifle our spontaneity."

Gordon rose from the chair and gently encircled her in his embrace. "Ever hear of leg irons?" he whispered in her ear.

Nila grinned. "You're a sexual gannet, you know."

"Gannet?"

"Another British term for your collection; a gannet's a large fish-eating seabird that can eat so many fish that it's temporarily unable to fly—and while digesting its catch, can be dashed on the rocks and killed."

Gordon slipped his hand between her legs. "You're wet already," he said.

"Afraid it's becoming a permanent condition." Nila grinned, dropped to her knees, and slid his patterned swim trunks to his ankles.

~*~

Gordon hadn't bothered to dress. He was sprawled on the office carpet with an imitation zebra-skin pillow under his head.

"They're still playing with their interlocking blocks," Nila said, tiptoeing into the office. She, too, hadn't bothered to put her clothes back on. She sat down on the carpet next to Gordon's legs and began to massage his left foot.

"That feels so good. Who taught you massage?"

"No one, really. Della and I used to massage each other when we were little—guess it's something that comes naturally."

"You're full of surprises today—nice surprises. Thanks."

Nila giggled. "I think it was my turn, wasn't it? I didn't finish telling you about Mary's call. She—"

"Sorry I forgot to tell you about the Concord house," he said, interrupting her. "A while ago, before you and I met, I got Susan, Karen's stepsister, to check out the place. I think I told you—Susan owns a real estate agency."

Nila nodded. "You did tell me."

"I wanted Susan to start the process to sell the place and also to see if there was anything in the house that she might want—Karen's personal things, or any of the furniture or decorations. Some of the furniture came from Karen's parents' house. They were things that had been passed down through her family: antiques, paintings, and an old grandfather clock. I wanted Susan and Karen's stepbrother Todd to take whatever they wanted. Anyway, when Susan went through the house, she decided that she'd like to buy it for herself and her husband, and made what I thought was a fair offer. Except for my clothes and other personal things—my desk, books, and the Hale family documents and papers in my office—I sold it fully furnished: curtains, furniture, dishes, pots, pans, and everything."

"You were that positive you wanted to put all that behind you? When did this happen?"

Gordon groaned with pleasure. "Please don't stop." He moved his right foot close to Nila. "You're so good. Right one next, please."

She shifted to her left and took Gordon's foot between her knees.

"That's almost as good as sex. Especially when you do the arch—oh, that's it, wonderful...Where was I?"

"You decided to sell the house."

"I made that decision when I took Karen's ashes back to Concord and slept at the house. Mary wanted me to stay with her and Milt, but I was determined to see if I still felt the same about the place as I did before Karen and I left. The thing is, it was Karen's house—I never really liked the place, with its old furniture, low ceilings, and creaky floors. Never liked it at all.

The house was built around 1800; it had been well maintained over the years and was still structurally sound. The family who sold the house to us had the bathrooms and kitchen modernized and replaced the electrical system, the heating, and the roof. It had just gone on the market when Karen and I announced our engagement. Karen loved old things—anything charming and old. I was in on the decision—well, sort of. I guess if I'd seriously objected we would have bought a different style of house, but I didn't object. Don't misunderstand me; Karen and I were very happy for the brief time we lived there. It's just that once she was gone, I knew that I never wanted to live in that house again."

"It's been sold, then?"

"Officially, next month. The email from Mary is the inventory of everything that stays with the house. I have to sign off on that; it's the last step before closing."

"Actually, Mary's call wasn't really about the house. She said her husband has volunteered to design my wedding dress and Della's dress, too. He's good, this Milton, I gather?"

"'Good' isn't the correct adjective for Milt. I don't know anything about women's fashions, but Milt is world-famous. He did the inauguration ball gown for one of the first ladies—I can't remember which one, but it's in the Smithsonian."

"Crikey! He's that famous?"

"Yes, that famous. He's done some gowns for your royals, as well."

"Fancy that! Little Nila Rawlings in a wedding gown by the famous Milton—what's his surname?"

"Ashton. Milton Ashton. Milt does the creative work and Mary runs the business—a very profitable business."

Nila frowned. "You wouldn't mind about the expense for the dress?"

"Like I told you—I want this wedding to be the most special event in your life. Besides, I'm sure it will be Mary and Milt's wedding present."

"How exciting! Then you wouldn't mind if we go to Miami week after next? Mary and Milton are hosting a wedding show at one of the big hotels and Mary said that Milton can fit me and maybe Doo-Doo too, if she can fly over. Plus, Della can meet you and the girls, and I'll meet Milton. How exciting!"

Gordon sat up, his back against the couch. He smiled at Nila's enthusiasm. "It's a wonderful plan, but there's a problem. I've got less than two weeks to prepare for the bar exam—I don't think I can spare the time. But that's no reason to keep you from going."

"This exam is important, isn't it?"

"Not exactly a matter of life and death, but it is important. I'm an almost-partner in one of Boston's top law firms, so it would be a big embarrassment to everyone if I didn't pass first time around and had to retake the test."

Nila stood and retrieved her top, shorts, panties, and Gordon's swim trunks from the carpet. "I suspect that I don't really need to go to Miami. Mary said that Milton could work from photos and measurements for Della's dress, so I guess he could do the same for mine."

"I'll drive you and the girls over. It only takes about three hours to central Miami. I can drop the three of you off, say hello to Mary and Milt—and Della, too, if she can make it—and be back here in the late afternoon. Then you and the girls can hang out with Della for a couple days and maybe have dinner with Mary and Milt. I'll come get you after the exam. It'll give me something to look forward to after all the studying. Whadya think?"

"You wouldn't mind the driving?"

"No problem."

"How exciting! Let's call Della. I hope she can organize to come at such short notice. I'll call Mum, too."

"Don't you think you ought to get the dates squared away with Mary and Milt before you call Della and your mum? Why don't we call Mary together?"

"I guess we should dress first," Nila said with a smile as she handed Gordon his swimsuit. "Oh—I nearly forgot the reason I invaded your privacy. I wanted to tell you that I talked to Beverly when I was shopping at Kopel's this morning. She asked if we'd seen Myra Silk's obituary in the *Sun*. When I told her we had, she said that she'd heard the new owner of the big house was getting ready to move in soon and asked if we'd met her."

Gordon shook his head. "No need to read the paper when we've got Beverly."

"Beverly says the owner's hired a house-clearance company to clean out the place, as well as a decorator and a contractor to redo the inside. The contractor told Beverly he's only talked with the new owner on the phone but that she sounds young."

"Actually, I noticed there have been a lot of vans and trucks parked in the driveway in the last few weeks. It'll be nice to have someone younger in the neighborhood. Is she married? Any children?"

"Beverly didn't know anything more except that her name is Devon Sinclair. Devon, like in England."

Gordon pulled on his swim trunks. "Devon, huh? She was mentioned in the obituary. It doesn't really matter how old she is, or if she's married or not. Any new neighbor would be a big improvement on Myra Silk."

19

Thierry was in the shower. He was shouting over the hiss of the spray and the metallic squeal of the barely functioning ceiling-exhaust fan. "You won't believe these two girls I met at the pool this morning. Freakin' gorgeous, swimming topless—perfect bodies, great tits, pretty faces. I mean, real classy stuff."

"Whores?" Bruno asked.

"Not likely," Thierry shouted over the noise of the fan. "They spoke to each other in English, but used perfect French with me when they realized I was from France."

"Doesn't mean much—top Russian and Czech whores speak lots a languages," Bruno replied.

"Paco says the women flew in on a private flight last night from the BVI and are booked for spa treatments every day this week. Whores don't stay here—way too expensive."

Bruno grinned. "Then what in hell you doin' here?"

"I'm an employee—just like you. Difference is, the hotel pays you and the ladies pay me. That's why they come here, of course—lookin' for a lot more than a suntan. This place would close down without some young, hard, masculine bodies for rent—yours as well as mine."

Thierry stepped out of the shower stall, switched off the noisy fan, and began to dry his mass of brown ringlets with a thick hotel towel. He was six feet tall, with a well-proportioned, tanned, athletic body, and expressive brown eyes. "The older of the two is the type you like," he said to Bruno. "Maybe forty, tall, very white skin, with light-red hair and a hard, muscular body. Haven't seen a body like hers around here in a long while."

"How about the other?"

"She's probably a model—slim, with long legs, short brown hair and bright-blue eyes. Probably in her thirties." Thierry tossed the damp towel into a wicker basket. "Not much chance either of 'em pays for sex. But then, money isn't everything—eh, Bruno?"

"I'm on massage today. I'll see that I get to do whichever of them is signed up. Women love to talk about physical stuff during massage—I'll check how she responds to a bit of subtle flirting. Talk to you this afternoon. What's your aunt got you up to today?"

Thierry moved to the small bedroom, took a pair of worn canvas boating shorts from a cardboard box at the foot of one of the twin beds, and pulled them over his slim hips without unzipping the fly. "Still workin' on the diesel. Chuckles said the parts I ordered came yesterday. If the Cro-Magnon at the marina got the order right this time, I should finish today."

Bruno smirked. "Better be careful. The girls in the restaurant know that you call your Aunt Catherine 'Chuckles,' but if she found out she'd be steamed. You know she doesn't have a sense of humor—especially when she thinks she's being disrespected. Don't want to lose your free room an' board, do ya?"

Thierry looked around the small room and scowled. "Not much of a room. This economic collapse is really cuttin' into my tips. Those teachers from Aix only gave me two hundred euros—two hundred for two nights humpin' the both of 'em. Pretty sad. You remember Hanna, that rich, sixty-ish Swede who always comes in June? Paco says he doesn't have a reservation for her. I mean, I can always count on Hanna for a grand—and mostly just for being her companion. You've been sleeping in the room most nights—you haven't been doin' much business, either?"

"Not really, but I'm okay. Between what your aunt pays me and the tips I get at the spa, I've put away enough so's I don't have to look for other work when the resort shuts down at the end of the summer. I could do with a few more sleepovers. That Corsican couple—the older guy with the wife half his age—was my last. Kinda kinky. She wasn't a beauty but had a nice, firm body—and after some champagne, was full of enthusiasm. The old guy stripped off, sat in a chair, and watched us go at it. When I was finished, he gave me two hundred, pointed to the door, and took my place. We did an encore the next afternoon—I figure he wanted me to get her pregnant."

"You and me could write a book." Thierry pulled a clean, but paint-spattered, T-shirt over his head and slid his feet into a pair of worn flip-flops. "Talk to you tonight. I should be back and cleaned up by four. Meet you here or at the pool. See what you can find out about the new girls."

"Yeah, right," Bruno replied as he switched on the annoying fan and stepped into the shower.

~*~

Le Cap Sud was the most exclusive boutique spa-hotel in Martinique and one of the more expensive in the Caribbean. Except for the August/September months when it was closed, Le Cap's twenty-four spacious, expensive suites were nearly always booked months ahead. However, the sputtering economy in Europe and the US had resulted in vacancies all through the winter high season. Mid-season was down as well. April was only half-booked, and May was even worse. If it weren't for the eight women from Wisconsin who'd booked as a group for two weeks in June, Catherine Bizzot, Le Cap's owner, would have closed the spa a month early and spent the extra time with her boyfriend in Provence.

Devon sprawled on her belly on a poolside lounge chair, reading a French fashion magazine. She was thoroughly covered in SPF 50 sunscreen, with two umbrellas completely shading her nearly nude body from the morning sun. As soon as Hattie went for her ten o'clock massage, Devon planned to move into the direct sun for an hour to begin restoring some color to the hospital-pale skin that she'd inherited from Maggie. Dr. Ponder's big nurse had warned Devon about the risks of exposing her milk-white, and surgically altered, skin to the intense tropical sun, but Devon was sure that an hour's exposure in the morning and then again in the late afternoon wouldn't be a problem. Hattie didn't agree. Since Tortola, she'd resumed the role of Devon's watchful acolyte, a role she'd abandoned during the years she'd spent as the nurse for old Myra Silk. But now, Hattie would fuss over Devon's well-being. Like the dominant partner in a long-enduring marriage, Devon would pretend to listen and then ignore her.

"Pardon the interruption, Mademoiselle," the pretty, round-faced young woman said. "I am the manageress of the hotel restaurant and would like to speak with you about the culinary options here at Le Cap Sud. Would it be possible for me to take a few minutes to discuss this with you now—or would you prefer another time?"

Devon put down her magazine and leisurely rolled onto her back. Her bare, enhanced breasts and flat tummy reinforced the young woman's speculation that Devon was an actress or a model.

Devon raised her sunglasses. "Culinary options? What culinary options?"

The young woman clutched a large menu to her chest. "We like to make sure each guest will enjoy their favorite foods and beverages prepared to their specific tastes. Depending on the fresh ingredients available to him each day, our chef prepares exceptional menus—but if there are dishes that are your particular favorites, we'll make every effort to obtain the ingredients and prepare them to your requirements."

"Oh—like what?" she asked.

The young woman brushed her sandy-blonde hair away from her forehead and smiled. "We've satisfied our guests' requests for any number of things: Maine lobster, Sydney rock oysters from Australia, or French Creuse oysters, Iranian caviar,

California abalone, wild boar, antelope steaks, shark fin soup, and suckling pig. There are flights to Martinique from several North America cities every day, and from France every other day. With the internet, it's no problem obtaining most anything within a day or two. We have an exceptional wine collection in our refrigerated and humidity-controlled storage units, but we can order any specific wines, unusual vodkas and spirits, or even beer. I'd advise against flying in older vintages of red wine—the sediment gets stirred up during transport and there isn't usually enough time after it gets here for the sediment to resettle. The wines can turn out muddy."

Devon extended her hand. "Let me see the menu," she said.

"And the wine list?"

Devon nodded.

The manageress bent at the waist and held out the menu. "This is today's lunch menu. The fish were all caught this morning and the meats and poultry have never been frozen. Chef hasn't yet finished the menu for this evening, but it will be available shortly. The breakfast buffet was to your satisfaction?"

"Breakfast was fine; my companion and I eat lightly in the morning." Devon scanned the lunch menu. "This will do for us." She placed the menu and wine list on her lap. "In the evening, my companion eats only meat as her main course—any sort of meat that is cooked very little."

The manageress nodded. "I'll inform the chef."

Devon flipped through the pages of the wine list. "The man who was here by the pool this morning—a tall man with curly brown hair and green eyes. Is he an employee, or a guest? Do you know who I mean?"

The young woman nodded. "Thierry. I'm sure you mean Thierry."

"His accent was *provençal*; I'm quite sure of that."

The manageress smiled. "You're very good with accents. Are you French?"

Devon shrugged. "No, but in the past, I lived in France for long enough to recognize regional accents."

"Thierry is from Provence—from Antibes. Actually, he's neither an employee nor a guest. His aunt is the owner of Le Cap Sud and Thierry visits for several months each spring. Madame Bizzot also owns the marina at the end of the bay. Thierry's a skilled mechanic. He works on her charter boats and gets them into shape for the high season. He also services the refrigeration and air-conditioning units at the hotel."

"He's a bit of a handyman, then?"

The young woman couldn't suppress a smile. "You could put it that way, yes."

Devon reached into her bag on the low poolside table. She removed a twenty-euro note from her wallet and tucked it between the pages of the wine list before she returned the list to the manageress. "With lunch, we'll have the Batard-Montrachet—not overly chilled. Also, the catch on my favorite necklace is broken. Perhaps this handyman could have a look at it? Perhaps you could ask him to call me?"

"With pleasure, Mademoiselle. He usually finishes at the marina by midafternoon. I'll have him call you when he comes to the hotel. Please let me know if there is anything else I can do to make your stay more pleasant."

"I'll let you know."

The young woman nodded, turned on her heel, and walked briskly toward the restaurant, just as Hattie emerged from the masses of bright red bougainvillea and palms that formed a visual border between the pool area and spa buildings.

"You stayin' out a the sun then?" Hattie asked. She was wrapped in a silken robe with Le Cap Sud embroidered on the breast pocket.

"Of course," Devon replied, and rolled onto her stomach. "I'll have lunch at one in the restaurant. You'll be done by then?"

"I don't know—I'm gettin' a manicure after. You're not doin' the spa today?"

"No, not today—I'm relaxing. I'll start tomorrow."

"Shall I sign you up for a massage?"

"It's taken care of," Devon replied. "When we checked in, remember?"

"Oh, yeah. Well, I'm off. Don' wait for me at lunch. There's a health food and juice bar inside the spa; maybe I'll just be healthy for a change."

Devon turned onto her side. "You may not see me for dinner. If I'm not at our table by eight, you're on your own."

Hattie put her hands on her hips and grinned. "You take care. That body's had plenty a experience, but it's been well over a decade since your mind's had an orgasm. Take it slow."

"Goodbye, Hattie."

"Uh huh."

~*~

The coroner peeled off the rubber gloves and untied the rubber apron, then dropped them all into a plastic bin. He washed his hands, wrists, and forearms. "Myocardial infarction: a heart attack. Specifically, cardiogenic shock. The septum—the wall that separates the left and right ventricles—was severely ruptured."

The uniformed policeman was scribbling in his small notebook with a stump of a pencil. "How ya spell that myocardial thing?"

"Just like it sounds. Look—I'm the coroner, not a journalist. You'll get my report when I'm finished."

"Drugs?" the policeman asked without looking up from his notebook.

"Not really. A trace of marijuana—nothing more."

"So, he just had a heart attack and died. Young, strong guy."

"Appearances can be deceiving. I don't have access to his medical records, but I'd bet he had a preexisting condition called Prinzemetal's Angina. It probably wasn't diagnosed—most likely, he never even knew he had the condition. I didn't see any evidence of earlier scarring. I suspect intense physical exertion exacerbated the condition and drove the heart into an uncontrolled spasm, triggering the heart attack. Perhaps something stressful that happened to him at the hotel."

"Oh, like what?"

"Put your notebook away. What I'm gonna tell ya won't be in the report and I'll deny I ever said it but—I think this guy may have been screwed to death."

"You're kidding!"

The doctor shook his head. "It's my guess that the cardiogenic shock that blew his heart apart and killed him resulted from an extended period of intense physical exertion and nervous tension. His penis was inflamed and his testicles were all shriveled up. They looked like walnuts—he must have ejaculated multiple times over a relatively short period to get 'em like that. His back was all scratched up, like it had been gouged by fingernails."

The policeman whistled. "Girls at the hotel told me he was always hitting' on them and on the hotel guests, as well. The cook said that some of the guys who work at the spa have a regular stud service goin' for the female guests, and that our boy was probably part of it. Nothin' unusual, nothin' illegal. It happens at all of the spa-resorts—women on their own looking for more than a tan and a backrub. We get more than a dozen complaints every season from foreign bimbos who say the young guys that they invite to their rooms help themselves to jewelry or cash when they leave."

The doctor shrugged. "Guess we're in the wrong line of work. You said they found his body by the pool?"

"Yeah. He was in a lounge chair. He'd been smokin' a cigarette and it'd burned all the way down to his fingers. Security found him about midnight—there's no telling exactly how long he'd been out there. I'm sure the woman who runs the restaurant knows which guest he was with, but she didn't wanna say and I didn't think it mattered, so I didn't press her. I mean, it was one of them mycardi-infection things that killed him, right? Like you said, a heart attack? Nothin' suspicious—nothin' more I should investigate?"

The doctor removed his glasses and put them in his shirt pocket. As he pushed through the morgue's swinging doors, he called over his shoulder, "Myocardial infarction resulting in severe cardiogenic shock—that's what's goin' on the death certificate."

The policeman nodded, closed his small notebook, and then put it and the pencil into his back pocket.

20

Carrie Trumble had owned the house at 1 Holland Park Road for eighteen years. When she returned from Ghana with her two young girls, but without Hubert, her husband, Carrie had purchased the house from her uncle's estate. It was a terraced house—the first in a long row of attached, three-story town houses. Although it wasn't particularly large or imposing, it was located in a desirable section of London, one block from Kensington High Street, around the corner from her travel-bookings business. It was also conveniently located a few blocks from Tube stations on two different underground-railway lines. Since she'd owned the house, real estate in West Kensington and also neighboring, once-seedy, Notting Hill had become trendy and expensive. She'd raised her two daughters in the house and had been perfectly content to remain there until three years ago, when her sciatica made climbing the two flights of stairs progressively more painful. Reluctantly, she was about to put her house up for sale when her boyfriend Nick surprised her with an unusual birthday present—a compact, single-passenger elevator.

Carrie was 44, attractive, and trim, with large dark eyes and naturally blonde hair. She was regularly pursued by men a decade her junior. For the last five years, Nick had been the only man in Carrie's life, and—though Nick was thoroughly devoted to Carrie—for reasons only the two of them understood, they never married. Nick owned an engineering company in Dorset, a three-hour drive from West Kensington. He lived in Dorset from Monday morning until Friday afternoon and then drove up to London to spend weekends with Carrie.

Carrie was halfway between the second and first floors in the claustrophobic, one-person, compact elevator that Nick had engineered and installed, when she heard the doorbell. She pressed a button and spoke into the intercom. "I'll be there in just a minute," she shouted over the hum of the elevator's motor. The descent complete, she stepped from the door-less box into the space that, before the elevator's installation, had been the kitchen pantry, and walked to the front door.

"Mrs. Rawlings?" the slim, well-dressed, dark-complected woman asked.

Carrie was momentarily taken back—she hadn't been addressed as Mrs. Rawlings for years. "Trumble," she replied. "Carrie Trumble. Rawlings was my married name—I've been divorced for a long time."

"I'm sorry—I should have known." The woman extended a business card toward Carrie. "I'm with the Ghanaian High Commission. My name is Helen Morticum."

Carrie took the card from the woman's hand and glanced at the embossed Ghanaian gold seal. "Helen Roth Morticum—Head of Chancery Section, Belgrave Square," the card stated.

"Years ago, when I was married and applied for a visa, the commission was in Highgate," Carrie said. "I see you've moved to pricier digs?"

Helen Roth Morticum smiled. "Consular section is still at Highgate; Belgrave Square is the high commissioner's residence and the executive offices."

Carrie quickly looked Helen Morticum over. She was young, probably less than thirty-five, slim, very pretty, and dressed in a tailored, dark-blue business suit and high heels. Carrie also noticed the chauffer-driven Jaguar parked at the curb across the street. "Since I haven't applied for a visa recently, I assume you're here on another matter, Ms. Morticum."

"Actually, I've come to see you at the request of your former husband, Hubert Rawlings. Hubert's wife, Morowa, is the high commissioner's sister."

Carrie opened the door and stepped back. "I see," she replied, unable to hide the apprehension in her voice. "Won't you come in?"

Helen Morticum smiled and entered.

"Please come through to the kitchen. I can make some coffee—or tea, if you'd prefer."

"Thank you—either would be lovely."

Carrie led the way down the long hallway to the recently modernized kitchen. "Please take a seat. The kettle's already warm. How is Hubert? I haven't heard from him in years."

"Actually, I've never met Mr. Rawlings. At the high commissioner's request, I spoke with him on the phone last week."

Carrie nodded. "Coffee all right? I'm afraid it will have to be instant."

"That's just fine. Thank you."

"Let me just fix the coffee and I'll join you."

While Carrie spooned the powdered coffee into two mugs, Ms. Morticum took a small notepad from her purse and set it on the table. "Lovely place you have here. I'm quite impressed with your conservatory—is it a recent addition?"

"We added it on at the same time we redid the kitchen—about two years ago. I was thinking about selling the house, but when I decided to stay on, we did the kitchen over and added the conservatory."

"It's lovely," Ms. Morticum repeated. "So open and bright—you must spend a lot of time in the conservatory."

Carrie shrugged. "I have a business in the High Street. I'm not really home that often."

"I understand. Between my job and all of the social commitments that come with it, I'm seldom at home. My husband says we should move to a hotel."

Carrie placed the two steaming mugs on paper napkins she'd laid on the wooden table and sat. "Sorry—did you need milk or sugar?"

"No, thank you."

Ms. Morticum took a small sip of coffee and then opened her notepad. "As I said, Ms. Trumble, I'm here at the behest of your former husband, Hubert Rawlings. To come directly to the point, Mr. Rawlings would like to meet with you here in London. His mother, Juba Rawlings, recently passed on and there are some matters regarding her estate that he needs to discuss with you. You knew Juba Rawlings?"

Carrie was startled. It had taken her years to push the memories of her former mother-in-law into the far recesses of her mind, walling them off as a spider might do with an insect in a silken cocoon. And now, with a few words from a total stranger, those memories were released—Juba's face, her large mouth, startlingly white teeth, and enormous brown eyes once again loomed in Carrie's consciousness.

"Ms. Trumble—you did know Juba, Mr. Rawling's mother?"

"What? Yes," Carrie nearly whispered. "When we lived in Ghana, years ago. She's dead, you say?"

Helen Morticum flipped through her notes. "Last month—she died last month, Mr. Rawlings said. I'm sorry to have surprised you with the sad news. He didn't tell me the cause of death."

Carrie stared through the glass wall of the conservatory into the small, well-tended garden. "Doesn't matter," she said, more to herself than to Helen Morticum. "Makes no difference to me how or when Juba Rawlings died. We never got on, you see. No, actually it was more than that—we detested each other. Do you understand?"

Carrie turned, placed her elbows on the table, and looked Helen square in the face. "You do understand?"

The atmosphere in the kitchen was suddenly tense and unfriendly, and Helen Morticum became uncomfortable. She was anxious to conclude her assignment and be on her way. Helen stared at her notes. "Ms. Trumble, Mr. Rawlings is here in London, and asks if you could meet with him tomorrow or the next day. He's suggested that the meeting take place in Belgrave

Square, in the offices of the High Commission. Will that be possible for you?"

Carrie slowly shook her head. "I can't imagine why Juba's estate could have anything to do with me," she said. "There's no possibility she'd leave anything to me."

"I'm sorry, Ms. Trumble. I wasn't clear. The issues around Mr. Rawling's mother's estate are in regard to your eldest daughter, Naki Rawlings, not yourself."

"Nila," Carrie forcefully replied. "Her name is Nila, not Naki. Nila is her baptized, Christian name."

"I'm sorry—I wasn't aware. Mr. Rawlings referred to her as Naki."

"Well, it's Nila, not Naki."

"I understand: it's Nila. Then, in your daughter Nila's interest, could you meet with Hubert Rawlings tomorrow afternoon at the High Commission? I'll send a car for you, if you wish."

Carrie stood. "I don't know, Ms. Morticum. Please tell Hubert that I'm not sure I want to see him. I'll need to have a think and call you later this afternoon. I'm afraid this meeting has been quite upsetting to me. I don't wish to offend you, but I'd like you to leave, now."

"I'm so sorry to have caused you discomfort, Ms. Trumble. I'll show myself out. My cell number is on the card; I'll await your call."

Carrie heard the front door close and mechanically resumed her seat. She placed her elbows on the table and buried her face in her hands. Carrie didn't cry—she was far too angry for that.

21

"She specifically said that she wanted the girls to come and that Hattie, her housekeeper, would help look after them. You've met Hattie?"

"Yes and no," Gordon replied. "When the EMTs were getting ready to take you to the hospital, Myra Silk and her nurse came to the house. I was too frazzled to notice much, but I think they stayed with the twins 'til the female cop arrived. Hattie was very pale and tall—that's all I remember."

"You don't remember Hattie from your childhood? Wasn't she with Myra Silk back then?"

Gordon shrugged. "I don't know. You'd have to ask Mary. She was older and her memory's better than mine."

"Doesn't really matter," Nila replied. "I met Hattie only once, just before Myra died. I was taking a walk along the driveway. Not the sort of woman one could easily forget. As you said, she's tall and unusually pale—likely an albino—with pinkish eyes. She seemed to be in her mid-fifties. But when I bumped into her at the post office yesterday, she seemed ten, perhaps fifteen years younger. And her eyes were pale green, not pink—obviously contacts. She could have been her own younger sister."

"But it wasn't her younger sister?"

"No, it was the same Hattie. She came right up to me. No doubt my confusion about her age showed on my face, even though I tried to cover it up. 'I thought you'd gone back to Louisiana with Myra Silk,' I told her.

"She was quite chatty, and told me that the reason she and Myra had rushed off so quickly was to meet with Myra's lawyers in New Orleans. Hattie said that something had happened with Myra's money—something Hattie didn't understand—and that Myra had been wiped out. Myra was now broke and in debt. The only asset Myra still owned was the big house."

"Those things do happen—crooks taking advantage of an old woman. But what's that got to do with this person, Devon, moving into the big house?"

Nila held up her hand. "Let me finish Hattie's story. Hattie said that Devon Sinclair's parents were Myra and Hattie's longtime neighbors in New Orleans. Devon's mother was an alcoholic and she and Devon didn't get on. Devon's father was always away on trips. So, during Devon's adolescence, Myra became her closest adult friend—maybe even her surrogate parent. Last year, Devon's mother and father were killed in a car accident and Devon inherited lots of money. Hattie said that Devon's mum was driving drunk."

"This was in New Orleans?"

"Yes. And when Devon found out that Myra was dead broke, she offered to buy the big house from Myra and pay off Myra's remaining debts. Just after they had completed the purchase, Myra had a stroke and died. Hattie said it was from the stress of her bankruptcy. When Devon found out that Myra was gone, and Hattie was going to be both penniless and homeless, she offered Hattie a job as her companion."

"So, Devon and Hattie are both gonna live in the big house?"

"Hattie said that Devon wanted to get away from New Orleans—that's what the trucks and the workmen were all about. Devon's had the big house all tidied up so that they can live there—new bathrooms and kitchen, and new furniture, too. Her party is at three o'clock—a housewarming, she called it. Devon apologized profusely about the last-minute invitation and said that she didn't know anyone was living at the beach house until Hattie told her about meeting me at the post office. It was a bit embarrassing—Hattie had told her that I was the nanny, so when she called, she only extended her invitation to you. I had to explain that our relationship had 'evolved' and that I was no longer your paid employee. Right away, of course, she invited all of us—the girls, too."

"Devon's not married, I take it?"

"Actually, Devon didn't say, but I suspect not. She kept using 'I' instead of 'we.'"

"You said we'd come?"

Nila frowned. "I thought maybe you wouldn't want to take the time away from your studies, so I said I'd have to discuss it with you and call her back."

"You wanna go?"

"If you can spare the time away from your computer. I'm curious to suss out Devon and see the inside of the big house."

"It's not a formal thing? I don't have to wear a suit?"

"She didn't say, but since neither of us have any adult, dress-up clothing, it'll have to be casual—at least for the two of us."

Gordon shrugged. "Okay. It will be a relief to get away from this computer for a while."

~*~

Although Gordon vaguely remembered Hattie from the time that she and Myra came to the beach house after Maggie's death, even Nila's recent description of Hattie hadn't prepared him for Hattie's appearance. Her exceptionally pale skin confirmed that she was an albino, but her light-red, natural-appearing hair, pale green eyes and a young, hard body that was trying to escape from her black, spandex jumpsuit seemed to belong to a different woman.

"Hello again, Nila from London," Hattie said as she embraced Nila and twice touched cheek to cheek, in the French manner, then settled on one knee in front of the twins' double stroller. Both girls were asleep. She stroked Janna's curls. "They're even more beautiful than when I first met them with your sister Mary," she whispered. "And my, have they grown!"

"They're fifteen months and walking everywhere now," Nila replied.

"Which means that we're constantly running," Gordon added.

Nila nodded. "They've just had lunch, and this is their normal nap time—so if we find a quiet corner, they're likely to stay asleep in the stroller for the next hour or so."

"Don't you worry none 'bout your two beauties. I'll park them just inside the dining room where I can keep an eye on them and where we can hear if they fuss."

Hattie stood and extended her hand to Gordon. "I'm happy to formally meet up with you, Mr. Hale. Last time at your place was real confusin'."

"Please, it's Gordon," he replied. "We didn't meet when I was a child, did we, when my mother, sister, and I came here to visit Mrs. Silk?"

Hattie frowned and shook her head. "I don't think that's likely." She withdrew her hand, slipped around Gordon, and opened the sliding doors to the dining room. "Now I'll just put this stroller right here inside and leave the door partly open. Miss Devon's in the kitchen with the caterer. She'll be along in jus' a minute."

Hattie grasped the handle of the stroller with one hand, while with her other, she gestured toward the sunroom. "Go right on in. I'm sure you'll recognize most of the guests."

Besides Nila and Gordon, only ten other people had been invited to Devon's housewarming, and all but one were from Castle Key. Gordon was pleased to find people he knew, such as Dr. Axel Quigley and his wife Susan, who were standing at the ornate bar in the sunroom, talking with Dale Connor, the local architect Gordon had commissioned to plan the renovation of the beach house. Since Karen's death, Gordon had seen Axel only once, when he and Nila had taken the twins to Axel's clinic for their one-year check-up. Susan assisted Axel's regular nurse at the clinic during the winter high season. She had been born and educated just outside London, so she and Nila had much in common, and after their first meeting, the women were quickly becoming friends.

Devon exited through the dining-room pocket doors while looking back at Hattie, who was hunched over the twins in their stroller. She soundlessly closed the sliding doors behind her, put on a full, beaming smile, and stepped into the sunroom.

Nila was the first to notice Devon's entry. Their gazes met as Devon walked directly toward Nila and Susan with her hand outstretched. "I'm sure you must be Nila from London. We spoke on the phone yesterday. Hattie's told me all about you—you and your babies." She turned to Susan. "Sorry to interrupt, Susan. I was anxious to meet my new neighbor."

Nila took Devon's hand and returned her smile. "Well, they're not exactly my babies—in the biological sense, that is."

"Yes, I understand," Devon replied. "They're absolutely gorgeous—I had a quick peek on my way through the dining room; they're sleeping. And this must be Gordon Hale."

Gordon turned from his conversation with Axel. "Ms. Sinclair, what a pleasure to meet you."

"Please—it's Devon," she said with a smile.

Gordon looked into Devon's astonishingly blue eyes and was momentarily hypnotized. He mechanically took the hand she offered and continued to stare without speaking.

Devon withdrew her hand. "Myra told me all about your family—how they once owned this house and all the surrounding property."

Gordon was thoroughly confused. It was as if he were meeting an old friend—someone he knew well, someone he knew he should remember but couldn't. Speechless, he continued to stare into Devon's brilliant blue eyes.

"Mr. Hale?" Devon asked. "Are you all right?"

Gordon was embarrassed. "I'm sorry to stare. You seem very familiar—I was just trying to place you. We haven't met before, have we?"

"I doubt it—have you ever been to New Orleans?"

"Only once. It's just that you remind me of someone I've known—someone I can't quite remember."

"I graduated from Louisiana State University. Maybe we met there?"

Gordon shrugged. "I've never been to LSU. I've only visited New Orleans at Mardi Gras, when I was in college. To be honest, that whole weekend is a blur in my memory." Gordon recovered his composure and looked around the sunroom. "You've made some big changes to this place—very positive changes. As a kid, I always dreaded coming into this room when my mother and sister and I visited Mrs. Silk for tea. The room was packed with dusty old furniture and smelled like a damp basement. It's much nicer now—light and open."

"Clarisse planned the remodeling of the house, selected all the furniture, and supervised the decoration—not one of my interests. I only saw what she'd done when I moved in. Clarisse is my decorator, my financial manager, my secretary, my best friend, and she's a talented artist. You haven't met Clarisse yet—she's the petite blonde." Devon nodded toward an elfin woman with sharp features who was animatedly reacting to Charlie Kopel, the owner of the mini-market, and his continuous stream of jokes.

Gordon pointed toward the window. "There used to be a black grand piano over there. My sister tortured us by playing it."

"Clarisse donated the piano to a nursing home somewhere off the island."

"And that wall next to the big doors was covered from top to bottom with pictures of women and girls."

Devon nodded. "Clarisse decided to keep Myra's art collection, and she's rehung it on the wall above the staircase outside the great room. I'm not sure if I'll keep Myra's pictures or not; they're sort of creepy."

"All I remember is that there were dozens of portraits—all

female."

"Come see what you think—they're just through this door." Devon turned to Nila and Susan. "Excuse me for a minute. I'm just gonna show Gordon what Clarisse has done with Myra's pictures."

Devon opened the door to the long hallway that led off the main entrance. A grand staircase rose before them. She motioned for Gordon to enter the hall.

"Good God! This looks like a museum. Do you know how many pictures?"

"I do," Devon said with a laugh. "Forty-two, counting Myra."

"Myra?"

Devon walked to the staircase and climbed to the fourth stair. "This black-and-white photo with the glamour-girl treatment—that's Myra. It says so on the back. It's not dated, but I'd guess she was in her twenties when it was taken."

Gordon joined Devon on the staircase and stared at the photograph of an attractive young woman. He shook his head. "There's no resemblance with the Myra Silk I knew. Hard to believe it's her—she must have been pretty hot in her day."

"Clarisse found Myra's photo in the sunroom on the old piano, with a picture hanger next to it. It looks like Myra was about to hang this up with the other portraits. You think I should keep 'em on the wall, or not?"

Gordon shrugged. "I don't know much about art. Some look like oil paintings, and could be old—maybe valuable. Perhaps you should get them appraised? It's curious—all of the women in the paintings have brilliant blue eyes, just like Myra's. Of course, you can't tell about the eyes in the drawings and old photos."

"Hmm," Devon said as she stepped to the bottom of the staircase and looked up at the wall of portraits. "You're absolutely right; I hadn't noticed. The eyes seem to be the one thing they have in common. But they don't really look like they're related, do they?"

Gordon shook his head. "No, they don't. Did you ask Hattie if she knew when Myra collected the portraits?"

"I did. She said the pictures were on the wall in the sunroom for as long as she could remember."

Gordon descended the stairs and stood in front of Devon. "Yours, too," he said. "Your eyes are brilliant blue, just like all the women in the pictures."

Devon turned away from the portraits. "This is getting way too creepy. I think I'll take your advice, get them appraised and out of here. I don't think I can handle all those blue eyes staring at me every time I go up to my bedroom."

Gordon grinned. "Yeah, I can see how those faces might start appearing in your dreams. When you're ready, Charlie Kopel can probably help you find an art appraiser. He's part owner of an art gallery in Naples."

Devon walked toward the door that led back to the sunroom. "He's the large man who owns the mini-market?"

"And a half-dozen other businesses around this county and the next. Speaking of Kopel's, make sure you never tell Beverly, the clerk there, anything private, unless you want the entire island to know about it."

"I see," Devon said over her shoulder as she stepped back into the sunroom. "That self-same Beverly told me that you're going to be setting up a law practice here in the near future. You're a lawyer?"

"Guilty," Gordon said with a smile.

"Perhaps you could refer me to someone local—a lawyer who handles questions about property documents? My purchase of this house from Myra happened so quickly—and then with her stroke, I never really got to review all the papers and closing documents. So my knowledge of the property lines between this house and your beach house, and the rights-of-way we share, are particularly vague."

"I'd be happy to have a look at your documents. Property law is my specialty. I can help you with the documents—that is, as long as there aren't any questions that might involve a conflict of interest."

Devon swiveled to face Gordon. "I'm sure that'll never happen. We're going to be the best of neighbors, and the best of friends. I'll make sure of it."

~*~

Nila had just finished a glass of wine when she heard the twins begin to fuss. She interrupted her conversation with Clarisse and Devon and set the empty glass on the bar. "Excuse me; I think the girls are awake."

Devon slid down from the barstool. "I'll go check on them," she said.

Nila was already moving toward the dining room. "No, no… you stay with your guests." Nila was almost to the dining-room door, when she heard a sneeze. She slid open the door and found Hattie bent over the double stroller. As the light from the sunroom spilled into the darkened room, Nila saw that Hattie was pulling Janna's fluffy sock back onto her foot. The sock back in place, Hattie started brushing Janna's dress with her hand.

"Dust fallin' down from that ol' lamp—that's what's makin' her sneeze." Hattie gestured to the large chandelier that hung above. "Don't wanna get your pretty party dress all dusty," she said to Janna. "I'm gonna have to get up there on a ladder tomorrow and wipe that old thing down. Painters shoulda cleaned it up, but they didn't."

Julie joined Janna in sneezing. Nila bent down and lifted Janna from the stroller. Julie reached out toward Nila and began to fuss. "I, too," Julie said. "I, too."

"Can you bring Julie into the barroom?" Nila asked. "Everyone's been wanting to meet the two of them."

Hattie nodded. "Sure thing," she said as she moved a small vial from her left hand into the cleavage of her jumpsuit and then lifted Julie from the stroller. "C'mon, honey—your admirers are waitin'," she said to Julie with a grin.

22

Hubert Rawlings was dressed in a dark-blue pinstriped suit, white shirt, and regimental tie. His jet-black hair was graying at the sides, adding a statesman-like finish to his trim, five-eleven frame. He stood facing the ornate marble fireplace, his hands clasped behind his back. Although it was June, a decorative gas fire danced among the artificial, glowing coals in the antique fire grate. With the exception of the gas fire, and the electric lights and lamps, the structure of the library was little changed from its mid-nineteenth-century origins. The built-in bookcases were filled with hundreds of mostly leather-bound volumes—books that were regularly dusted but never read. The awkward Victorian furniture that came with the house had long ago been replaced with more graceful—but historically incorrect—antique Georgian mahogany tables, chairs, an upholstered settee, and a large desk. Colorful Persian carpets covered the floor. Only the Ghanaian flag in a stand next to the desk, and the portrait of His Excellency, the president, which hung over the fireplace, indicated that the library was now part of the Ghanaian High Commission.

Hubert was uncomfortable. Beads of sweat had begun to collect along his lightly starched collar, and he repeatedly clasped and unclasped his hands. Although he'd planned for weeks what he would say, the precise words still eluded him. True to her nature, Morowa had prodded him to tell the unedited story from beginning to end, but he knew that wasn't a possibility—it would take courage to fully own up to the mistakes and failings of his life, and he was a coward. Juba, Hubert's mother, had dominated every aspect of his life. She had driven away Hubert's blonde, English wife and his two young daughters and then guided him through the process of securing a Ghanaian divorce on the fabricated grounds of abandonment.

She had hastily arranged Hubert's second marriage to Morowa, her cousin's beautiful young daughter, and then bitterly sulked each time Morowa produced a male child instead of the female she needed to preserve her family's ancient lineage. When, after bearing five healthy sons, Morowa announced that she was physically incapable of any further pregnancies, Juba had gone into a prolonged, deep depression that had only ended with a fatal stroke.

Although Hubert's mother had been dead for two months, here he was in England, still carrying out her commands, still acquiescing to her iron will.

There was a soft knock on the massive mahogany door. Hubert turned to face the door as it opened and Helen Morticum's unsmiling face appeared. "Mr. Rawlings, Ms. Trumble has arrived. Shall I show her in?"

Hubert nodded and swallowed hard. "Thank you, Ms. Morticum," he said, his voice louder than necessary. "Please do."

Helen stepped into the library, holding the door open. "Ms. Trumble, please come in," she said.

Carrie Trumble came through the doorway and then stopped. She looked briefly around the room at the furnishings and carpets and then fixed her gaze on Hubert. She was dressed in a gray pantsuit worn over a frilled, ivory-colored blouse. Her blonde hair was done up in a businesslike bun.

Helen Morticum gestured toward the upholstered couch. "Please take a seat, Ms. Trumble," she said. "There are pots of coffee and tea on the side table and I'll bring in some biscuits if you wish."

Carrie shook her head. "Not for me, thank you."

"No, thank you," Hubert said.

Helen nodded. "I'll be at the desk just outside the door if there is anything you need—Mr. Rawlings, Ms. Trumble." She closed the heavy door behind her.

The two stood staring at each other for several seconds, as if they were each trying to avoid being the first to speak.

Hubert lost. "Thank you for coming, Carrie, and at such short notice." He gestured toward the couch. "Won't you have a seat?"

Carrie remained standing. "Hubert, I suggest we skip the polite conversation and get straight to the point of this meeting. Why am I here, and what do you want of me?"

Hubert was taken aback by her directness. "Please, won't you sit down?" he asked.

"After all these years, you appear out of nowhere and expect me to sit and have a civil conversation? I don't think so. You've never shown the slightest interest in my life, or in the welfare of my girls, and I don't expect you to begin now."

Hubert lowered his head. "Carrie, you have every right to despise me. We both know that I am a coward and a weakling, and that I abandoned you and our children. It would be unthinkable for me to ask for forgiveness. I ask nothing from you. I am here only because there are things I must discuss with you about our daughter Nila's relationship with Juba, my mother, and about the provisions in my mother's will for Nila's benefit. Please, won't you sit down? I promise this will be a short, businesslike meeting."

Carrie stepped to the white upholstered settee and settled tentatively on the edge. "As you wish. Your mother's death was recent?"

Hubert sat down across from the settee in an uncomfortable-looking mahogany armchair. "Last month; it was a stroke. She was paralyzed for three days and never recovered consciousness."

"I imagine she thought she'd live forever. She certainly acted that way."

"After my father's death, Juba was never comfortable with life. She died a bitter, unloved woman. Only now can I truthfully say that although I never loved her, I felt sorry for her. She did, however, anticipate her death and left a most specific will—a will that includes Naki." Hubert lowered his head. "Please forgive me; I meant to say, a will that includes Nila. Morowa always refers to Nila by her tribal name and I must admit that I think of her that way as well."

Carrie was about to say, "Oh? I'm surprised that you think of her at all!" but decided to keep her sarcasm to herself. Instead, she asked, "How is the lovely Morowa?"

"Morowa is well, and sends her best wishes."

"I always liked Morowa. Your mother made a good choice for you."

Hubert stared at the floor. "Yes, she did."

"I understand that you have four boys?"

"Five; Peter is the youngest. He was born two years ago."

Carrie leaned back on the settee and crossed her legs. "So, you wanted to tell me about Juba's will—Juba's will, and Nila."

Hubert looked directly into Carrie's eyes. "Specifically, my mother left Nila four valuable pieces of jewelry: one orange-colored diamond ring, two diamond pendants, and a necklace. I've had the jewels appraised here in London, and the combined value is close to a quarter of a million pounds. Since the exceptional quality of stones, caret sizes, cuts, and antique settings are unique and irreplaceable, the insurance value would be considerably higher—as much as double that estimate."

Carrie frowned and shook her head. "Why?" she asked. "After completely ignoring her firstborn grandchild for almost twenty years, why would she leave her such valuable possessions? I don't understand."

Hubert quickly reviewed the mental gymnastics he'd struggled with since he'd read his mother's will and met with Ringwald. What, exactly, should he tell Carrie and Nila? How could he attempt to account for Juba's bizarre life and hurtful behavior?

"Let me try to explain what I can," he began. "Much of what I will tell you about my mother I only learned after her death.

Frankly, I'm still not sure what to believe. You remember that Juba was of the Ashanti?"

"Yes," Carrie said.

"Even though he was fully integrated into Ghanaian society, my father privately regarded the Ashanti, and the other West African tribes, as heathen. Don't misunderstand me—his opinions had nothing to do with race. The Rawlings have been genuinely color-blind for generations."

"And because of your father's wishes, you were raised Church of England—I remember your stories."

"And that's why I learned so little Ashanti history and lore; my father forbade it. However, I knew that within the Ashanti, my mother's family was of an ancient, high-caste lineage, the equivalent of royalty. Of course, the oral history of the Ashanti goes back thousands of years—probably as far back as the Greeks or Romans."

Carrie smirked. "You're saying because she believed she was of an ancient, royal lineage—that explains your mother's self-centered rudeness?"

"No, not at all. What I've recently been told is that Juba believed she had special, magical powers—powers to combat evil forces that walk the earth today, and that these powers had been passed to her through her mother, her grandmother, her great-grandmother, in an uninterrupted matriarchal line that extends back to the first humans, and the gods who created those first humans."

"Voodoo, you mean? Voodoo powers? I think I vaguely remember that the Ashanti practice voodoo."

Hubert shook his head. "No, not voodoo—the Ashanti know nothing of voodoo. In the seventeenth and eighteenth centuries, the Arab slave traders focused heavily on what is now West Africa, and thousands of African tribal peoples, including large numbers of Ashanti, were captured and sold to plantation owners in the New World. Some of these Ashanti women may have possessed ancient powers, or thought they did, and that's likely the origin of voodoo in the Caribbean and the Americas. Voodoo is a New World invention, not African."

"So Juba thought she had inherited special powers from her female ancestors. What's that got to do with Nila, and with Juba's diamonds?"

"You remember my Uncle Ringwald, Juba's brother?"

Carrie leaned back. "Your Uncle Ringwald? No, I don't think so. Was he the farmer who always showed up at your mother's house on holidays?"

"Wearing wellington boots?" Hubert asked.

"Exactly."

"That was Ringwald. He managed our teak plantations. After Mother's death, I visited Ringwald and he explained that Juba believed that she had inherited primeval powers—specifically, powers that enabled her to battle the destructive force of an ancient female monster that attacks children."

Carrie laughed. "And you believed that nonsense?"

Hubert shook his head. "Of course not, but what I believe is of no consequence. It's what Juba believed that's pertinent—and, according to Uncle Ringwald, there was no doubt in her mind that she possessed these ancient powers. Further, Juba believed that it was her sacred mission in life to preserve those powers and to pass them on to the next generation—to a daughter, or, failing the birth of a daughter, to her nearest female blood relative." Hubert intensely focused on Carrie's eyes. "Since Morowa and I never had a girl child, Juba's closest female relative would be..."

"Nila," Carrie whispered.

Hubert nodded. "Specifically, in order of strength of her matriarchal line, Juba's choices would have been: first, the daughter she never had, and then, since Morowa and I are second cousins, the granddaughter Morowa and I never produced, then Nila, and, lastly, Della."

"And this is why you dragged me here—to tell some fantastic

story that would explain your mother's obsessive, hurtful behavior? After all these years, do you think I really care why your mother behaved as she did toward me?"

Hubert shook his head. "No, not at all. I asked to see you because I need your help. I need to know what to do about Nila and the diamonds."

"What sort of help?"

Hubert rubbed the back of his neck with his right hand. "When my mother tattooed Nila, that tattoo was her *mark*—a mark that signified that Nila was provisionally designated as her successor."

Carrie sprang up from the settee. "So that's why she mutilated Nila? It was some dreadful voodoo rite?"

Hubert stood as well. "No, not voodoo. An Ashanti tribal practice, not voodoo."

Carrie was visibly upset and paced in front of the settee. "Why, in the name of God, didn't you get us away from your mother's vile superstitions? How could you let her disfigure your child? What kind of man are you?"

Hubert sat down hard and lowered his gaze to the floor. "That is the question that never leaves my mind."

Carrie moved directly in front of the seated Hubert. "When I returned home from Ghana with the girls, I was furious with you for several years. It was the kind of fury that eats away your heart, fills your mind with poison, and destroys your life. Once, I really loved you, treasured you, bore your children, and expected us to live a contented life together, right through to the end. My fury, my anger, is what sustained me. It became the reason to get up in the morning, to care for my daughters, and go to my office every day. Then, a few years on, Della was sick in bed with a high fever. When the fever broke, Della told me that in her dreams she'd been in a pleasant place, a place where I was happy again—just like I used to be. I hadn't realized how obvious it was to my girls that anger was destroying me.

Later that day, I looked in the mirror and I saw your mother peering out at me, and I realized that she was the one who was destroying me, not you. Della got well and so did I. Hubert, I don't think about you at all, and I don't care what kind of man you are. Are we finished here? I need to get back to my office and my life."

Hubert continued staring at the floor. "There's just one more thing," he said in a flat, emotionless tone. "The last thing I must do to fulfill my mother's will and free myself of her control—I must deliver the jewels to Nila. Will you help me do that?"

Carrie returned to the settee. "Nila lives in America now. She's marrying an American soon."

"I see. Where does she live—which state?"

"She lives in Florida."

"Miami?"

"No, not Miami, but she *will* be staying at a hotel in Miami for a few days."

"Will you tell her about Juba's jewelry?"

"If you wish; I can call her cell phone," Carrie replied.

Hubert nodded. "If she agrees, will you help us to meet? I can get a flight to Miami right away—either tonight, or tomorrow. I have a diplomatic passport and won't need a visa."

"I'll tell her about this conversation."

Hubert reached into his shirt pocket and produced a card. "She can call anytime on this cell number, or at Grosvenor House. I wrote the hotel number on the back. If Nila would rather I call her, you could give me her number in Florida."

Carrie stood. "I'll call her. Then it'll be up to Nila, won't it?"

23

Gordon raised his voice. "I missed the last thing you said—I must have passed through a cell dead-zone. Say again?"

"The DNA sample taken from Margaret Cartwright's corpse before it disappeared matches the DNA found on the liquor store clerk's throat wounds. The dead clerk up near the border."

"What? You're messin' with me?"

"They're positive about the DNA match," Deputy McGill repeated. "The sergeant said that the odds of an error would be one in millions. Don't remember the exact number but it was lotsa millions."

"Hold on a minute," Gordon said, as he exited from the interstate to a rest area and pulled into the first open parking spot. "My God," he said softly. "This is getting weirder and weirder."

"Not to mention disgusting," the deputy responded. "Also, the Pennsylvania authorities are sticking with the story that Amy Cartwright died from a heart attack and that the trauma to her neck was caused by rats and occurred after death. The body was released to the family and has already been cremated. That case is closed. It appears the Cartwright family has lots of influence, as well as money."

"Remember—Nila told us that Maggie attempted to bite her throat, so there's a pattern here."

"Like I said, case closed. Heart attack or not, we'll never know what really happened to Amy Cartwright," the deputy replied.

"And still no trace of the missing corpse?"

"*Nada*—and nobody on this end wants to see anything more about either Margaret Cartwright or the attack in the media. I don't know how the powers-that-be are gonna spin the missing corpse story once it gets out—and it will get out. Since the attack on Miss Rawlings was widely reported, some pain-in-the-ass newsperson might try to get a follow-up story. Probably be best if you and Miss Rawlings didn't have anything more to say about Margaret Cartwright."

"Is that friendly advice, Mick, or an official request?"

"Look, Mr. Hale, there wasn't any authorization for me to tell you about the DNA match on the dead clerk. Since we've all been through this together, I figured you had a right to know." The deputy sounded hurt.

"Mick, I apologize. I'm really sorry I said that. If it weren't for you, who knows what could have happened to Nila and the babies!"

"No apology necessary, Mr. Hale. We're all getting weirded out by this thing. It's just that I overheard a reporter asking someone for information on where Miss Rawlings could be reached, that's all."

"I dropped Nila and the girls off at a hotel in Miami earlier this morning, and I'll be going to Tampa tomorrow and then joining Nila and her sister in Miami. There won't be anyone here for the newspeople to hassle for the rest of the week. But thanks for the heads-up. I'm on my way home now and will be around until tomorrow if there's anything else we should discuss."

"Right. And good luck with the bar exam, Mr. Hale."

"Great memory, Mick."

"That's not what Tyrece says," the deputy said with a chuckle.

Gordon closed his cell phone and headed for Castle Key and his empty house.

~*~

Devon placed her smartphone on the kitchen counter. "No delays on Alligator Alley or the interstate. He should be here soon—make sure you're ready."

Hattie opened the refrigerator door and removed a bowl. "And what if he doesn't want lunch? What if he stopped to eat on the way home?"

"Wouldn't matter—he's the polite, considerate type, so good manners will oblige him to eat your lobster salad. Not so many men are like that—most use their manners as camouflage for their ambition."

Hattie smirked. "What else is new?"

"This one might be different. I'll know more once I get control over him."

"What if he don't like lobster?"

"He's from Massachusetts, and at the party he told us a story about illegally poachin' lobsters when he was a kid. He'll eat the salad."

Hattie placed lettuce leaves on two plates and then spooned out the lobster salad. "Green plate for Gordon and white for Devon—got that?"

"Green for Gordon," Devon repeated, as she used an eyedropper to place six drops of clear liquid onto the lobster salad on the green plate. She replaced the dropper back in the small vial and then mixed the drug into the lobster salad with her index finger. "That'll do the job. After he eats the salad, he'll be drooling for sex and thinking with his dick instead of his brain."

"Where'd you get that stuff?" Hattie asked.

"I discovered the ancient formula a long time ago in Alexandria; it was an extract from a poisonous reptile. Worked well, but occasionally had lethal side effects. But back a hundred years ago, some scientists in Germany chemically synthesized a much better formula—a 'date-rape drug.' The compound has dozens of street names—Ecstasy is the most common. I paid a chemist to modify the formula to my specifications—to make a drug that provides the same sexually ecstatic, hallucinatory reaction as Ecstasy, but fades away in a shorter period. For a medium-size, adult male like Gordon Hale, six drops ingested with food will quickly get the results I want and wear off in about three hours. Most important, he won't remember what I did to him while he was drugged."

Devon rinsed the empty mixing bowl in the sink while Hattie returned the green and white plates to the fridge.

"Is this the wine you got?" Hattie took a bottle from the refrigerator.

"He knows a lot about wine, and this is a special bottle—I don't think he'll be able to resist."

Hattie examined the label. "Le Musigny," she said, with the correct French pronunciation. "The rarest and most expensive white wine of the Côte de Nuit. I'll open it now and leave it on the granite counter to stabilize. The fridge is way too cold to properly chill a great white wine."

Devon pulled Hattie close and lovingly fondled her butt. "Don't you mock me," she gently hissed. "You're an ignorant girl from New Orleans—stay in character." Devon kissed Hattie's lips and then stepped back. "Later," she said. "Later."

Holding the hem of an invisible dress, Hattie feigned a curtsey. "Yes, Ma-Ma," she girlishly giggled.

~*~

Gordon pointed to the date on the plot plan that lay open before him on the dining-room table. "1999: that's when my father sold the big house to Mrs. Silk and that's when this survey was completed. Actually, there are really only three aspects of the survey that require your understanding. The first is the southern property line between this house and the beach cottage, and the northern property line between the big house and the McClatchy estate—those appear to be straightforward. The second is the driveway and the right-of-way granted to the beach cottage. Third is the property line between the Gulf of Mexico, the beach, and the land you own—and that can be a legal quagmire. But most likely, it's also something that will never be an issue—

unless, that is, you have plans to extend the house toward the water, or to erect a fence, or another structure, between the house and the beach."

Devon shook her head. "Not likely that I'd ever need to extend the house. Four of the six bedrooms are unfurnished and unused. There's a lot more space here than I'll ever need."

Gordon grinned. "Never know—you could get married and raise a bunch a kids."

"Not possible," Devon firmly replied. "The kids, I mean—not marriage."

"In any case, my advice is to get a local property surveyor to do a current survey and plot plan. You've already done business with Dale Connor—I'm sure that he could recommend the best firm to use. If you have any concerns about access to the property and the right of way, Dale could also put you in touch with a local attorney. That probably won't be necessary, but I'm afraid that a potential conflict-of-interest would prevent me from rendering any opinion."

"I understand your position."

"As to the Gulf, the beach, and your property ownership and rights, I'd be happy to provide as comprehensive and boring a tutorial as you'd be willing to suffer through. I've just had to learn the Florida-specific, high-waterline beach laws for the bar exam and I'd enjoy sharing the pain."

"Thanks, but no thanks," Devon said with a smile. "I'm really not much of a beach girl—I prefer swimming in a pool to the ocean."

"In that case, you're welcome to use our pool while we're away."

"Thanks. I might just do that tomorrow. I enjoy a swim first thing in the morning. I've been toying with the idea of puttin' in a pool inside the walled garden. It'd be convenient and I wouldn't even have to put up a fence...or wear a bathing suit." Devon grinned. "So, I'll take your suggestion and get a new survey.

Would you be willing to look it over when the plan's done?"

"My pleasure. In fact, if you let me know who's going to do the new survey, I'll have my architect get them to do my cottage property at the same time. I think Nila told you that we're going to renovate the kitchen and baths, and add another bedroom to the old place—it won't be too long before the twins need their own rooms."

Hattie partially opened one of the sliding doors between the sunroom and dining room and inserted her head into the gap. "Excuse me interruptin' this important meeting, but your lunch is all set up in the great room an' I jus' need to know when to take the lobster salad outa the fridge."

"Hattie's made her special Louisiana lobster salad for you, Gordon. Kopel's got in fresh, live lobster especially for us and Hattie's been cookin' for most of the morning…You will stay for lunch, won't you?"

For a microsecond Gordon visualized the unappetizing baloney, yellow-mustard, and white-bread sandwich he'd planned to make for his lunch. "Great, I'd love to try your lobster salad—lobster's one of my favorites."

Devon stood and slid her chair back from the dining-room table. "Thank you so much, Gordon, for helping me understand all these papers. Daddy always took care of the financial and legal affairs for the family. Fortunately, I've had Clarisse to manage important matters for me since he's been gone. It's a relief to know that there's someone nearby whom I can trust."

"I'll go finish puttin' out lunch," Hattie said as she fully opened the doors.

"Don't forget the wine," Devon called after her. "I put it out on the countertop—it was gettin' too cold in the fridge."

"Right, Ma-Ma," Hattie laughingly called over her shoulder as she returned to the kitchen.

Gordon rose from his chair and smiled. "Your Hattie is quite a character. I don't think I've ever met anyone like her before."

"She is, isn't she? I've known her for years; Hattie and Myra were our next-door neighbors where I grew up in New Orleans. Mommy was an alcoholic and Daddy was always traveling and seldom at home—mainly to avoid fightin' with my mother. When I got fed up with my mother's drinkin' and carousin', Hattie and Myra were my support group. Actually, Hattie more so than Myra. Then, when I was a teen, sometimes Mommy would bring home some scary guy and I'd go next-door and stay in Myra's spare room 'til he left. I had my own key and, when Myra went to Castle Key during the winter, I'd stay at their house more than at my parents' house. Just before my parents were killed in the car crash, it got to the point where I had more of my clothes and things at Myra's house than in my own bedroom."

"You never came to visit Myra here in Florida, at this place?"

"Never—I was too busy at LSU to travel. I was—maybe still am—a pretty serious student, and had just begun my doctoral dissertation when my parents were killed. Then, Myra died. I had no siblings or blood relatives to share the trauma, so that kinda knocked the wind out of my sails. Hattie was destitute and homeless and I was a wealthy, confused orphan, so I decided to take the two of us to a horribly expensive spa in the Caribbean for the better part of a month. They did a great job toning up Hattie's body and an even better job on my mind. Let's go in for lunch and then we can talk some more."

Devon linked her arm into Gordon's and they walked through the sunroom to the entry hall and grand staircase.

"I see you've decided to keep Myra's picture collection on the wall." Gordon sounded surprised.

Devon nodded. "Still thinking about what I'm gonna do. I did take your suggestion and asked Mr. Kopel to get someone to appraise the pictures. His man is comin' over next week. If you're interested, I'll go over the appraisal with you when you get back from Miami."

"I don't know much about art, but I'd be interested to know

more about your collection. I'm sure Nila would be interested, as well. Did she tell you that she's an artist and an artist's model?"

"She never mentioned it—she does that as a career?"

"She's quite talented, but she's also very modest about her talent. I'll get her to show you some of the sketches she's done—they're really good. After our wedding, I plan on actively encouraging Nila to get more serious about her art—perhaps someday put on a one-woman show. I really think she's that good."

"At our little party, Nila told everyone that your wedding will be here, on Castle Key. Is that right?"

"We decided to do it outdoors at the Castle Hill Inn. She's started working with the inn's wedding planner and they've tentatively decided on sometime during the first two weeks of October, toward the tail end of hurricane season. You'll come, of course—and Hattie, as well."

"Why, thank you! We'd love to come to your wedding."

"Good. I'll make sure the two of you are on the guest list."

Devon turned to the imposing, eight-foot-high double doors at the end of the hall. They had been painted an antique cream, with the edges of the interior panels highlighted in gilt. "Do you recall what the great room looked like in your grandparents' day?"

Gordon shook his head. "I was very young when my parents and sister and I visited my grandparents—probably five or six. We always stayed at the beach cottage, so I don't have any solid memories of this old house. Later on, when Mother, Mary, and I visited Mrs. Silk for tea, I don't think we ever ventured beyond the sunroom. Wait—I do remember a few things. My grandmother always called the big room the ballroom, not the great room. On the far end, there were windows that looked out onto the beach and the ocean."

"Very good," Devon said with a smile. "Is that all?"

"No, I remember the floor. It was a dark wood and very shiny;

I used to slide on the floor in my stocking feet. It was almost like sliding on ice."

Devon reached for the gold-plated doorknob. "In all the time Myra owned the house, this room was never used. Clarisse sent me some photos before she started redecorating and it was pretty much as you describe. Come have a look."

~*~

The great room was the same rectangular shape and size as the sunroom wing on the opposite end of the house, but the ceiling was higher—twenty feet or so at the apex. Standing just inside the tall entry doors, Gordon looked around the room and then shrugged.

"Spectacular," he said, "but not at all what I remember. It looks like the lobby of one of those expensive boutique hotels, the kind you see popping up like mushrooms in New York and Boston."

Devon pointed to the west-facing wall. "You were right about the windows overlooking the beach and the water—the originals were much smaller. The new windows are impact glass, to protect against windstorm damage."

"Do you mean hurricanes?" Gordon asked.

Devon frowned. "I don't say that word. When you name a thing—say its name—you're calling it to come."

"Never heard that before."

"It's true," she said. "The ancients always avoided using the proper names of devils, because to use their names was to summon them. That's why there are so many substitutes for the name of the evilest of creatures: Beelzebub, Old Nick, Old Scratch, Lucifer, Mephistopheles—the list would fill a dictionary." Devon abruptly changed the subject. "And you got the dark-colored wood floor right, as well. I thought it might be mahogany, but the builder told Clarisse it's stained walnut.

She's covered over most of the flooring with carpet, but left the wood exposed over there in the back corner—a dance floor, for when I start giving parties. I love to give parties—you'll come, of course."

Devon turned toward the far corner that faced the large windows. "Let me show you my special place."

They walked around a grouping of chairs, tables, and couches, toward an oasis of tall palms in huge, ceramic pots.

"The trees are live?" Gordon asked.

"It's an experiment. We're waiting to see if there's enough light comin' through the new windows to keep 'em healthy. So far, so good. The men from the nursery are optimistic, but when the sun dips down lower in winter, we may have to put in some plant lights."

Devon circled around the palms and extended her arm toward the carpeted space between the windows and the trees. "Whadya think?" she asked.

"Impressive video monitors." Gordon nodded toward the three 120-inch screens abutting each other on the wall that ran perpendicular to the windows. "You must watch a lot of TV and movies."

"They're high-def monitors—mainly for Clarisse's light shows, but you can display movies and TV, too."

"Light shows?"

"I think I told you that Clarisse is an artist, as well as my decorator as well as my financial manager."

"You did, but I haven't seen any of her work on your walls. I take it she doesn't do paintings?"

"Clarisse does light shows—both live performance art and digitally synthesized audio/video displays. I'm her patron: I bankroll most of her expenses and am the primary sponsor for a show she does in Miami Beach during the annual art festival. While she's become well known in her field, her work isn't something the average person will ever encounter—nor is it ever gonna make her rich."

"It's none of my business—but you really are quite wealthy, aren't you?"

"I'm always havin' a competition with my trust fund," Devon said with a broad smile. "It seems to generate more money than I can spend. For as far back as I know, my ancestors have made their living from mining, mining for precious metals. I'm the principal owner of several active mines. We trade gold and silver for whatever currencies are in use when we need to buy anything. As I told you, Clarisse manages all our financial activities; she always has."

"Sorry I was so direct. I don't usually pry into other people's personal business."

"Pry away. I'm just a simple, rich, Southern girl who's trying to figure out what to do with the rest of her life." She pointed to the long, cream-colored, fabric-covered sectional that faced the windows and monitors. "Sometimes Hattie and I will watch a movie here in the evening, though not often TV. I find TV boring. We've gotten in the habit of having our afternoon cocktails, and sometimes dinner, here as well while watching the sunset."

"You two have an interesting relationship."

Devon moved to the small, circular table that was set for two, with a white-linen tablecloth, china, crystal, and silver. "Please sit right here by the green plate; green for Gordon," she said, smiling. "Hattie's gone to a lot of fuss to impress you; I don't think you'll be disappointed. And yes, you're right—Hattie and I have a most unusual living arrangement. When we're here alone together, we act like close friends—sometimes, even a bit like mother and daughter. We eat most meals together, but as soon as there's anyone else in the house, Hattie takes on the role of cook and maid. Understand—this is her choice, not mine. She has a clear vision of her place in the world and would be most uncomfortable changing. Would you like to pour the wine? I'm afraid I don't have a proper ice bucket yet, but I think you'll find the temperature about right."

Gordon reached for the bottle. "I don't think I should have any wine—I've got more reading to do this evening. There's just one more day before the bar exam. Let me pour for you." He held the bottle up and looked at the label. "My, my—this is really special: Le Musigny. I know what it is but I've never had the opportunity to taste it. It's quite a rare white wine and very expensive. You didn't buy this around here, did you?"

"I didn't buy the wine. My father had a large collection of fine wine, mostly French and Italian. He kept it in a secure, temperature-controlled warehouse and would call up to have bottles delivered to the house, or—more often—to his country club. I had the warehouse manager ship a dozen mixed cases here when I moved. He sold the other eighty or ninety cases at auction."

Gordon poured the golden-hued wine into Devon's glass. "I'm afraid I can't turn down the opportunity to sample this rarity. Just one glass shouldn't damage my memory any more than it already is." He filled his glass halfway and raised it to the light.

"To your success with the bar exam," Devon toasted as they clinked glasses.

~*~

Gordon used the last toast point to scoop up the remaining morsels of lobster salad on the green plate. "That was the best lobster salad I've ever had." He dabbed at his lips with a linen napkin. "The touch of hot sauce is unique—nothing like we'd ever do with lobster in New England. Your Hattie is quite a cook; you two should open a restaurant."

Devon grinned. "Maybe someday, when I'm ready to do something useful. More wine?"

"This burgundy is superb—so good, I wasn't able to stop

myself at just one glass."

"Let's finish it," she suggested, and without waiting for Gordon's response, divided the remaining golden liquid between their glasses.

"Of course, you do realize that if I screw up the exam, I'm gonna blame you. Hattie's lobster salad and your extraordinary burgundy led me to ruin—that'll be my excuse."

Devon laughed. "The jury won't buy it, Counselor—ignorance of the law is no excuse. Come on over here." Devon rose from her chair and moved to the sectional. "Bring your wine and I'll give you a quick preview of our system. I'm sure you'll enjoy the experience."

"Okay, but after all that wine and great food, I'm not sure I can move." Gordon followed her instructions, stepped to the far end of the couch, and clumsily set his wineglass on the side table. "Okay—made it this far."

Devon smiled. "Everything runs off this remote," she said, holding up a larger than usual television-remote-like device. "First, the background." Unseen recessed lights threw a soft indirect glow across the entire room. "Next, the shutters." Electric motors whirred and the external, slatted shutters slithered down, covering the large windows and canceling out all sunlight. "You're comfortable?" Devon asked.

"You designed thess?" Gordon slurred the words.

"Clarisse did, with some computer-science grad students. Now, the audio." The sounds of gently running water—a stream or brook—poured into the room. Then gradually, over several minutes, it built to the deafening roar of a waterfall. "Pretty cool, huh?" Devon shouted as the sound began to recede.

"Now the picture show." Devon still shouted, even though the sound level was at a more comfortable level.

The three large monitors filled with images of horizontal, multicolored lines, the images passing uninterrupted from one screen to the next. Almost imperceptibly, the lighting in the room gradually dimmed as the images on the monitors became more intense. For over five minutes, the horizontal lines changed colors, alternated between thick and thin, migrated from one monitor to another, and then took on jagged shapes, shapes of thunderbolts, saw blades, and a phallus. The lighting had completely shut down, and the only illumination was now coming from the three monitors. Sounds that had begun as a series of single, computer-generated tones followed the frenzy of the monitor images and gradually escalated in tempo and intensity to become dissonant music. Suddenly, the abstract, pulsing lines on the three monitors vanished and were replaced by rainbow-hued, kaleidoscopic clouds, shifting shape and color like Escher's dragons. The music became soft and melodic—cloud music.

"You okay?" Devon asked.

"I'm having trouble visually processing this," Gordon attempted to say but was unable to transmit those words from his mind to his mouth. He couldn't see Devon but sensed she was nearby.

"Big clouds," he said at last. "Big clouds." Gordon was confused. He closed his eyes, but incredibly intricate fractals continued exploding, growing, and twisting behind his eyelids. He saw bright neon colors, and shafts of light turning into complex, awe-inspiring hallucinations.

From somewhere in the now-dark room, Devon gave a deep, guttural laugh. "Time to begin our journey," she called to him. Then there she was—her face and shoulders filling the central monitor. The clouds crossed over from the left and right monitors to fill the space behind her head. The cloud music rose in volume and intensity as the camera pulled back to focus on her naked body, standing on a fine-powder-sand beach, with azure water lapping at her feet.

"You do remember, don't you?" Devon called. Gordon was unable to tell if she was speaking to him from the couch, or if her voice came from the image on the screen.

"You remember?" her screen image asked as her hands lifted her firm breasts. "You remember?" she asked again as she stroked her shaved vulva. "I was blonde then—blonde just for you." The image shifted from the beach to a bedroom. Devon was lying naked on silken sheets. The headboard and everything beyond Devon's immediate image was blurred and indistinct.

Gordon tried his best to focus on the monitor as the music became more engrossingly complex, driving the approaching psychedelic thunderstorm that was forming in his head. And then she was kneeling next to him on the couch, her lips next to his ear, and her fingers stroking his penis through his trousers.

"I took you in my mouth and sucked you dry. You remember, don't you?" She breathed heavily into his ear as she unfastened his belt and unzipped his chinos. She slid her hand under his jockey shorts and wrapped her fingers around his fully engorged penis. "You do remember?" she asked again.

The screen image echoed the cry. "You do remember, Gordy? We were so perfect together, our bodies joined like pieces of a jigsaw puzzle—on the beach, the sand packing into my butt, threatening to become sandpaper in my vagina; in the car, pounding against the old leather upholstery, its animal smell an aphrodisiac; in the urine-scented ladies room of the Sand-Dollar, the zipper of your jeans cutting into my thigh, with each thrust—cutting painfully, beautifully, perfectly. Then you went down on me on the sloping back of my Jaguar in the parking lot at two o'clock while the greasy truck driver emptying the dumpster watched. The truck's hydraulic, mechanical arms lifted the dumpster aloft, above the truck, reaching up as if in prayer above the driver's leering face in the cab, and then dropped the dumpster load into the truck's filthy maw. The driver watched us screw while he masturbated."

Devon's screen image in the bed was joined by a naked, slim man whose face was shadowed and unrecognizable. The same image filled the two side screens, but each from a different angle. The man lowered his head between Devon's legs and she leisurely began to flex her abdomen in waves of pleasure. Devon's image writhed in ecstasy on all three monitors as she approached orgasm, her partner's tongue and lips foraging in her vulva, searching out her clitoris. She grasped her partner's head, pulled him in even closer and began to moan. "Yes, Gordy! Do it."

Devon moved from her kneeling position on the couch to the carpeted floor, removed Gordon's boating shoes, and then pulled his chinos and undershorts down to his ankles and over his feet. Whatever attention Gordon had left was focused on the three screens until Devon slid back his foreskin, and then began to simultaneously stroke and kiss his throbbing penis. Gordon watched her red lips encircle his cock. Although he felt the pleasurable stimulation of her rough tongue rubbing against the underside of his hypersensitive glans, he found it confusing to accept that those sensations were real. Instead, he felt it was more likely that he and Devon were performers on a fourth monitor. He focused on the circular smudge that her bright lipstick had left around the circumference of his shaft as he approached ejaculation. Devon sensed his excitement and pulled back. "Not yet," she whispered. "I need you inside of me." She firmly guided Gordon's body from the edge of the couch onto the carpet.

Devon straddled Gordon's hips and guided his swollen organ inside of her. She unhurriedly rocked back and forth, while at the same time flexing her vaginal muscles, tightly contracting her vagina around Gordon's penis while she moved and then, seconds later, pausing and relaxing the muscles. Gordon intuitively responded by tightening his sphincter muscles each time she squeezed. Every tiny pressure was exquisite. With each thrust and movement, Gordon felt his psychic energy flow through his penis and into Devon's body. The outcome of their internal *pas de deux* was an extended period of near-ejaculation that lasted for minutes—finally ending, for Gordon, in a trembling psychedelic explosion.

Devon lowered her body to Gordon's chest, her sweaty breasts compressing against his, her mouth near Gordon's ear. They were both panting and out of breath. "You do remember?" she asked again.

And Gordon remembered. In his experience, there was only one woman who could so precisely control her vaginal muscles.

"Maggie," he whispered, breathing heavily. "Maggie."

24

"Wake up! We have to talk," Nila animatedly called as she rocked her sister's unresponsive body back and forth in the large bed.

"Get away, Ian! It's not morning yet," Della sleepily groaned. "I'm exhausted. We'll do it later, after I wake up."

Nila laughed. "Doo-Doo, it's me, not Ian—and you have to wake up, right now."

"Nila, what are you doing in my room?"

Nila pulled the blanket and sheet away from Della's naked body. "You're in Miami at a hotel and you have to wake up right this minute." She smacked Della's butt.

Della partially opened her eyes and looked around the room while Nila drew the drapes to admit the midmorning sun. The sunlight bounced off the crystals of a large chandelier and danced in rainbow colors on the beige walls and furniture.

Della pushed herself up on one arm and hesitantly lowered her legs over the side of the bed. "What time is it?"

"It's ten in the morning here in Miami. It's about four in the afternoon back at home. You've slept for nearly ten hours—Gordy's just left."

Della yawned and stretched. "My head's all fuzzy," she mumbled.

Nila smiled. "That's the jet lag and champagne, silly goose. You do remember the party—Mary and Milton, the models, Gordy, and the babies?"

Della's face brightened. "The babies! Oh yes, your darling babies—of course, I remember."

Della slid out of bed into a standing position and stretched upward on her toes. Although her complexion was several shades lighter than Nila's and her hair a pastel brown, there was a clear family resemblance between the sisters.

"You need to be wide awake. Mum called back a short while

ago and Dad's going to be ringing us at half-ten; there's not much time."

"Our dad?"

"Dad's here in Miami and he wants to meet with us."

"Our dad, really?"

"That's right—our dad." Nila grabbed Della's wrist and forcefully pulled her toward the bathroom. "You brush your teeth and put something on while I tell you what's going on."

"Okay, okay, don't pull," Della complained. "I'm wide awake now. Our dad, huh? Really?"

"Really—our dad."

Nila stood in the doorway while Della brushed her teeth. "First off, Mum said that our grandmother recently died and that in her will she left some valuable jewelry to me. Of course whatever it is we'll share."

Della spat out the toothpaste and rinsed her mouth. "Our gran's been dead for years."

"Not that grandmother, the one in Africa. Mum said her name was Juba."

"Oh, that one. I don't remember anything about the grandmother in Africa. Are you sure?"

"You were a tiny baby when we left Ghana—you wouldn't remember. I was older than you, but don't recall much about a grandmother, except that she was the one what put the cat tat on my belly and got Mum all steamed."

"Oh yeah, your cat tattoo—I remember the story about where you got the tattoo."

"So, Dad just went to see Mum in London and told her about his mother dyin' and her jewelry. He said that before she died, his mother made him swear that he would personally deliver the jewelry to me and that's what he wants to do. He's come to Florida and is staying at a hotel in Miami. Mum called and asked if it would be okay for her to give him my phone number. I agreed and so she set it up for him to call us at half-ten. That's in exactly thirteen minutes. He wants to arrange a place where we can meet later today, Mum said."

Della hastily grabbed a hotel robe from the back of the bathroom door and walked to her suitcase, which was lying open on a chair. "I guess I should feel excited about meeting my father for nearly the first time in my life." She shrugged. "But somehow I'm finding that I don't really care." She pulled on underpants and an old, worn Rolling Stones tour T-shirt from a long-ago concert at Wembley Arena. "Ian gave me his prized shirt not long after we met. It was to commemorate our mutual loss of virginity, he said—romantic, he is!"

Nila laughed and helped Della with the robe. "You're still happy to be living together?"

"Ecstatic. Ian's the most gentle, randy, loving man I've ever known—and funny, too. Sometimes when he gets me laughin' I can't stop, and wind up wettin' me knickers. I think it's likely we'll marry; he wants to get a book published first and then quit his temp jobs. I don't mind, though. I'll have him just as he is."

"We'll take the call in the other room," Nila said. "I asked Mary to join us, because she knows Miami and might be able to help us choose a place to meet if we have to. I asked her not to speak; I think Dad's only expecting to talk with us."

Della entered the sitting room and plopped onto a couch with her legs drawn up under the robe. "What's he like, our dad?"

"Don't really know. Mum destroyed all the photos she had of him and of us with him when we lived in Ghana. I did see a wedding photo, once; it was tucked into a book of poems in Mum's closet. I don't think she knew the photo was in the book. He was likely about the age I am now, with a darker complexion than mine. As I recall, he was good-looking—but that's all I remember."

There was a soft knock on the door. Nila opened it and found Mary with a finger held to her lips.

"All clear," Nila whispered. "He hasn't rung yet."

Mary embraced Nila, quickly stepped to the couch, and sat next to Della. "This is so exciting!" she gushed, wrapping an arm around Della's shoulders. "And so mysterious."

Nila's cell phone chirped. "I'm setting this to speaker," Nila said. "Mary, there's paper and pen on the coffee table if you want to ask a question. You two ready?"

Della and Mary nodded in unison as Nila pushed the talk button.

"This is Nila Rawlings," she said in a higher-pitched voice than normal.

"Nila, this is Hubert Rawlings—your father."

"Hello, Dad. Mum said that you'd be ringing me up. I'm very sorry to hear about your mother. Della is, too."

"Della's there with you?"

"Uh huh."

"Hi, Dad—it's me," Della called.

"Your mother didn't tell me that the two of you were together in Miami."

"We're getting fitted for our wedding dresses this afternoon—both of us."

Hubert sounded surprised and confused. "You're both getting married in Miami?"

"No, Dad—it's just me gettin' married. Della's my maid of honor and the wedding's at Castle Key—that's an island on the other side of Florida. Not 'til October, though. We're getting our gowns made by a famous designer who's here in Miami."

"I see; your mother didn't say. She told you about your grandmother's passing and about her will?"

"She said that my grandmother left me some jewels and that you'd promised her you'd deliver them to me."

"Yes—her name was Juba, your grandmother. I have four pieces of jewelry for you. They're quite valuable and are in the hotel safe. I'm staying at the Madison, in South Beach. Do you know where that is?"

"I don't know where anything is. We only arrived yesterday."

"Maybe you could come to the Madison this afternoon; any taxi driver will know where it is. Then I can get the jewelry out of the safe and tell you about your grandmother's will."

Mary took up the pen and furiously printed in large letters on the hotel stationery: NO! PRESS MUTE NOW!

"Hold on a second, Dad. Someone's at the door." Nila pressed the mute button and looked toward Mary.

Mary shook her head. "No way, girl," she said. "You don't even know what this guy looks like. He could be anybody—someone who's not your father. This could be a scam. Tell him to come here and meet you in the lobby at three."

Nila nodded and pressed talk. "Sorry, Dad. That was my fiancé's sister at the door—she's looking after my babies while we're having this conversation, but she can't continue to care for them this afternoon. If you want to meet with us today, I'm afraid it will have to be here, at the hotel where Della and I are staying."

Nila shrugged and gestured questioningly at Mary. Mary gave her the thumbs-up.

"Your babies?"

"Mum didn't tell you?"

"Only that you were living in America and that you're marrying an American. Nothing about babies."

"Okay. I'm marrying an American named Gordon whose wife died. He has twin girls that, after our marriage, I'll be adopting. The babies are here with me in Miami and I already think of the two of them as mine. Della lives with her boyfriend in London and will probably be getting married soon, as well. That's probably all you need to know about us."

Della turned on the couch toward Nila and echoed Mary's thumbs-up.

Hubert paused. "All right—I'll come to you. What's the name of your hotel?"

"The Mandarin Oriental."

"The address?"

Mary pointed to the address on the hotel stationery.

"500 Brickel Key Drive. We'll meet you in the lobby at three."

Hubert cleared his throat. "It's only you, Nila, whom I need to meet with. Not Della."

Della frowned and stuck out her tongue.

"Sorry, Dad. That's not the way it's gonna work. Whatever you have to tell me, you'll tell Della, as well. We'll be in the lobby at three and each have a flower in our hair so that you can recognize us."

"If you insist." Hubert's voice had taken on a hard tone.

"I do."

"Is there somewhere private where we can talk?"

Nila looked at Mary. Mary mouthed *here,* and pointed to the floor.

"We can use our suite. We'll go up after we meet."

"We'll meet at three then, in the lobby of the Mandarin Oriental," Hubert said and hung up.

"Good job," Mary enthused. "This whole thing smells fishy."

"Fishy?" Della asked.

"A man who says he's your father—a man who neither of you remembers or would recognize—wants to meet Nila, and only Nila, in a South Beach hotel best known for its bedroom ceiling mirrors. He says he'll give Nila some valuable jewelry left to her by his dead mother from Ghana, whom neither of you can remember. Got it? Smells like a day-old fish left out in the sun."

Della laughed. "When you put it that way, there is a rank odor about it."

Nila frowned. "Mary, what should we do?"

"Here's a plan. Milt and I bring lots a business to this hotel every spring and so they take especially good care of us. I'll get the management to have hotel security keep an eye on the two of you down in the lobby. If you feel any threat, or think you're in danger, just wave your hand in the air and security will come a-runnin'. If you think this man calling himself Hubert is legit and agree to a private meeting, bring him up here, to Della's suite. I'll wait in the bedroom and if there's any trouble, all you have to do is shout for help and I'll call security."

Nila frowned and shook her head. "Actually, I'm sure Hubert is our real father and that he has no intention of harming or scamming either of us, but I've heard the horror stories of what can happen in Miami to naïve girls. So, okay. We'll do as you suggest."

~*~

Nila checked her watch for the second time in a minute; it read 3:10. She looked at the middle-aged man coming through the hotel entrance. "Don't think so; this one's quite gray, likely too old."

The man in the tailored leather jacket and designer jeans noticed the girls' flowers and puzzled expressions. He smiled and strode toward them.

"Nila!" he enthusiastically called as he approached the couch that was strategically placed to face the main entrance of the hotel.

"Dad, it's really you!" Nila stood, ignored his outstretched hand, and embraced him as one might greet a friend. Hubert turned toward Della, who stood but opted for a handshake.

"Hello, Dad," Della coolly stated. "Long time no see."

"I guess you could say that," Hubert said with a grin. "You didn't need the orchids in your hair. The resemblance with your mother is remarkable—you especially, Della."

"You've seen our mum in London?" Della asked, although she knew the answer to her question.

Hubert nodded. "I got into Miami yesterday evening. I'm feeling quite fresh, though. I think it's the anticipation of seeing the two of you as young women. This is quite a magnificent hotel—much better than the place I booked from the airport help desk."

"My almost-brother-in-law is a fashion designer who's hosting a wedding show here tomorrow. He's designed our wedding gowns and did the measuring and fitting just now—it was quite a process. Our suites were comped."

Hubert cocked his head. "Comped?"

"That means given free, and since our measurements are nearly identical, we can just swap dresses when it's my turn to be the bride," Della added, with a grin and a moderate thaw to her initial coolness.

"You said your fiancé's young children are staying with you?"

"Yes, my almost-sister-in-law is babysitting them in my suite. We can use Della's suite so we won't be interrupted. You did say you wanted to have a private conversation?"

Hubert nodded and patted the breast pocket of his jacket. "I have the jewels with me. I suggest that you put them in the hotel safe after we talk. As you'll see, they're very valuable."

Della gestured toward the reception desk. "The lifts are just over here," she said.

While the group silently waited for the elevator, an athletic-looking young man in a dark suit joined them. He entered the car last.

"Which floor?" he asked.

"Twelve, please," Nila replied with a smile and a discreet wink. They all exited at the twelfth floor. Nila, Della, and their father turned left while the athletic young man strode down the hallway in the opposite direction.

"It's just here," Della said. She inserted her key card and opened the heavy door; Hubert held the door while the women entered.

Della stood in front of a wall mirror and plucked the orchid from her hair, while Nila settled on the upholstered couch.

Hubert removed his leather jacket and extracted a thick, white envelope from the inside pocket. "Could you find a small towel where I can lay out the jewels?"

Della nodded and went through the bedroom to the bathroom for the towel. She found Mary sitting on the bed with her cell phone in hand. Della smiled, gave Mary an okay sign, and returned to the lounge.

"There's coffee if you'd like," Nila offered.

Hubert declined the coffee. He opened the white envelope and took out four clear plastic sleeves, each tied at the top with an old-fashioned cord wrap. Della spread the hand towel on the coffee table in front of Hubert, who placed the plastic sleeves on the towel and leaned back into the couch. He hung his head and bit his lower lip before speaking. "I realize this meeting is awkward for both of you. I'm your natural father, and yet I'm a stranger. We share DNA but have little else in common. For much of my life, I behaved badly toward your mother. And toward you two, as well. Although it was your mother's choice to leave Ghana and return to England, I'm really the one who deserted the family. I don't ask for your understanding or your forgiveness, nor do I have expectations of any change in our relationship. My life is what I've made of it and I will die with the pain I have caused the three of you on my conscience."

Della sat on the carpeted floor at the end of the coffee table nearest her father and stared, wide-eyed, into his face. "Our mum never told us much about you, or why you two broke up. All she told us was that she wasn't able to live in Ghana and had to bring us home to England."

"And that our grandmother put the cat tattoo on my belly without Mum's permission in some sort of voodoo ceremony," Nila added. "She said that really was the last straw; it totally freaked her out."

Hubert shook his head. "That tattoo didn't have anything to do with voodoo. Let me explain. My mother descended from the

Ashanti, an ancient African people with a complex, sophisticated history. For thousands of years, until the final military conquest by the British in about 1900, the Ashanti were the dominant force in West Africa. They controlled the lands that today are called Ghana and the Ivory Coast. Ashanti culture was ancient, rich, and complex, but because the Ashanti had an oral, rather than a written, history, the Europeans chose to marginalize the Ashanti as savages. Since my mother was of the Ashanti, all three of us have Ashanti blood flowing in our veins and—"

"What did she look like? I've never seen a photo," Della interrupted him.

"Juba was a tall, slim woman. I take after her—except for her darker skin."

"And you have a wife and children?"

"My wife's name is Morowa—she too is African and of the Ashanti. And yes, Morowa and I have five sons—Joshua, the eldest, is sixteen and Peter, our youngest, is two."

"So, your sons are Nila's and my stepbrothers. Isn't that right?"

"Della, I think it's half-brothers, not stepbrothers—can you please let Dad get on with what he was telling us?"

"Okay, but I'd really like to see their pictures—my five stepbrothers."

"Della, please? Go ahead, Dad."

"As I was saying—Juba, your grandmother, was of the Ashanti and came from a high-status family. In Europe, the family would be considered royalty. From her childhood, she was taught that she had inherited special powers, powers she could use to protect her family, and to ward off malevolent forces. These special powers had been passed down through the women of her family all the way back to the time of creation."

"You mean like a good witch? You've seen her use these powers?" Della excitedly asked.

Hubert shook his head. "Never," he said. "I seriously doubt

that she actually had powers of any sort—but she believed that she did. And, like her mother, grandmother, and all the women of her family who had preceded her, she firmly believed that it was her solemn duty to pass these powers on to her daughter—or to her closest female blood relative."

"But you're an only child, aren't you, Dad? Your mother never had a daughter?" Della asked.

"Exactly," Hubert said. "Since she had no daughter, Juba believed that she had to pass her powers to her closest female descendant—and that, of course, would be you, Nila."

"Wow!" Della nearly shouted. "Nila, her first granddaughter—that makes you a good witch, Nila."

Hubert nodded. "That cat tattoo on your belly is your grandmother's mark. She placed her mark on you to signify that upon her death, the ancient powers she believed she possessed would pass to you. However, Morowa and I are second cousins. So, if we had had a daughter, then that child would be closer in the bloodline to my mother than you, and would supposedly inherit my mother's powers. But Morowa and I only had boys, no girls."

Nila grinned. "That's silly. I haven't felt any differently—no ancient powers. When did Juba die?"

"Two months ago."

"So you'd think I'd know by now if anything was different."

"As I've told you, I never saw any evidence that my mother had special power—but there is one more piece of the puzzle." Hubert picked up one of the plastic sleeves from the table, opened the string closure, and then removed a small velvet pouch. "This is one of the four pieces of jewelry that Juba left to you in her will. It's a ring," he added, as he opened the velvet pouch and held the gold and orange-diamond ring toward Nila. "A diamond—a three-caret, orange-colored diamond. Orange-colored stones of this size and quality are extremely rare, the appraiser said. He's given the ring a retail value of eighty thousand pounds."

Della gasped. "That's enough to buy a house...well, not in London."

Nila reached out with a trembling hand and took the ring between her thumb and index finger.

"Look at the color," she whispered, holding the ring up to the light. "It's as if it's glowing from inside the stone."

Nila extended her hand to Della, who took the ring and slowly slid it onto her ring finger. "It's magnificent. I've never seen any stone this luminous before. If you're planning on wearing it, Nila, you'll need to get it sized down. It's too large to safely wear."

"According to my uncle, who was the family historian, this stone in its raw, uncut form was the property of the Ashanti for thousands of years," Hubert said. "When the stone was cut, and set into the ring, it was passed to someone in our family—likely my great-great-great-grandmother—and it's been in the family ever since. My uncle said that the diamond was a 'power stone.' He couldn't exactly remember why it was called that, but said it had more to do with the powers of the person wearing the ring than powers within the stone itself. My mother loved to wear her jewelry, but I never saw her wear this ring. I'm reasonably sure that she never felt that she needed to use the protective powers she believed she had inherited."

Della removed the ring from her finger and passed it to Nila. Nila held the stone to the natural light from the far window.

"It's heavy for its size," she said. She held the ring by the sides and slid it onto the ring finger of her left hand. "Actually, this fits perfectly. It doesn't need to be sized down at all."

"That's not possible," Della said with a frown. "Your hands aren't any bigger than mine and the ring was obviously way too big for me. Here, let me try it on again."

Nila twisted the ring and tried to remove it from her finger but couldn't. "That's odd. It went on easily enough, but now it doesn't wanna come off." She stood and continued to pull and twist the ring. "Soap and cold water should do the trick—let me go into the bathroom."

"Make sure to close the drain first," Della cautioned her.

"Wait a minute," Hubert said, tapping his fingers against the plastic sleeves on the coffee table. "You've got three more spectacular pieces to see. Sit back down and afterward I'll help you get the ring off. Then we'll put all four pieces into the hotel safe."

"Right," Nila agreed and resumed her seat. She turned to Della and smiled. "Check 'em out and pick the one you want for yourself."

"Really?" Della exclaimed.

"Yes, really. I'll keep the ring—maybe it'll be my engagement ring. Then we'll sell the other two pieces and I'll split the money with Mum. Somehow, I don't think she'd want any of Juba's jewelry. Is that okay with you, Dad?"

Hubert cleared his throat. "I don't have a problem with your selling the necklace and pendants. They were things my mother purchased during her lifetime, but I hope you'll keep the ring in the family. It's been with the Ashanti for so many centuries that it would be a tragedy not to continue to pass it on."

"I understand—but with twin girls, it might be complicated to pass on a single ring. Then again, there's the distinct possibility that I'll have a few babies myself—maybe a beautiful daughter who'll continue the Ashanti bloodline. Is that what you'd want, Dad?"

Hubert nodded. "That's exactly what your grandmother would wish—and my late Uncle Ringwald, as well."

~*~

"Me do," Janna exclaimed, as she placed the square red block on top of another block of the same shape and color.

"Yes," Julie agreed. "This!" she said, placing a rectangular yellow block on its side, perpendicular to the two red blocks. Janna grunted and covered the rectangular block with another of the same shape.

The twins were dressed in matching pink coveralls and frilly white socks, without shoes. They sat side by side on the plush carpet. The colorful blocks were their current favorite plaything. They took turns placing the remaining blocks together until all of the wooden toys were stacked three levels high. After Julie had placed the final block, a cone, on top of the two rectangles, Janna lifted up onto her knees and, with her small hands, quickly flattened the creation. Both girls squealed in delight and then proceeded to take turns building another structure. During the hour that Nila and Mary had left the girls in DiDi's less-than-attentive care, the twins had built and razed a dozen or more structures, and showed no sign of losing interest.

DiDi was lying on her back on the carpet in front of the upholstered couch, her cell phone pressed against her ear. The babies were building their creations on the other side of the carpeted room, about thirty feet away. DiDi was in her early twenties, tall, and fashionably emaciated. She wore a white spandex tank top with denim Daisy Dukes, and yellow-tinted, half-frame glasses. At the septum of her nose, a small, bone-shaped piece of silver pierced the cartilage. The hair surrounding her right ear had been shaved and a circle of red-and-blue tattoos of miniature flowers circled her ear and extended down to her neck. DiDi was an aspiring model, and an assistant to the wardrobe mistress who managed the garments displayed in Milt's fashion shows. Mary had given her some extra money to watch the twins while Nila and Della met with their father in the hotel lobby.

DiDi was totally absorbed in a heated argument with her about-to-be-ex boyfriend. Her angry voice grew progressively louder and the expletives more anatomically specific as she repeated the details of his recent, cocaine-fueled bedroom feats as graphically described in an earlier call with her ex-best-girlfriend.

"The fat cunt said she was calling to apologize for having sex with you. But it wasn't an apology! She called to brag about getting to suck your dick and how much you loved it." DiDi's voice rose to a scream. "She said you told her how terrific it was to screw a woman with real tits, instead of a bag-a-bones."

Julie and Janna were startled by DiDi's wild screams. They pushed back from their blocks and stared, wide-eyed, at the fuming, foul-mouthed woman. Julie moved close to Janna and whispered in Janna's ear. Janna listened intently and then nodded.

Although both girls were now able to walk reasonably well, when on carpeted or smooth, wooden floors, they still preferred to crawl. Janna crawled to the end of the couch, stood, and then pulled her small body up onto the seat cushions. She scrambled to the opposite end of the couch, directly above DiDi's head, awkwardly stood, tottering on the spongy cushions, and then tumbled forward from the edge of the couch onto the babysitter's face. DiDi shrieked as the twenty-pound human cannonball dropped, but it was too late to raise her hands or arms to ward off the pink missile, and Janna's knee scored a direct hit on DiDi's nose.

"Aaaggh!" DiDi cried out and threw down the phone, as bright-red blood began to flow from her likely broken nose. She raised her hands to her face and tore off the eyeglass frames that had snapped into two pieces from the impact of Janna's knee. One end of DiDi's sharp, silver nose piercing had been driven into her upper lip, adding to the copious blood flow. She cried out again when she saw her hands covered with blood.

After the impact with DiDi's face, Janna rolled onto her hands and knees and quickly scooted across the room to Julie's side. DiDi's nose piercing had punctured Janna's knee and the resulting small gash left blood smears across the carpet.

Just as Julie put her arm around Janna's shoulders, Mary opened the door and began to call out a greeting, which she stifled when she saw DiDi's blood-covered face and the bloody handprint she'd left on the carpet when she raised herself to a sitting position against the couch.

"What in hell!" Mary shouted.

"They attacked me," DiDi shrieked. "The monsters jumped on my face!"

Mary looked across the room, and—after quickly deciding that the twins were in no immediate danger—dropped to her knees next to the blubbering young woman.

"I can't see," DiDi squealed. "It's my left eye—I'm blind!"

DiDi was a mess. Her damaged nose was swollen and already beginning to bruise. The silver, bone-shaped piercing had been torn from her septum, and the end was stuck in her upper lip. A sharp edge of the broken eyeglass frame had cut into the soft flesh to the side of her left eye. The blood that flowed from her nose had already begun to clot, and globs of red mucus hung from her nostrils and gathered on her lips.

Mary stood. "Don't try to wipe your face. Just stay still until I get a wet towel and clean you up."

As Mary moved to the bathroom, the twins turned their gaze from the blood-covered DiDi to each other. They both grinned, and then burst into excited squeals of laughter.

25

Nila was frustrated. "He's not answering. I've tried his cell, the landline, and even the car phone. He always has his cell turned on—I can't understand why I can't get hold of him."

Della shrugged. "It isn't really all that important, is it? You told me the doctor said there's nothing wrong with Janna. It's just a superficial puncture—no stitches and likely not even a scar. All he did was apply some antibiotic cream and a plaster—isn't that what you said?"

"Band-Aid," Nila corrected. "They call 'em Band-Aids, not plasters. But that's not the point! Janna is Gordy's daughter and I'm responsible for her safety. I'm not the mum yet. He needs to know Janna was injured—even though it wasn't serious."

"Maybe he drove up to Tampa early. Maybe his cell ran out of charge—that's happened to me often enough."

"If Gordy were driving, he'd answer the car phone—that seldom gets used, but never runs down."

"You texted him?"

"Uh huh, but no response. It's just not like him to be out of communication—that's all."

"Listen, Nila—surely there's a reasonable explanation. You left messages for him to call back?"

"Of course. I'm sure he'll call as soon as he gets a message; Gordy's a very responsible parent. I need to tell him about the bruise on Janna's foot, as well."

Della looked puzzled. "Bruise?"

"I didn't tell you? When the doctor was examining Janna's leg, he discovered a tiny black mark on her right foot in the space just between her big toe and the next toe. It looked like the number 7. He said it was just a bruise and nothing to be concerned about. The babysitter's face is a mess. Her nose and lip are swollen and they had to put a few stitches between her nostrils where the silver piercing was ripped out. But the good news is that her nose isn't broken and in a few weeks, she should be back to normal—if normal is a possibility for a creature like her."

Della smirked. "Have you and Mary sussed out what actually happened? That baby-minder was in quite a state when you all left for the hospital. She kept insisting that the twins attacked her."

"She calmed down some after they gave her a sedative in the emergency room. What we've pieced together is that DiDi was lying on her back on the floor in front of the couch, talking on her cell and not paying any mind to the twins. It would seem that Janna crawled up onto the couch, lost her balance, and fell onto the girl's face." Nila began to sob. "It gave me quite a scare when we came in and saw all that blood on the couch and carpet, and no babies."

Della embraced her sister and wiped the few tears from Nila's cheek with her fingers. "Put it out of your mind. Mary handled the situation perfectly and your babies are just fine—they've both been fed and are sleeping. I've rung up room service and ordered a pizza and margaritas for the two of us—they'll be here any minute. It's been quite a day—a day of surprises. We should probably make an early night of it."

Nila continued to tightly hold on to her sister. "Maybe you could sleep here tonight? The bed is certainly big enough for the two of us, and I'd rather not be alone."

"And we could tell scary stories of witches and dragons, just like when we were wee tykes and shared that creaky four-poster bed in our gran's spare room?"

Nila laughed and released her hold on Della's body, but continued to clasp her hand. "We've had enough scary experiences for one day. Perhaps we could do our game—you remember, don't you?"

"Mmm hmm," Della replied with a grin. "But wouldn't that

be wicked, now that we're grown women?"

"I don't see why. After all, we *are* loving sisters."

Della squeezed Nila's hand. "Just like your babies."

Nila nodded. "Just like my babies."

~*~

The bedroom shimmered with dazzling morning sunshine—the intense light common to tropical regions and deserts. Gordon had gone to bed in the dark and failed to notice that the drapes weren't drawn. He rolled from his stomach to his back, stretched, and then fumbled about on the bedside table, his fingers searching for the cell phone. It was early—the screen read 6:20.

Gordon had a headache. He was confused and ravenously hungry. He remembered reviewing Devon's documents at the big house the previous afternoon: the amazing monitors, and huge palms in the great room. He remembered the lobster salad and the superb wine and the conversation with Devon. He remembered waking after dark in the hammock by the cottage pool, but couldn't remember driving the Lincoln back to the beach cottage. "Really bad," he said aloud as it came to him that he had been too drunk to drive. He continued thinking. *I'm gonna have to reconsider drinking. Maybe I'm an alcoholic like Father and Mother. If I had left the property and driven out on the road, I could have really screwed up bad.* He violently shook his head from side to side, making the pain in the back of his head worse. "Later," he said aloud, "gotta concentrate on this friggin' exam right now."

He was about to return the phone to the night stand when he noticed that he'd had several messages. He immediately recognized the calling number—all were from Nila. The last call was at 10:35 the night before. He pressed the voicemail icon and lifted the phone to his ear. After retrieving the most recent message from the mailbox, he heard Nila's distinctive accent and smiled. "Hi, it's me again. I've been trying to reach you for several hours without success and am going to bed now. It's been quite a day. Della is staying with me and the girls for the night. The thing is, there's been a minor accident involving Janna. No need for concern—she's just fine. She has a tiny wound from a fall off the couch in my suite. The doctor treated her with some antibiotic cream and a Band-Aid, so obviously, it wasn't serious. Nevertheless, I feel so responsible for the girls' welfare that I had to share this with you right away. There was so, so much more that happened today—things I need to tell you about. Mostly positive things—at least, I think they were positive. Please come and get us soon. I love you very much and I'm feeling randy as hell tonight. Oh, best of luck with the exam, of course. We all love you. Wait—what was that? Oh, Della says she loves you, too. Night-night." Nila made kissy noises, and then rang off.

Gordon's immediate thought was to call Nila back. The twins usually woke with the sun and so Nila was likely to be awake, but she'd need time to get them and herself washed and dressed. He decided to take care of his own personal needs and then make the call. Like Nila, Gordon usually slept nude, and when he rolled from the bed, his penis rubbed against the cool, satin sheets. It was especially sensitive and the edges of the foreskin were irritated. He and Nila had made love yesterday morning before he left the hotel, but, with the babies asleep in their cribs in the same room, they'd been more restrained than usual. He was surprised at the extent of irritation on his foreskin. In the bathroom, he soaked a cotton ball in mouthwash, rolled back his foreskin and dabbed at the irritated areas. Gordon grimaced. From experience, he'd anticipated the alcohol's sting and quickly pulled the foreskin back in place to minimize the discomfort.

He looked in the bathroom mirror and decided to shave. Gordon had a light beard, which was the same color as his sandy-blond hair, and didn't shave every day. But, he reasoned, if he shaved this morning, he wouldn't have to bother again until after the bar exam. He was about to turn on the bathtub shower but instead decided to use the outdoor shower by the pool. Showering naked, outdoors, in the sunshine and breeze, was one of the small hedonistic pleasures that Gordon had discovered during his early teen years at the beach house. He'd arise with the sun, before his mother could force him to put on a bathing suit, and then enjoy a soapy, masturbatory massage under the warm water. On occasion, he'd see girls in bathing suits having an early morning stroll on the beach, a hundred yards away, and then he'd fantasize that they were watching him and becoming wet with excitement.

Gordon returned to the bedroom and retrieved the phone from the pillow where he'd tossed it. The phone said 6:58—he was sure Nila and the girls would be up by now. She answered on the third ring.

"Hi!" Nila nearly shrieked. "I was just about to call you again. I've been quite worried about you. Called the house, your cell, and even the car, I did."

"Sorry to worry you. After I got back from Miami, you'll remember that I'd promised to look over Devon's legal documents. When I finished, Devon insisted that I stay for a late lunch. Along with Hattie's lobster salad, I drank several glasses of an exceptional white burgundy they offered. Afraid the wine really did me in. When I came back to the house, I decided to have a nap in the hammock out on the lanai. With lots of assistance from the wine, I'm afraid my nap turned into serious sleep and I never heard the phone, or cell from inside the house. I think all the driving the last two days, along with the two or three glasses of wine, finally got to me. When I woke it was dark and too late to call. You're okay, and Janna's okay?"

"Like I said in my message, all it took was a Band-Aid and some cream to patch her up. This morning, Julie pulled off Janna's Band-Aid, and we discovered that the cut has just about healed."

"She fell off the couch, you said?"

Nila replayed the adventures with DiDi, and Hubert's surprise visit to the hotel. With Gordon's frequent questions and Della's in-the-background interruptions and additions, the stories took a while to tell.

"Good thing Della was there with you."

"Mary, too. She cleaned up the babysitter and took her to the hospital with Janna and me. She is such a strong woman; I can better understand now how you depended on her when you were a child."

Gordon chuckled. "*And* she's raising her own two boys—I can tell you there's been lots of blood and tears in that experience."

"The ring," Nila interrupted. "I need to tell you the rest of the story."

"Oh, what about the ring?"

"As I said, it's absolutely fantastic. The orange diamond glows as if there were some sort of fire inside. While I haven't tried too hard, I haven't been able to get the ring off my finger since I slid it on. I was thinking that if you agreed, perhaps we could make it my engagement ring. It's beautiful and valuable and also we wouldn't have to shop for a ring."

"If that's what you'd want, I don't think I'd have any problem with you using your family ring as our engagement ring. That used to be a regular custom in the old days. Let's talk about it when I get there, okay?"

"Fine. Milt and Mary are leaving on Thursday morning. Della's flying out on a late afternoon flight, as well. Pity you won't get to spend time with her."

"Well, at least we got to meet. Now she won't be a stranger when she comes back for the wedding. I like Della a lot; she's like a smaller, fairer, more talkative version of you."

Nila chuckled. "Considerably more talkative; I'd almost forgotten how she goes on. I love her dearly and it's been such a joy to have her with me for a few days and to finally have her meet you and the girls. She thinks you're handsome and wonderful and that the babies are the most clever, beautiful children in the world."

Gordon laughed. "Della is clearly a young woman with excellent judgment. I've decided to drive to Tampa this afternoon and get settled in. I've come to the conclusion that I've done more than enough prep for this exam—I really don't think it'll be that difficult."

"It takes two days, you said, the exam?"

"Wednesday is an essay and Thursday is a general overview common to most states' bar exams. I've already taken the second part in Massachusetts and pulled some strings to wangle an exemption."

"You sound quite relaxed."

"I am. If the drive from Miami up to Tampa were shorter, I'd come join you today and then drive up from Miami."

"Milt's show starts this morning at eleven. I don't think you'd want to sit through forty or fifty evening gowns and bridal dresses worn by emaciated, flat-chested models."

"Right!—as I said, it's a long drive. I'll call you tonight when I get to Tampa and then again on Wednesday after the exam's over."

"So, you'll come get us on Thursday?"

"Possibly late Wednesday night. I could stay over; it'd be great to see everyone again before they leave. It really depends on how long the exam takes and how tired I am afterward. I'll call you tonight from Tampa."

"Gordy, I gotta go. Della and I are taking the girls to a preshow breakfast in Milt and Mary's suite with a lot of fashion reporters and critics, and we all need to get ready."

"Give our girls a kiss from me and one for Della and Mary, as well. As for you, you'll have to wait until I can guide you out of your panties and kiss what we now know to be your witchcraft tattoo: your cat—or maybe it's a pussy?"

Nila laughed. "Maybe both," she replied. "Love you, kiss, kiss."

~*~

A white-haired couple was walking a black Lab along the water's edge. The large dog was leaping joyously in and out of the surf. Gordon thought they might be the McClatchys—the family who owned the estate on the other side of the big house. Although the couple was likely too far away from the beach house lanai to notice that Gordon was showering naked, he reflexively turned his back to the beach and saw Devon standing on the lanai, just outside the kitchen sliders. She was dressed in a knee-length, pink terry robe and flip-flops, her brown hair pulled back in a short ponytail. She held a coffee mug.

"You make good coffee," Devon said. "You do remember that you said we could use your pool while you were away? I thought you were leaving last night."

"Whoops," Gordon said as he reached for the shower-control valve on the wall.

She slid out of her flip-flops. "Don't turn off the water. I always shower before swimming." She set down the coffee mug on the pool bar, untied the terry-cloth sash around her waist, and then slipped the small robe over her bare breasts and onto a bar stool.

Gordon appreciatively gazed at her full breasts, the sexy curve of her abdomen, and her long, straight legs.

She smiled and nodded toward Gordon's now fully erect penis. "I guess I won't need this," she said as she pulled the string on the side of her thong bikini bottom and let the swimsuit fall to the tile floor.

~*~

Gordon was softly snoring in the big bed. The suppository Devon had gently inserted into his rectum during foreplay had done its job. He'd had a crashing orgasm, rolled onto his back, and fallen into a light sleep. Devon smiled. Unlike the previous afternoon, this time she wanted Gordon to remember—to remember not just the sex but to remember that Devon, not Maggie, had been his partner.

"Ready?" Hattie called from the hallway outside the master bedroom.

"Come on in," Devon replied. "We've got about ten minutes before he wakes up."

Hattie opened her colorful, beaded bag and handed Devon a two-inch-long needle with a black T-shaped handle. "Between the toes?" she asked.

Devon shook her head "Too obvious. He wears flip-flops or sandals most of the time. We'll do it on the back side of the scrotum, near the top. Even though he and Nila are intimate, she's not likely to notice my mark back there."

Hattie nodded, rolled Gordon's slumbering body to his stomach, and then spread his legs apart. "You want me to do it?"

Devon pulled herself onto the bed and knelt between Gordon's legs. "No. I'll enjoy this." Devon spread the soft skin above Gordon's testes with the thumb and index finger of her left hand, while, with the needle's black T-shaped handle secure against her right palm, she expertly pricked out the pattern of her mark. She extended her hand with the needle.

"Wipe," she said. Hattie exchanged the needle for a sterile, alcohol-infused pad, which Devon used to remove the blood that had gathered on Gordon's skin.

"The power," Hattie said, placing a small, plastic, eye-dropper-like bottle in Devon's hand.

Devon tilted the bottle over her needlework and dripped a few ink-black drops onto Gordon's skin, then blotted the excess liquid with the used wipe.

"Good?" Hattie asked.

"Perfect." Devon grinned and moved her hands away so that Hattie could admire her handiwork. "Now he's mine."

The inky liquid had stemmed the blood flow and the new, half-inch tattoo was precise. At first glance, it appeared to be a capital L, but closer inspection showed that, unlike an L, the bottom leg of the mark was tilted upward.

"Anesthetic," Hattie said as she handed Devon a fresh wipe and another dropper bottle. "That mark's likely ta sting for a bit."

Devon dripped on the clear liquid and then blotted the tattoo with the fresh wipe. "Okay, now you set up the Du-mon on the window ledge outside the children's room. I need to get outta here before Gordon wakes up."

Hattie laid a small, black, felt-covered package on the bed. She rolled back the cloth and removed a brightly painted figure. The one-piece icon stood no more than ten inches tall. Its torso was a sphere that was painted to mimic a bloodshot eyeball, with a bright red iris. Two separate heads extended from the eyeball. One head had a leering, cruel smile, and the other was painted in violent colors and twisted with rage, its jagged teeth bared.

Devon grasped the Du-mon and pressed it firmly between her breasts. "That'll wake it up!" she hissed.

Hattie dropped the bottles and needle into her beaded bag and zipped it tightly. "After all these years, I still don't like to mess with that slimy thing."

"The Du-mon is my alternate consciousness—my proxy. When I transfer power to the Du-mon, I get total control over the mind of anyone who bears my mark—the babies and now Gordon. Soon, we'll mark Nila and add her to our little family. Then the Du-mon can rest until I need it again."

Hattie shook her head. "You really wanna have them all hangin' round? I mean, you haven't never done this family stuff before."

"You stupid girl! Nila and Gordon are breeders. If something happens to the twins and they die or are disfigured before we can take their bodies, we'll need other babies. Nila and Gordon are young and healthy. They can make us lots more baby bodies if we need 'em."

"Brilliant—jus' brilliant," Hattie said with a chuckle.

26

It was a small mouse. The mouse had been attracted by the smell of stale, shelled peanuts that had long ago become lodged between the wooden baseboard and the concrete floor in the space that, before the mini-lift was installed, had been the kitchen pantry. Unable to coax out the few tightly wedged peanuts, the mouse turned its attention elsewhere and squeezed through a ventilation opening in the lift's motor enclosure. It sniffed at the grease on the gears.

Carrie stepped into the lift and pressed the up switch. The electric motor whirred into action and the gears caught hold of the mouse's tail, quickly pulling its body into their sharp teeth. In an instant, the mouse's soft body became a clot of blood, fur, and gore, but when the gear teeth encountered and crushed the tiny creature's skull, the resilient bone fragments logged in the spaces between the gear teeth and caused the electric motor to strain, sputter, overload, and then stop. Carrie peered down. The single-passenger elevator had traveled only five feet above floor level before jerking to a halt, and the light flowing into the kitchen from the conservatory was still clearly visible at the base of the elevator shaft. She pressed the down button. Nothing happened. Then she pressed the up button—still nothing. The small ventilator fan at the top of the wooden car continued to whirl away and the lights on the control buttons glowed brightly; it was clear that a power failure wasn't the cause of the stop. She pressed the up and down buttons again—there was no response. Carrie was aware that she was beginning to breathe rapidly and forced her lungs to slow down. Months before, just before she'd taken her first ride, Nick had explained the safety features of the single-passenger lift, but in the excitement of that initial brief journey, she hadn't taken in much of that information. All Carrie could recall was that Nick had said there were rubber friction strips in the shaft that would slow the fall of the car should it become separated from its cable—friction strips that would gradually arrest the fall before the car could crash onto the concrete floor below. She looked at her watch; it was 6:20 in the evening. Fortunately, Margaret, her assistant, would still be at the office and could call for help. Carrie reached to the right-rear pocket of her jeans for her cell phone. It wasn't there.

"Damn," she said aloud. In her mind, she could see the phone lying on the kitchen table where she'd left it after talking with Nick. Beads of sweat started to form on the back of Carrie's neck and she forced herself to sit on the triangular seat that Nick had built into the left corner of the box. The seat was shallow, barely deep enough for both butt cheeks—more a package shelf than a real seat. "Okay, what to do?" she asked herself and reviewed her situation. Nick would be calling between nine and ten to finalize their weekend plans for a Saturday overnight, and Sunday picnic, on his brother's boat. Nick would be surprised that she wasn't in. He'd guess she'd probably gone around the corner to Razza's convenience store to buy milk, or something else she needed for breakfast. She was sure that Nick would realize something was wrong when he called a second time and she failed to answer. Although it would be late by then, she felt confident he'd call Stella, her longtime next-door neighbor, or Margaret. She was equally sure that when Nick spoke to them, either Stella or Margaret would come to the house. Both of them had door keys, and could call 999 and get the fire brigade to rescue her. Carrie looked at her watch once. "Half-ten," she said aloud—four hours from the present time. She knew that would be the most optimistic timeframe for her release. Carrie felt sure she could survive the claustrophobic imprisonment of the box—her wooden coffin—for four hours. But what if it took longer? What if Nick decided it was too late to call? He was always considerate of her work schedule and knew she would be rising at six for work. She kicked off her high heels, knelt, and tried to find a reasonably comfortable position on the carpeted floor. The floor was nearly square, but she discovered that, with her feet under the corner seat and her body curled toward the open front, she'd be able to rest, if not actually sleep.

Carrie stood, stretched her arms to either side of the car, and tried to force herself to relax. Nick would call—she knew he would call. "Don't quit yet," she said aloud. "Maybe I can get this thing unstuck." She stood shoeless in the middle of the car and jumped up as high as she was able. As her feet impacted the floor when she came back down, the car seemed to descend a fraction. She jumped again but nothing happened. Carrie tried three more jumps and then gave up. The intercom! She'd forgotten about the intercom that connected to a small speaker that was set into the wooden trim next to the front door of the house. She pressed the call button, and the light lit; it was working.

"Help!" Carrie called. "Help me! I'm stuck in the lift." She called again and again until her face was damp with perspiration and her throat was raspy. She looked at her watch and decided it would make sense to wait until she heard noise from a passing pedestrian near the front door before calling out again. The sciatica in her lower back and left leg was beginning to throb. Carrie realized that she wasn't too far from panicking and started to sob.

~*~

Nila was bored. The clothes and the models were all beginning to look the same and the dresses and gowns displayed on the catwalk were styles she had never worn and knew she never would. After the experience with DiDi, Nila wasn't about to leave the twins with a hotel-supplied sitter. The girls had both been very quiet but were losing patience and beginning to fuss. Nila had hoped that they would fall asleep, but the pulsing music, and constantly changing lighting, along with the steady applause from the enthusiastic, well-dressed, mainly female audience, prevented the girls' boredom from turning into sleep. Nila had strategically placed herself and the twins in the back of the room, next to the main exit, and now she stood and quietly pushed the new double stroller toward the door. Mary had placed Della in a prime-viewing seat in the first row along the catwalk. Della was clearly caught up in the uniqueness of the event and was obviously enjoying herself. She turned her head toward the departing Nila and frowned. Nila smiled and waved her hand in a gesture she hoped Della would read as, "Stay and have a good time." Della seemed to understand and returned Nila's smile. A tuxedo-clad hotel-staff member held the door open for Nila as she guided the stroller into the hallway.

"Drink," Janna called loudly. Nila stooped in front of the stroller, and Julie echoed Janna's request.

"How about some ice cream? You two have been so patient that you deserve a reward."

"Icekeem," Julie enthused.

Nila stood and wheeled the stroller toward the lobby snack bar.

"Icekeem, icekeem," the twins repeated in unison.

Two young women having coffee at a table by the window overlooking the street were the only other people in the snack bar. Nila arranged the chairs at a small table to accommodate the stroller, placed her bag on the table, and turned toward the service counter.

"Sit down, honey," the frizzy-haired Hispanic woman behind the counter said to Nila. "I'll come to you."

"Icekeem, icekeem," the twins called.

"Same as yesterday?" the waitress asked Nila.

Nila grinned. "I guess you'll have to ask them—it seems like they're doing the ordering."

The waitress stroked Julie's dark hair. "Two ice-cream cups comin' up. Coffee for you, honey?"

"How about some iced tea—unsweetened, with lemon?"

"You got it," the waitress replied and returned behind the counter. "These-here ice-cream cups are frozen pretty solid. You want me to soften 'em up in the microwave?"

Nila nodded. "Good idea. I'm gonna let them feed themselves, so get the ice cream rather soft, if you would. Oh—and better bring some extra serviettes."

"Serviettes?" the waitress asked.

"Sorry—paper napkins."

Nila's left hand was resting on the table when her ring suddenly pulsed, the gold band gently contracting around her finger. She looked down at the ring and spread her fingers wide. It happened again, and this time the orange diamond flashed in unison with the ring's contraction. Nila twisted the ring with her right hand—the ring swiveled but wouldn't come off. It pulsed again—this time, the contraction was stronger.

The waitress arrived with the ice cream. "It's nice and soft," she said. "Do you want me to give the cups to the girls? I brought plastic spoons and paper napkins. Napkins are servilletas in Spanish—I should have known what you wanted."

"In England, we say serviette. Sure, let's let 'em have some fun; they've been angels all morning." Nila flipped up the plastic tray on the front of the stroller and the waitress placed an ice-cream cup in front of each twin while Nila stuck in the plastic spoons.

"Ouch!" Nila called out, and pulled her left hand away from the tray.

"You pinch yourself on that tray, honey?" the waitress asked.

Nila held up her hand. "It's this ring—it's uncomfortable on my finger and I'm getting cramps."

The waitress held Nila's wrist and inspected her hand. "Gorgeous ring—can you take it off?"

"It's not especially tight, but I can't seem to get it over my knuckle."

"Butter," the waitress offered. "That always works. Let me get some and you can try it."

The ring pulsed and flashed again.

Nila twisted the ring and peered into the central facet—the flat face that jewelers call the table—where she saw a bright image. The image wasn't actually displayed on the surface of the stone—it was more like the diamond was projecting an image through Nila's eyes to her consciousness. The image was perfectly distinct, clearer than a photo on the screen of her iPhone. It was her mother, who was lying, unmoving, on her side in a near-fetal position. Nila gasped and turned the ring away from her gaze.

"You all right, honey?" the waitress asked.

"I—I don't know," Nila stammered. She refocused on the orange stone. "She's still there," she whispered, more to herself than to the waitress.

"I'll get some butter and we'll get that ring off your finger."

Her heart pounding, Nila reached into the pouch on the side of her leather purse and removed her phone. She nervously selected her mum's cell number from the list and pressed the call button. Nila was breathing heavily while the connection moved through the international gateway to the UK network. Before Gordon had presented her with the new iPhone, he'd had it programmed to allow her to dial directly to her family and friends at home. At last, she heard the familiar European ringtone.

The frizzy-haired waitress returned and placed two pats of foil-covered butter on a paper napkin. "This'll do it," she said with a smile. Nila didn't notice the waitress or the butter. Her eyes were fixed on the image of her mum on the floor of the lift.

"Here you all are," Della called as she entered the snack bar.

Nila continued to hear ringing. She held up her free hand toward Della. "It's Mum—something's wrong."

"Hello, this is Carrie. I can't answer just now—please leave a message and I'll ring back as soon as I can. Cheers."

"Mum, this is Nila...I think you're in some kind of trouble. Call me right away—I need to hear your voice."

"Something's wrong with Mum?" Della asked. "What's going on?"

"I think Nick's mini-lift is stuck with Mum inside." Nila set her phone down on the table and raised her left hand to Della's face. "Look into the ring—you can see for yourself."

Della grasped Nila's left wrist and pulled the orange diamond closer to her face. "I don't understand—what am I supposed to see?"

"Mum!" Nila shouted. "She's on the floor of the lift." Nila turned her wrist and stared at the pulsing stone and image of her mother. "She's there—can't you see her?"

Della searched the ring. "Nila, there's nothing. I can't see a thing."

"Right there!" Nila pointed to the image of the mini-lift that she saw hovering in the air above the ring. "You can't see Mum lying on the floor?"

"I don't see anything, except your ring."

"See how the stone's pulsing?"

"No, I don't."

Nila shook her head. "We've got to get help. You've got Stella's number in your cell? You know—Mum's next-door neighbor?"

Della nodded. "Yes, but what..."

Nila retrieved her phone. "Give me her number; I can dial straight through on this phone."

Della fished in her shoulder bag for her cell phone. "I don't understand why you want to call Stella."

"Just give me her number—I'll explain afterward."

"Okay, I got it."

Della called out the number and Nila dialed. "Come on, come on," Nila impatiently muttered as the call was routed through the international gateway.

"Seven-seven-three-nine-four-two-one," Stella answered after the first ring.

"Stella, it's Nila Rawlings. There's a problem with my mum and I need your help."

"Nila, I thought you were in the States."

"I am, but I need your help. Mum's stuck in her new mini-lift. You still have her latch key, don't you?"

"What? Well, yes—I'm sure it's on the rack with the other keys but..."

"Please, Stella—go next-door and check on my mum. I'm positive she's in trouble."

"All right, if you say so. I'll just slip on a coat and take the phone with me. Nila, you're sure about this?"

"Please, Stella—Mum needs help."

"Okay. Stay on the line."

Stella quickly located the key; it was attached to a small plastic, advertising give-away from Carrie's travel agency. She pulled a tan raincoat over the lacy, baby-doll nightie that clung to her generous curves—Dennis would be arriving at any moment, and the sexy nightie was a surprise for him.

"Okay, Nila. I'm going next-door now."

Stella knocked and then pressed the doorbell. The intercom crackled to life. "Help me! Please help me!" Carrie shouted in an exhausted voice. "I'm trapped in the lift!"

"Good God!" Stella called out as she turned the latch key in the lock.

~*~

Della was kneeling beside the double stroller, trying to wipe up the sticky globs from the tile floor. "I'll need some more napkins, please," she called to the frizzy-haired waitress. "I doubt that they actually ate any of this ice cream—it's all over their hands and faces, as well as on the floor."

"Leave the floor to me, honey," the waitress called. "I got a wet mop back here—we get spills all the time."

Della stood and shifted her clean-up focus to the girls and the stroller. The twins both reached out to Della. "Go walk!" Janna called. Julie bounced excitedly in the seat. "Up!" she cried. "Me up."

Nila pivoted toward Della, her cell phone still pressed to her ear. "I've got Dennis on speaker; they got Mum out of the lift. Dennis arrived home at the same time Stella was entering Mum's house. Dennis called 999 first and then, since he knew Nick had built the lift, he called Nick. Nick told him to have Mum press the up and down buttons at the same time and hold them in for ten seconds. It worked; the lift came right down and Mum's safe. Dennis says Mum looked upset, but none the worse for wear. She was desperate for a pee and ran for the loo just as the lads from the fire brigade arrived. He says to hold on until our mum comes out of the WC and the medics check her out. It's quite noisy that end—I could hardly hear him."

Della lifted Janna from the stroller. "I think I'm gonna laugh," she whispered to the baby. "Or maybe I'm supposed to cry?"

Nila tilted the phone away from her ear. "You said you didn't see anything?"

"What?" Della asked.

"Mum in the lift—the image from the ring."

"Not a thing."

"But you saw the ring flashing—didn't you?"

"Nila, I didn't see a thing. Just you holding out your left hand and telling me that you saw Mum trapped in Nick's lift. That's it."

"But I saw her! I saw her lying on the floor of the lift—it wasn't an illusion. Stella and Dennis found her trapped in the lift, didn't they? It wasn't my imagination—the image was as clear as day."

"It's what our dad told us: you've inherited our grandmother's powers—her powers and her ring. That's why you knew Mum was in trouble."

The phone in Nila's hand crackled. "Nila, Nila, are you there?"

"Mum!" Nila and Della cried out in unison. "Are you okay?"

~*~

Della came into the lounge from the bedroom. "The babies are clean. It took a while to get their hair unstuck. I put the pram under the shower—there's ice cream all over the seat and straps."

Nila was sprawled on the couch. She sat up and smiled. "They had a good time—that's what matters. You checked their nappies?"

"Mmm hmm. The pull-ups were sticky on the outside, but the girls were dry. They've caught on to potty training very quickly. Is that normal for their age?"

"Not really; they're ahead of schedule. It was the same with feeding themselves. I'm sure they're unusually intelligent—unfortunately I can't take any credit for that. Are they back in their cribs?"

"Lying on their backs but not looking sleepy." Della plopped onto the carpet at Nila's feet in an approximation of a yoga position. "Okay, like I was saying—we need to contact our dad to see if he can help explain the ring and your visions."

"I don't expect that's a good idea; I think Mum wouldn't approve. Besides, I don't have any contact numbers for Dad."

"I do. He gave me his card before he left, and I gave him my email address. Dad promised he'd send pictures of his sons—our half-brothers—and of Morowa, his wife. I'm anxious to see what they all look like. Just because he and Mum had a nasty break-up shouldn't mean that I can't have any contact with him. I mean, there's no need for our mum to know—is there?"

Nila held out her left hand and twisted the orange-diamond

ring. "I'm so confused. This ring isn't uncomfortable on my finger, or too tight, and yet it won't come off. When it started pulsing and contracting, it was as if it was announcing an incoming telephone call—a cry for help from Mum. You really didn't see a thing?"

Della shook her head. "And neither did the waitress, when she was trying to help remove the ring. You're the only one who saw the image of Mum in the lift. It's you, Nila—like Dad said, you've inherited our grandmother's white-witch powers and somehow that ring is connected with those powers. We have to talk with—"

Nila's ringing phone interrupted Della. Nila removed the phone from the pocket of the hotel bathrobe.

"It's Gordy!" she told Della and pushed talk.

"Hey, you! Where are you?"

Gordy's voice was flat and subdued. "Tampa. The hotel. I think I got the flu. I'm achy, feverish, and have been erupting at both ends ever since I checked in."

"Gordy, you need a doctor. Call the front desk and see if the hotel has a doctor on call."

Gordon sneezed. "I already called Axel Quigley and he's faxed a prescription to the CVS here—the pharmacy is in the same complex as the hotel."

"What are you gonna do about the bar exam? Can you get them to reschedule because you're sick?"

"No—no way. I got some Imodium from the lobby shop; it should start working on the bottom end soon. I'll go down to the drugstore when we finish talking. If Axel's medications can control the nausea and vomiting and I can get some sleep tonight, I think I can do the exam."

"You said yourself that the exam isn't a matter of life and death. Why don't you rest and then drive home when you feel up to it? You can do the exam another time—right?"

"I think I can do it tomorrow. The thing is, it may take an

extra day before I'm able to drive the six hours to Miami to get you and the girls."

"Not a problem. There's a car-hire desk here in the hotel. I'll hire a car and drive the three of us home. Better still, I'll drive up to Tampa tomorrow, drop off the car, and then drive all of us home in the Lincoln when you're well enough for the trip. I'm sure I can work it out with your hotel to put us all up for an extra night or two."

"No—I don't want you to cancel your plans with Della. It's her last full day and I know she's really looking forward to the special dinner with you, Mary, and Milt. Here's what I think we should do: I'll try to make it through the exam tomorrow and then I'll spend the night here in the hotel. You and Della check out the beach scene and then have the dinner you planned. You reserve a rental for Thursday, drop Della off at the airport, and then drive yourself and the twins home. I'm sure I'll be able to get home by Thursday night. If there's any change to my condition, I'll call you and we'll re-strategize. We better communicate by text for the next day—if I can fall asleep, I'd rather not be woken up by a phone call."

"If that's what you want," Nila agreed reluctantly.

"Gotta run, literally—call you tomorrow."

"Take care of yourself. We love you," Nila called into the dead phone line.

~*~

Gordon set his iPhone on the bedside table and rolled into the center of the king-size bed. He pushed up onto one arm and grinned. "You think she bought the story?"

Devon nodded as she turned from the window. The afternoon sun that was streaming into her bedroom accented the white triangle the micro-bikini had left on her tanned lower belly.

"Oh, yes. How could she possibly question such a pathetic

story?" She pressed her knees into the side of the mattress, arched her back, and pulled her brown hair back into a short ponytail.

"Nila's such a pretty, innocent thing; she'll make a lovely addition to our little family," Devon said.

27

Deputy Sheriff McGill was holding a large Styrofoam cup in one hand, with a 'Little Debbie' packaged cake balanced on the lid. He bent down and opened the door of the squad car with his free hand just as Nila pulled the rented Nissan SUV into an adjacent parking space. She waved through the open window.

"Mick—how lovely to see you. Now I know I'm safely home."

"You're just getting back from Miami?"

"I am." She turned her head toward the child seats in the back. "These two urchins screamed and shouted the whole trip—never slept 'til we came to the toll bridge. They're zonked out now. I've got a raging headache—I hope Kopel's has some aspirin."

"I know they have Aleve and Excedrin."

Nila opened the door and stepped out.

"Mick, I realize that you're on duty, but could I possibly impose on our friendship and ask you to keep an eye on the twins while I run in for something for my headache and a bottle of water? I never leave them on their own in a car, but I'd rather not wake them up and restart the howls—they're teething, you see. Won't be a tick!"

"No problem—I'm on coffee break. I'll just have my coffee next to the car while you go in. This a rental?"

"Yes, it is. I got it at the hotel. Gordy drove the Lincoln up to Tampa for the bar exam. He got the flu or something and wasn't able to come pick us up. He should be back home tonight or tomorrow morning."

The deputy shook his head. "No, he's already back. I passed the Lincoln about a half hour ago down by Aracetti's lounge. He had a passenger—nobody I recognized. But I'm sure it was Mr. Hale driving."

"That's strange—I haven't been able to talk with him today.

No phones allowed in the examination room."

"I'm positive it was Mr. Hale in the Lincoln."

Nila frowned. "I'll be right back. Can I get you anything?"

"No, thanks—I've got my coffee. You know about the storm, right?"

"Just what I heard on the radio. I've never been in a hurricane, but the radio said it wasn't going to be serious."

"It's just a tropical depression right now. Could become a tropical storm later. It's predicted to run up the coast tonight and come ashore around the Tampa Bay Area tomorrow. It'll probably get pretty windy around here later this afternoon and evening. Nothing to worry about, but best you plan on staying home tonight. There are likely to be branches down on the roads, and possible intermittent power outages. You've got flashlights and batteries?"

"There's an emergency generator. Gordy said it will go on by itself if the electrics go off. Maybe I should buy some milk. You don't mind waiting an extra minute?"

"No problem—there was nobody in the store just now."

"Thanks. Be right back."

~*~

Beverly was bent down stocking shelves, out of Nila's view.

"Hello, anyone here?" Nila called out to the empty store.

"I'm back here. Be right with you as soon as I can straighten up. Oh, it's you, Nila—didn't hear you come in. That door buzzer died this morning. Just like me, nothing works the way it used to do. Mr. Hale forget something?"

"Sorry—forget something? I don't know what you mean."

"Mr. Hale was in about one. Bought some food and milk—in case the storm gets worse than anticipated, he said. Your new neighbor, Miss Devon, was with him; she stocked up on wine."

"So he *is* back," Nila said, more to herself than Beverly.

Beverly noticed the surprise on Nila's face. "'He's back,' you said. Back from where?"

"It's nothing, really. Gordy was in Tampa and I wasn't expecting him until later. Must have gotten away sooner than he anticipated. Do you have something for a splitting headache—aspirin, perhaps?"

"We don't carry aspirin. People don't want aspirin anymore—they hear about these painkillers on TV and that's all they want. Aleve is pretty good. You can take two right away and then another before bed if that headache hasn't gone away by then. I take it when my arthritis flares up."

"I'll take the Aleve—and a small bottle of water, as well."

"Water's next to you in the cold case. I hope there's nothing wrong with Mr. Hale."

Nila placed the water bottle on the counter and stared into Beverly's face. "He's fine. Don't give it another thought."

Beverly silently returned Nila's change and nodded.

As she walked down the ramp to the parked cars, Nila struggled with the cap on the bottle of Aleve. "These pill bottles are too clever by half," she blurted in frustration.

"Your phone's ringing," Deputy McGill called out.

Nila quickly pulled open the SUV door, tossed the Aleve and water bottle onto the seat, and retrieved her cell phone from the console. She saw Gordon's number on the screen and quickly pressed talk.

"Hey, you! Where are you? I've been trying to reach you all day."

"Things got all changed around," Gordon replied in a quiet tone. "There was some kinda security incident in the building where the bar exam was scheduled. The officials evacuated the place and the exam had to be postponed. Don't know yet when it will be rescheduled."

"You're okay? Feeling better?"

"The prescription that Axel faxed to the pharmacy in Tampa

worked great. Fixed me up in just a few hours. I slept well. I'm feeling a little weak, probably from the terminal diarrhea, but otherwise all right."

"So, no one was hurt in the building?"

"I don't think so; not that I could see. There were lots of cop cars, ambulances, and fire engines, but no smoke or signs of a fire or explosion and no obvious casualties. I never got into the building. Hung out in front for half an hour with some others who were scheduled for the exam until a woman with a bullhorn shouted out for us to go home and check our email for further instructions."

Nila turned from the SUV and looked at the deputy.

"Gordy's okay," she mouthed to the deputy. "Where are you now?" she asked Gordy.

"I drove back home this morning. Tried to call your cell but you didn't pick up."

Nila grinned. "Not surprising. After I dropped Della at the airport, the twins were cross that she'd left them and decided to scream and fuss the whole journey across Alligator Alley. I tried to drown out the screams, turned my Adele CD up full volume, and sang along at the top of my lungs. Never heard the phone. Why didn't you leave a message?"

"I must have been more disoriented than I realized."

"I see. Are you at home now?"

"Actually, I'm at the marina. I'm trying to get some propane in case we need the emergency electric generator. Where are the three of you?"

"At Kopel's—Mick's here too."

"Mick? Why's Mick with you?"

"He's on duty and stopped at Kopel's for his coffee break."

"Oh. Don't bother getting any food, Nila. I stopped by earlier and stocked up for a few days—just in case this storm gets worse than predicted."

Nila forced a chuckle. "I know. Guess who told me?"

"Beverly, no doubt. She probably also told you that Devon was with me. Her car is being serviced and she wanted to get some food in."

"More like getting some wine in, right? Beverly doesn't keep secrets. I'm leaving now—we should be home in ten minutes."

"I just have to finish loading the propane—be there soon."

"Okay. Can't wait to see you. I love you," she said into a dead line. Nila placed her phone back in the SUV's console and retrieved her water and pill bottles from the car seat. "Do you mind?" she asked the deputy as she handed him the miniature pill bottle.

"You have to push these tabs together—it's a safety thing." He handed the bottle back to Nila. "Mr. Hale's okay, he said?"

As she swallowed the pills, she nodded. "Gordy said that there was some kind of security incident at the place where he was supposed to take the bar exam this morning. Lots of police cars and fire engines. They sent everyone home. Guess they'll have to reschedule."

"This was in Tampa, right?"

"Yes, Tampa—but I don't know where. Gordy didn't know anything more about what had happened."

"Haven't heard anything on the highway-patrol radio. Probably a false alarm. I'll give you a call if I find out anything important."

Nila slid into the SUV and closed the door. "Thanks for watching the twins, Mick. I better get 'em home before they wake up and start howling."

~*~

Gordon set his cell phone on the sunroom table. "Nila stopped at Kopel's. She knows that I'm on the island. She'll be arriving at the cottage in a few minutes."

Devon shrugged. "So, we'll just have to speed up the plan.

You told her you were here?"

"I told her I was at Clifford's Marina, getting propane for the emergency generator."

"Good—that'll buy us some time. Let her get the babies settled before you go over. She'll probably give them something to eat and then put 'em to bed. They'll likely be tired from the car trip."

"Maybe we should wait until tomorrow? She might be too tired for sex this afternoon."

"Nila hasn't seen you for days. You know she won't be too tired. You've got the suppository?"

He pulled a tiny plastic bag from the side pocket of his jeans. "Right here."

"Okay. Immediately after you insert the capsule, she'll experience about fifteen minutes of intense sexual arousal, followed by an extended orgasm. Then she'll close her eyes and be zonked out for about half an hour. That's when Hattie and I will come into the bedroom and mark her."

Gordon scowled. "It won't hurt her?"

Devon laughed. It was more a cackle than a laugh. "You should know. It didn't hurt when I marked you, did it?"

He shrugged. "I don't remember."

"Right—and neither will she."

28

When Nila pulled the rental car into the driveway that the beach cottage shared with the big house, the palms on either side of the drive were swaying in unison. She noticed that the high clouds were moving rapidly.

"Juice box," Janna called out. "Juice box!"

Nila looked into the rearview mirror. "Okay, so somebody's awake." Julie was wiggling in her car seat. "Make that two somebodies. We're home! I'll have you out in a minute."

Julie joined in the chant. "Juice box!"

"Okay, okay. I hope Daddy remembered to pick up some juice boxes. I'm pretty sure we were all out."

Nila pulled the SUV up to the kitchen door and then lifted each girl from her car seat. "I'm amazed you're dry," she said to Janna as she checked her pull-up.

"Potty," Janna responded. "Go potty."

Nila led the girls to the door and began to rummage in her purse for the key when she noticed that the security alert was glowing green. "Odd—not locked," she said aloud. Since the confrontation with Maggie, both she and Gordon always set the new security system whenever they left the house. She pushed open the door and the girls trotted directly to the nursery bathroom. Nila removed Janna's pull-up and Janna immediately squatted into the wood-and-plastic potty chair next to the toilet. When she turned to help Julie, Nila was surprised to see that Julie had already tugged her pull-up down to her ankles.

"Me do it," Julie said. "Big girl."

Nila smiled. "Yes, big girl."

The ringing of Nila's cell phone was clear, but distant. "Whoops, left the phone in the car," she called out. "Must be Daddy! Be right back." She moved quickly to the SUV and grabbed her phone from the center console. "Hey! We're home," she shouted as she moved back to the kitchen.

"Nila, it's me—Mick."

"Oh, Mick. I thought you were Gordy." She tried not to sound disappointed.

"Mr. Hale's not there, then?"

"No, not yet. We just arrived. Is something wrong?"

"No, nothing, I just wanted to check with him about the problem in Tampa at the exam site. I thought that Mr. Hale would want to know what happened, so I called a precinct sergeant up there, a guy on my softball team, to see if he knew anything. He checked, and there was no record of any emergency services call-out anywhere in the area. Kinda strange, huh?"

"Sure is," Nila replied.

"His exam was definitely in Tampa, right?"

"Definitely in Tampa. Gordy was staying at a hotel a few blocks from the exam location. I talked with him on the phone when he was at the hotel."

"Must be some kinda misunderstanding. But now I'm curious. Can you get Mr. Hale to give me a call when he gets in? No hurry—I'm sure we can figure this out. Okay?"

"Okay. Thanks, Mick. I'll have Gordy call."

"How's the weather there?"

"Getting blowy and a bit misty," Nila replied.

"Still no change in the forecast. Just a tropical depression moving up the coast. Should pass in the next few hours. No big deal, but best if you remain indoors. Stay safe."

~*~

"Eeeeeee!" Janna screamed.

Nila dropped her phone onto the kitchen counter and ran for the nursery. "What's wrong?" she shouted as she entered the room.

Both girls had shed their pull-ups and were naked, squatting close together in the middle of the carpeted floor. "Eeeeeee!" Janna screamed again while excitedly beating her hands against the floor. Nila quickly dropped to her knees. Julie lifted her right hand and Nila saw that they had captured a gecko—a small, harmless lizard that had found its way from outside into the house. The gecko was frantically trying to run, to escape from Julie's chubby fingers, but was veering to the right and making little forward progress.

"Toes!" Janna shouted as she held out the gecko's dismembered, but still wiggling, front leg for Nila's admiration. "More toes," Julie squealed in delight as she grasped the gecko by the torso and tore away its remaining front leg.

"That's monstrous!" Nila shouted. "Stop it! Stop it this minute." Nila pulled a tissue from her pocket, covered the still-struggling lizard in Julie's fingers, and squeezed the tissue and the gecko into a ball. She felt nauseated, and tasted acid rising in her throat and mouth.

Julie frowned. "Mine," she called, holding out her open hand to Nila.

"Good God, no!" Nila replied. She stood and quickly walked the few steps to the nursery bathroom, where she flushed the tissue and gecko remains down the toilet and then washed and dried her hands.

When Nila turned back into the nursery, she saw that the twins were standing by the window. They had pulled the red-and-white-striped curtains to the side and were gazing up at the windowsill.

"Kayba! Kayba!" Janna shouted as she began to jump up and down.

"Kayba!" Julie joined Janna in the chanting and energetic jumping.

"What are you imps up to now?" Nila asked. Her question died on her lips when she saw the object of their attention—an icon glaring into the room from outside the open, but screened, window. The torso of the small icon, a vivid, brightly painted eyeball, was iridescently pulsing in time to the girls' jumping. Two grisly heads emerged from either side of the eyeball torso—one with a face twisted in rage, the other with a cruel, cynical grin. The two heads alternately screamed and cackled.

"Bloody hell!" Nila whispered. She reached out to grasp and close the curtain, but Janna yanked the drape from her hand.

The children's chanting increased in volume as their jumping intensified. Both twins were jumping vertically three inches or more off the carpeted floor. The lurid colors of the icon's eyeball body—red, yellow, orange, blue, and purple—pulsed brilliantly in cadence with each jump.

Nila rushed from the nursery, out the kitchen door, and quickly turned the far corner of the beach cottage, toward the nursery window. A light, misty rain had begun to fall and the wind was increasing.

The plants below the nursery window had clearly been freshly trampled. Someone had recently placed the disgusting idol on the nursery windowsill. Nila's mind raced—who would do such a sick prank, and why? Her senses were on overload. She looked at the icon from the rear and saw that, unlike the torso and eyeballs, the back of the icon was a slimy gray that seethed like a ball of worms each time the front-facing heads wailed and snarled.

Without hesitation, Nila reached out, grasped the ten-inch-high icon with her right hand and forcefully tore it from the windowsill. The icon's cries increased in both volume and intensity. Nila felt a sharp stinging and saw that her hand was bleeding. Each of the icon's two heads had bared snake-like fangs and had pierced Nila's hand. She screamed, "Filthy beast!" She grabbed the icon with her left hand and tried to pull its fangs from the webbing between her right thumb and index finger, but the icon held fast. The bleeding increased. Blood was now flowing around her wrist, down her forearm, and dripping from her left elbow. Nila felt faint and was approaching complete panic. In an effort to free herself, she twisted the icon with her right hand, inadvertently pressing the power-stone ring on her left hand into the icon's luridly painted, pulsing torso. A silent, bright-orange flash obscured Nila's vision. She heard the icon emit a shrill, animal-like squeal as it released its snake-like grip on her hand. She hurled the now-silent and motionless effigy to the sandy ground at her feet. As her vision cleared, she grasped her right hand where the fangs had pierced her skin—but found no injury, no bleeding, and no blood on her hand, wrist, or arm.

The icon lay on its back, facing skyward at Nila's feet. She stared as the luminous paint covering the vile creature's body began to melt, liquefy, and then stream away up into the air. Paralyzed by both terror and relief, she stood, hulking over the melting icon for some time, as the loathsome monster slowly degenerated into a clump of colorless dust. She examined her hands once again—no injury, and no blood. She kicked at the pile of dust that moments before had been the gruesome icon. The increasing wind picked up the heap of powder, carrying away all traces that the icon had ever existed. Nila began to doubt her sanity.

The cat tattoo on her belly grew pleasantly warm—it seemed to offer reassurance of her mental stability. *Della was right,* she thought—*I am a witch. The tattoo my grandmother placed on my belly, Father's descriptions of the Ashanti legends, the power-stone ring that refuses to leave my finger, and the images of Mum trapped in the mini-lift, images that only I could see—they all prove that I'm a witch.* Nila's ring pulsed and then contracted, snapping her out of her trance-like state.

She turned toward the house and peered through the window back into the nursery. The room was empty—the twins had disappeared.

"My babies!" she cried.

Nila rushed into the house, shouting for the children. "Janna!

Julie! Come here this instant!" She rushed from room to room in the small cottage: guest room, master bedroom, living room, kitchen, and even Gordon's little office. "Janna! Julie!" she called. Then she had a terrible thought.

"Oh my God, the pool!" she shouted. As she raced to the sliding kitchen doors that opened to the lanai, a vision of two tiny bodies floating, face down, in the swimming pool fueled her panic. When she saw that the child-safety fence separating the pool from the surrounding patio was closed and locked, she was momentarily calmed. Her relief dissolved, however, when she saw the open screen door to the beach noisily banging in the wind. As Nila looked out through the lanai screening, she saw two tiny, naked figures on the beach, hand in hand, walking toward the wind-whipped waters of the Gulf.

"Janna! Julie!" Her anxiety turned the cry into a fearful shriek.

29

Devon slid the Lincoln key-fob across the granite kitchen countertop. "Time to go."

Gordon placed his hand over the fob. "I don't wanna do this," he whispered, rapidly shaking his head.

Devon glared, her face a cruel mask. "Now, you go now!" she shouted. "You'll do what I tell you. You bear my mark; you're mine. Go now, and text me when Nila's unconscious...You've got the suppository?"

Gordon patted his front pocket. "It's still where it was last time you asked."

"Understand? As soon as she's unconscious, you text me. Hattie and I will come into the bedroom and I'll mark her. It won't take more than a few minutes. Go now."

Gordon nodded and wordlessly exited the house through the sunroom. His head was spinning—gauzy images of Nila and the twins hovered in the air in front of his eyes. A distinct, dark visage displaced the image of Nila, a laughing, cackling face, Devon's face. As quickly as it had appeared in his consciousness, Devon's image began to burn and then explode. At the same time, Gordon felt a stab, a searing pain to his testicles. "Aaaggh!" he screamed. The burning pain subsided and vanished as quickly as it had occurred. He stumbled to the Lincoln, disoriented and profusely sweating, the echo of his beating heart pounding forcefully in his ears.

Gordon struggled with the car door and finally managed to drag himself into the driver's seat. He backed the big car from the garage and then drove the hundred-yard loop to the beach cottage, where he parked next to the rented SUV. He looked through the side window into the back seat—the child seats were still in place, a backpack and diaper bag sat on the floor, and partially eaten cookies littered the seat. Nila hadn't unpacked yet.

The rain increased from a trickle to a steady shower.

The cottage's security entry light blinked green. Gordon's thoughts were chaotic. He was anticipating a joyful reunion with Nila and his daughters and at the same time fearful that the events of the past two days might have damaged his loving relationship with Nila.

"Nila," he called from the kitchen. Anticipating that the babies might be in their cribs, he peered into the nursery from the hall. No babies. He checked the master bedroom, and the living room. No Nila, no children.

"Strange," he said aloud, moving back to the kitchen. The sliding doors to the pool were partially open, and the gusting wind was making the lightweight nylon curtains near the pine table flutter. As he reached out to close the doors, Gordon saw movement on the beach, near the waterline. The rain distorted his vision, but he clearly saw figures along the tideline where the normally placid Gulf waters had become wind-driven whitecaps. The long hair of the largest figure was blowing out like a banner.

"Nila!" he shouted through the partially opened doors, but the wind drove the words back into his face.

~*~

Devon was bent over the kitchen sink. She clasped her neck with both hands and forcefully vomited a stream of yellow bile into the drain.

"My Du-mon," she choked through the foul mucus that covered her mouth and dripped from her chin. "My Du-mon's destroyed."

Hattie ripped a handful of paper towels from the spindle on the counter. She held the towels to Devon's face and turned on the water.

"Destroyed? How you know that?" she shouted.

"The powers I transferred to the Du-mon are gone. Gone! I hurt all over," Devon cried.

Hattie tore off more paper towels, tossed the disgusting, used towels into the trash bin, and continued to clean Devon's face with fresh, wet towels. She pulled a chair close to the sink.

"Sit down here, Lilith, while I clean you up."

Devon sat, rocked from side to side, and moaned. "My Du-mon is gone. Destroyed. Vanished. Everything I created is undone."

Hattie drew the plastic waste-bin near, in case Devon needed to vomit again. She massaged Devon's shoulders and back and, after several minutes, Devon's breathing calmed. Devon stood, grasped the rim of the sink for support. "Get me a glass, so I can wash out my mouth." Devon splashed tap water on her face and washed her hands, while Hattie handed her a water glass.

"Rinse out your mouth with this water, but don't drink none. That'll get the nasty taste outa your mouth."

Devon rinsed her mouth, spitting the foul yellow residue into the steel sink.

Devon's cell on the counter vibrated. Hattie checked the screen. "This is blank; it don't say nothin'."

Devon retched twice, but failed to bring up more bile.

"I hurt!" she struggled to say. She turned her head toward Hattie. "Let me see that phone."

Hattie stared into Devon's face. Her jaw dropped and her eyes grew wide.

"Oh, shit!" she called out. "How could it happen now?"

Devon saw the shock and astonishment on Hattie's face. "What's wrong with you, you stupid girl?"

"Lilith! The transformation's begun!"

Devon shook her head. "That's not possible—I have years before this body will need to be replaced."

Hattie cast around the kitchen for a mirror. Seeing none, she stepped to the side of the stove and pulled a wide stainless-steel knife from the wooden knife block. She held the broad, flat side of the knife in front of Devon's face. Devon reached out and grasped the knife, her hand around the blade.

"Impossible!" she screamed as she saw the reflection of her face in the polished metal.

Blood dripped from her hand where she grasped the knife blade. She sprang from the chair and rushed to the large decorative mirror in the dining room. Devon dropped the knife to the wooden floor.

"No!" she moaned. "No!"

"Your skin!" Hattie cried.

"The Du-mon, the Du-mon—my power!"

Devon ran her hands over her face, leaving behind stripes of blood from the knife wound on her fingers. Her skin was quickly turning gray and her teeth black.

Hattie was horrified as she watched clumps of Devon's brown hair fall to the floor, leaving open, raw sores on her rapidly balding scalp.

"Do something!" Devon screamed, as black claws began jutting out from beneath her fingernails and toenails.

Hattie grasped her own forehead and pitched rhythmically backward and forward. "The druggie whore—the violent, druggie whore; you should have listened to me! That filthy woman was pure evil. But you had to have that body, and that face. Her evil is hatching inside your body, Lilith. Jus' like a horde of maggots crawlin' out from rotting flesh! You gave that vile Du-mon your powers an' now they're gone—an' you can't protect yourself! Tha's what's happening to you."

"Daughter—help me! Help me!"

"We gotta get ya out of that sick body, so you can start over again. We did this once afore—long, long time ago. You remember? You move into my body and share it with me 'til we can get you out and into a new one again."

"Do it! Do it now!" Devon screamed. "The pain! The pain!

Don't wait!"

Hattie picked up the knife that lay at Devon's feet. "This gonna hurt a lot," she said, slowly articulating one word at a time. Hattie stepped back and forcefully plunged the large blade into Devon's throat, twisting it back and forth and thrusting again until both carotid arteries were severed and crimson blood spurted from the broad wound.

~*~

Gordon didn't notice when the cell phone dropped from his hand and broke apart on the tile floor. His senses were concentrated on the figures by the shoreline. Everything else surrounding him seemed frozen in time. It was as if the last two days he'd spent with Devon had never happened. He slid his hand into the side pocket of his jeans and removed the tiny plastic bag with the suppository that Devon had intended for Nila. He dropped the bag to the floor and squashed it with his shoe, twisting his toes as one would do to kill a cockroach.

"Nila! My babies!" he yelled as he dashed through the lanai and onto the beach.

Gordon raced toward the shoreline, wet sand flying in his wake. The warm rain was matting his hair and flowing into his eyes. The figures he'd seen from the cottage came into focus—they were unmistakably Nila and the twins. The three girls were holding hands and running toward the breaking waves. All three were naked and dripping wet: naked, wet, and laughing.

Janna was the first to see him. "Daddy!" she called, jumping up and down, her small arms outstretched. Julie unclasped from Nila's hand and ran to Gordon. "Daddy! Daddy!" she echoed. "Come play escape!" Gordon gathered Julie up in a bear-hug, while Janna locked her arms around Gordon's leg.

A broad smile on her face, Nila stepped back while she delighted in the twins' outpouring of affection for their father.

"We're escaping from the waves," Nila shouted over the crashing surf.

Gordon wrapped his free arm around Nila's shoulders and pulled her close. The four of them held tight to one another, transfixed by the protective love that sprang from Nila and enfolded her family.

The rain had become a downpour. "We best go inside before we drown," Nila said, laughing. "Let me get my sodden clothes and shoes." She trotted around the nearby sand dune to her balled-up, brightly colored dress and sandals. The twins followed after her.

"Mama, look!" Janna nervously cried. Julie ran to Janna's side and pointed to a mass of bloated flesh and limbs, a body lying face up, partially covered by the blowing sand. The vultures had clearly discovered the corpse, torn out one of the eyes, and started to rip the soft lips and breast tissue.

Nila edged closer to the decomposing corpse. Her eyes were drawn to the savage throat wound. The body's scalp was covered with raw, open sores randomly spaced among the remaining wisps of brown hair.

"Devon!" she breathed. "My God, what's happened to her?"

30

"That's finished," Clarisse flatly stated, rubbing her palms together as she entered the immense, penthouse, great room. "I don't know why you insist on having me tack those scruffy pictures on the wall every time you change houses?"

Lilith, now in Hattie's body, slowly turned her gaze away from the panoramic, floor-to-ceiling windows. From the spectacular, penthouse view, twenty-one stories above the earth, the dark waters of the Atlantic Ocean seemed to merge with the distant sky and paint every spatial dimension a different shade of blue.

Hattie's eyes, as well, were intensely blue. After Lilith's mind had fled from Devon's festering body and entered Hattie's body, Hattie's albino, pink eyes had changed to Lilith's otherworldly blue.

Lilith turned to face Clarisse, her face showing her annoyance with Clarisse's question. "Those pictures are of my ancestors, my family, you stupid woman. Other than you and this daughter I'm now trapped inside of, they're my only family."

"You could at least allow me to reframe all of the paintings and photos into a single coherent collection. Better still, I could paint the images into a family portrait; a party or picnic scene. I'd paint all the women an identical size but retain their period clothing, hats and jewelry?"

Lilith grinned. "I'll think about it...You've put up the photo of Devon with the others?"

"Against my better judgment. The nude photo stands out like a hooker at a PTA meeting."

Lilith laughed loudly. "You'll remember that after I took over the bodies of the women in those paintings and photos, not one of them remained an innocent for long. I made sure of that, didn't I?...Enough about the pictures. When will she arrive?"

"I just checked my phone; the flight from Dulles is on time.

It's scheduled to touch down in just under an hour. She should get her here about 7 to 7:30. Flying Raven in on a private jet and the limo pick-up at her apartment was an excellent move. It convinced her of your serious commitment to financially back her campaign. Congressional staffers never get the ego pampering their bosses receive...Raven's excited about meeting you; 'a politically kindred soul with lots of money' was how I described you to her."

Lilith chuckled and settled on the white leather sectional. She patted the cushion next to her, summoning Clarisse to sit. "You think she has a real chance of winning the primary?"

Clarisse slid in next to Lilith. "I do," she forcefully stated. "The pundits all agree that the seat is ripe for turning. Raven's draped herself with the appropriate political ideology for the current atmosphere, she's articulate and intelligent, and she has a likeable, wholesome personality. In all the important ways, she's the opposite of the worn-out incumbent. All she needs to win is money. With your financial backing she'll be able to buy exposure, and the media will fawn all over her. I have no doubt that she'll run away with the nomination and have strong momentum going into the general election."

Lilith nodded. "You've served me well, Clarisse. Your research in selecting a new body for me has been flawless."

"Thank you, Lilith." Clarisse's elfin-like face beamed. She lowered her head. "You do remember the film clips and photos of Raven that we reviewed? Unlike Maggie Cartwright or the young Myra Silk, Raven Cortez isn't a sexy beauty. Raven's young and attractive in a fresh-faced way, but hardly glamorous."

Lilith pressed her head back into the couch, then forcefully inhaled and slowly exhaled. "I understand," she said with a nod. "I've thought this through quite carefully." Lilith sat up straight and turned to face Clarisse. "This episode of life will be about power, not sex or mischief, but power. Once Raven is elected to Congress, I'll use my resources to buy and accumulate influence—the muscle needed to open closed doors. No telling what opportunities for power Raven will find on the other side of those doors: senator, cabinet secretary, president?"

"I understand your plan," Clarisse nervously whispered. "Raven will be here soon. Please, one more time, Lilith. Can we walk through what I'll need to do to help get you out of Hattie's body and into Raven's?"

"Of course, my little one," Lilith softly cooed as she lovingly stroked Clarisse's cheek. "You'll do fine, little one; trust me."

FANTASY, SCI-FI, HORROR & PARANORMAL

If you prefer to spend your nights with Vampires and Werewolves rather than the mundane then we publish the books for you. If your preference is for Dragons and Faeries or Angels and Demons – we should be your first stop. Perhaps your perfect partner has artificial skin or comes from another planet – step right this way. If your passion is Fantasy (including magical realism and spiritual fantasy), Metaphysical Cosmology, Horror or Science Fiction (including Steampunk), Cosmic Egg books will feed your hunger. Our curiosity shop contains treasures you will enjoy unearthing. If you have enjoyed this book, why not tell other readers by posting a review on your preferred book site.

Recent bestsellers from Cosmic Egg Books are:

The Zombie Rule Book

A Zombie Apocalypse Survival Guide

Tony Newton

The book the living-dead don't want you to have!

Paperback: 978-1-78279-334-2 ebook: 978-1-78279-333-5

Cryptogram

Because the Past is Never Past

Michael Tobert

Welcome to the dystopian world of 2050, where three lovers are haunted by echoes from eight-hundred years ago.

Paperback: 978-1-78279-681-7 ebook: 978-1-78279-680-0

Purefinder

Ben Gwalchmai

London, 1858. A child is dead; a man is blamed and dragged through hell in this Dantean tale of loss, mystery and fraternity.

Paperback: 978-1-78279-098-3 ebook: 978-1-78279-097-6

600ppm

A Novel of Climate Change

Clarke W. Owens

Nature is collapsing. The government doesn't want you to know why. Welcome to 2051 and 600ppm.

Paperback: 978-1-78279-992-4 ebook: 978-1-78279-993-1

Creations

William Mitchell

Earth 2040 is on the brink of disaster. Can Max Lowrie stop the self-replicating machines before it's too late?

Paperback: 978-1-78279-186-7 ebook: 978-1-78279-161-4

The Gawain Legacy

Jon Mackley

If you try to control every secret, secrets may end up controlling you.

Paperback: 978-1-78279-485-1 ebook: 978-1-78279-484-4

Readers of ebooks can buy or view any of these bestsellers by clicking on the live link in the title. Most titles are published in paperback and as an ebook. Paperbacks are available in traditional bookshops. Both print and ebook formats are available online.

Find more titles and sign up to our readers' newsletter at http://www.johnhuntpublishing.com/fiction

Follow us on Facebook at https://www.facebook.com/JHPfiction and Twitter at https://twitter.com/JHPFiction